THE FIRST REALITY-BASED ROMANCE™

Judith Arnold
MEET ME IN MANHATTAN

Health Communications, Inc.
Deerfield Beach, Florida

www.hcibooks.com

Library of Congress Cataloging-in-Publication Data

Arnold, Judith.
  Meet me in Manhattan / by Judith Arnold.
    p. cm.
  ISBN-13: 978-0-7573-1533-6
  ISBN-10: 0-7573-1533-X
  I. Title.
  PS3551.R4852M44 2010
  813'.54—dc22

                                                      2010024956

Publisher: Health Communications, Inc.
          3201 S.W. 15th Street
          Deerfield Beach, FL 33442–8190

TRUE VOWS Series Developer: Olivia Rupprecht
Cover photo ©Getty Images
Cover design by Larissa Hise Henoch
Interior design and formatting by Lawna Patterson Oldfield

Praise for TRUE VOWS

"What better way is there to prove romance really exists than to read these books?"

—**Carly Phillips**, *New York Times* bestselling author

"Memoir meets romance! In the twenty years I've been penning romances, this is one of the most novel and exciting ideas I've encountered in the genre. Take a Vow. It rocks!"

—**Tara Janzen**, *New York Times* bestselling author of *Loose and Easy*

"An irresistible combination of romantic fantasy and reality that begins where our beloved romance novels end: TRUE VOWS. What a scrumptious slice of life!"

—**Suzanne Forster,** *New York Times* bestselling author

"The marriage of real-life stories with classic, fictional romance—an amazing concept."

—**Peggy Webb,** award-winning author of sixty romance novels

MEET ME IN MANHATTAN

In memory of my father,
who loved living in Manhattan

Dear Reader

AS A NOVELIST, I'M USED TO MAKING THINGS UP. I invent, I tell stories, I lie. I create characters who do my bidding. So when Olivia Rupprecht and Michele Matrisciani approached me on behalf of HCI Books with the idea of writing a love story based on actual people, I was hesitant.

Then I learned about Ted Skala and Erika Fredell. Their story transported me like the very best romance fiction. Two teenagers deeply in love yet too young to know how to deal with their wild-fire emotions extinguish that blazing love . . . or try to. Years pass, they build strong, successful lives for themselves, but a stubborn ember of their long-ago love refuses to die. Can they fan the ember back into a flame? If they do, will it burn them and destroy everything that matters to them now?

I'm enormously grateful to TRUE VOWS Series Developer Olivia Rupprecht for having given me the opportunity to write this glorious, passionate story, to TRUE VOWS Series Creator Michele Matrisciani for her sensitive guidance, support, and all-around brilliance, to Veronica Blake for suggesting to her HCI colleagues to enter the romance genre, and to Peter Vegso, the President and Publisher of HCI Books, for his open mindedness and encouragement as we developed the entirely new concept of "reality-based romance," and most of all, to Ted and Erika Skala for entrusting their wonderful story to me. I hope you enjoy reading it as much as I enjoyed writing it.

I love to hear from my readers. You can reach me through my website, www.juditharnold.com. And I encourage you to visit the official TRUE VOWS site: www.truevowsbooks.com, to interact with the couples and novelists, learn the latest news on the TRUE VOWS line, read about the upcoming books in the series, and even have the opportunity to tell HCI Books your true love story for a chance to be the subject of a future TRUE VOWS book.

One

RELAX, ERIKA TOLD HERSELF. *IT'S JUST TED.*

Standing in the drizzle on a busy SoHo corner outside Fanelli's Cafe, Erika Fredell acknowledged that there had never been anything *just* about Ted. And ordering herself to relax didn't make her nerves stop twitching. She'd raced here from the gym after working out, showering, and blow-drying her hair—a lot of good that did, since it was raining—and putting on some makeup so she'd look good, even though it was *just Ted* she was meeting. Fanelli's was only a few blocks from the gym, and she'd covered those blocks at a trot in an effort not to be too late. Halfway there, she'd realized that she'd left her wallet at home.

Relax. Yeah, right. She was really relaxed, she thought with a sarcastic laugh.

Fanelli's had been a good choice for her reunion with Ted. A bright yet cozy establishment, the one-time speakeasy attracted a cross-section of patrons: artists, professionals, locals, anyone who preferred a good hamburger and a cheap beer to pretentious ambience and inflated prices. It was her kind of place.

Sixteen years had passed since she and Ted had been a couple, and she no longer knew whether Fanelli's was *his* kind of place, or, for that matter, what his kind of place was. But he was inside

1

the neighborhood pub right now, waiting for her—assuming he wasn't running even later than she was. She was supposed to have arrived half an hour ago, but time had slipped away from her. Maybe he'd given up and left already, figuring she'd chickened out. Maybe he'd concluded that she'd stood him up, that she was only going to break his heart again.

Oh, please. That had been so long ago. Teenagers' hearts get broken all the time. Then teenagers grow up, their hearts heal, and they move on. If Ted hadn't grown up, healed, and moved on, he wouldn't have contacted her out of the blue and suggested they meet for a drink.

She gave herself three seconds to check her reflection in the rain-streaked window beneath Fanelli's red neon sign, adjusted the stylish chunky necklace circling her throat above the scooped neckline of her tank top, then decided *what the hell* and entered the pub. Anxious last-minute fussing wasn't going to improve her appearance. She looked how she looked. Sixteen years older. Her hair was long again, the way she'd worn it in high school. Not the short, playful style she'd been wearing when they'd had that painful, awkward meeting at the airport in Denver, after she'd started college. Back then, she'd been pretty sure he hadn't liked her short hairdo. Back then, she hadn't cared what he thought. She'd wanted a new look to mark the start of a new phase of her life. No more New Jersey. No more high school. No more horses.

No more Ted.

But now her hair was once again long. She wondered if this time *he* would be the one who didn't care. She wondered why *she* cared whether *he* cared.

She commanded herself to get a grip. She reminded herself that she and Ted were two old friends who happened to have both landed in New York City and were meeting for a drink on a drizzly

June evening. They weren't ex-lovers. They weren't high school sweethearts. They were grown-ups, living their own lives. Nothing more. She had no reason to be nervous.

Right. Tell that to her stomach, which at the moment was performing acrobatics like an Olympics gymnast hoping to score a ten.

Inhaling deeply for fortitude, she squared her shoulders, pushed the door open and stepped inside. A wave of raucous chatter washed over her; every person in the place seemed to be talking at once. And there were a hell of a lot of people crowding the tables and hovering near the bar. Maybe the boisterous crowd would buffer them, diluting the intensity of their meeting.

Not that it would be intense. Just two old friends meeting for a drink.

She surveyed the room but didn't see him. A waitress tried to stop her as she worked her way through the crowd, but she mumbled something about meeting a friend—"An *old* friend," she'd said because defining her and Ted as old friends soothed her bristling nerves—and then she spotted him, seated at the far end of the bar, a glass of beer in his hand.

He looked terrific. Damn it.

He'd always looked terrific, of course. But he'd changed so much from the lanky, gangly boy she'd been infatuated with that summer after high school. He was still lean and muscular, but more solid. His face had filled in a little. His dark hair was shorter, the tumble of curls tamed, and he'd acquired enough facial hair to grow legitimate, neatly trimmed sideburns. In his preppy cords and collared polo shirt, he looked crisp and fresh, impervious to the sultry heat of New York City in June.

He must have seen her the instant she saw him. His eyes widened, his smile widened, and he tilted his head slightly. She strode the length of the bar, spotting the empty stool next to him, and slid onto it. Bar stools at Fanelli's were at a premium, especially on a busy night like this. She wondered if he'd had to fight people off to save it for her. He'd always been a scrapper in high school, willing to fight if he had to. More than willing, sometimes.

But maybe he hadn't fought to save the stool for her. Maybe it had been vacated only a moment ago. Maybe some other woman had been sitting with him. A beautiful woman. Erika was so late, he might have chosen to make the most of her absence.

The notion shouldn't have bothered Erika. They were *old friends* meeting for a drink, after all. Not old, *mature*. Surely she was a great deal more mature than she'd been the summer she'd spent mooning and swooning over him, and trying to figure out what love was all about.

"Hey," he greeted her, then shook his head. "Wow."

"I know. Wow," she responded, wondering whether they were wow-ing the fact that they'd both landed in the same city, or that they were both sitting at the same bar, or that after all this time, all these years, there they were, face-to-face. Her wow reflected her opinion of how fantastic he looked, but she wasn't about to tell him that.

So there they were. Were they supposed to hug? Air-kiss? It occurred to her that if they were truly old—or mature—friends, she would know what to do. But the truth slapped her in the face. Sixteen years after Ted had told her he wanted her out of his life for good and forever, they could never be *just friends* any more than he could ever be *just Ted*.

Her stomach executed a vault worthy of a gold medal. "Listen," she said, smiling nervously. "I know it's been forever since I've seen you, but I don't have any money on me." *Oh, God,* she thought, *I am such an ass. And a nervous wreck, even though this is* just Ted.

He grinned. "Don't worry about it. We'll be fine."

She managed to smile and prayed he wouldn't notice how flustered she was—even more flustered because he seemed so damned calm and collected. He gestured toward the bartender, then thought to ask Erika, "You want a drink?"

God, yes. The bartender moseyed over, gaunt and fashionable, emanating unemployed-actor vibes like eighty percent of the servers in New York. Rather than have Ted order for her—that would imply something other than friendship—Erika requested a beer. If Ted was drinking Budweiser, she would drink Bud, too.

The bartender turned to Ted. "You ready for a refill?" he asked, nodding toward Ted's glass.

Ted appraised his glass and shook his head. "Not yet," he said, then took a drink. He set his glass down and Erika watched the residue of foam drip down its sloping sides. For some reason, it was easier than looking at Ted.

"So," he said. "How are you?"

She laughed, partly to shake off her tension, partly because the question was so banal, and partly because she wasn't sure how to answer. How was she now? How had she been last year, or five years ago, or ten? How had she been the day she'd left New Jersey for Colorado? The day she'd seen him in the airport? The day he'd told her he would never love her again?

"I'm fine," she said. "And you?"

"I'm also fine." He grinned. "Thank God we got that over with."

Okay. Maybe this wouldn't be too awkward, after all. Maybe they'd be able to chat—not like old times, but like two people who shared some pleasant memories. If they could both chuckle about the awkwardness between them and the stilted start of their reunion, she could survive this encounter.

She'd survive it a lot better if she had her beer. "I'm sorry I'm late," she said. "I hope you didn't have to wait too long."

He shrugged as if to reassure her that her tardiness was unimportant, then gestured toward the crowd mobbing the front room. "I had to fend off hundreds of people to hang onto that stool."

"Hundreds?"

"I'm lying. It was really thousands."

She smiled. All those years ago, she'd fallen in love with his sense of humor as much as his intensity, his energy, his native intelligence, his sexy green eyes, and his mop of tousled curls. The curls were gone, but he still exuded intensity and energy. And his eyes were still terribly sexy.

Her smile grew pensive. In sixteen years, she'd never met another man who could make her feel the way Ted had once made her feel. She was fine with that. She loved her life. She wasn't one of those desperate thirty-something single women, willing to settle for any guy just so she could get a ring on her finger. She'd never fallen in love after she'd ended things with Ted, and she'd never felt that this was a tragic deficit in her life.

But . . . being Ted's girlfriend all those years ago had been sweet.

"How's your family?" she asked, deliberately steering her thoughts in a new direction.

The bartender materialized in front of them with her drink, and Ted waited until he was gone before answering. "They're good," he reported. "My folks are still up in Maine."

"Your dad always loved it up there," Erika recalled.

"Yeah. East Machias." He shrugged. "Most older people head south to Florida when they retire. I guess those New Jersey winters just weren't cold enough for my parents."

"And your brothers?"

"Still obnoxious," he joked. "They're all good. Married, raising families, doing the usual stuff. My sister's hanging in there, too. How's your family?"

"They're doing well." Erika recalled how in awe she'd been of Ted's big, boisterous family. Four boys! She'd always felt kind of sorry for Ted's absurdly outnumbered younger sister, although she supposed a girl with four older brothers boasted a certain cachet. The Skalas had lived in Chester, a small town on the rural outskirts of Mendham, in an antique house that had once been the site of a cemetery, according to Ted. He'd insisted the place was haunted. She imagined that any creaks and thumps heard in that house were most likely caused by five athletic kids storming up and down the stairs.

"And work?" he asked. "What are you doing to pay the rent these days?"

"As a matter of fact, I just got a new job with one of the big international banks."

"Yeah? Doing what?"

"I'm—" she hoped he wouldn't think she was bragging "—a vice president."

He looked not surprised nor impressed but oddly satisfied. "You were always so smart. I figured you'd be running the world by now."

"It's a job," she said, which it was. A good job, a high-paying job, a prestigious job. She'd been excited enough when she landed the position to splurge on a Cartier watch for herself, and she'd booked a celebratory vacation trip to St. Bart's. She'd felt powerful, successful, proud to be a vice president at a major financial corporation.

But as she was learning, even a VP at a huge financial company could feel wobbly and anxious sitting at a bar next to her first boyfriend sixteen years after they'd broken up, after they'd broken each other's hearts. No exalted title or humongous salary could change that. "How about you?"

"I work at East River Marketing."

"Doing what?"

He gave her a smug grin and lifted his beer. "I'm a vice president," he said before drinking.

A warm bouquet of emotions flowered inside her. Delight that he'd achieved so much, because back in high school he hadn't been all that ambitious. Pride that he'd risen so high without— at least, the last she'd heard—a college degree. Relief that he wouldn't find her own fancy title intimidating. Bewilderment that she should feel relieved.

"Are you still doing art?" she asked.

"Well, there's some art involved. I'm in charge of design and production. I design environments that reflect the clients' brands. We try to find intuitive ways to brand the client, subliminal ways to communicate what the client is all about to the customers they're trying to reach. It's pretty creative."

"You were always such a talented artist."

At that he scoffed modestly. "I drew cartoons."

"Wonderful cartoons. And other things, too. Gorgeous stuff." She almost blurted out that she'd saved every drawing he'd ever given her. But she wasn't entirely sure why she'd saved them, and she decided it was best to avoid that subject. "You were very talented," she assured him. "Obviously, you still are."

He shrugged. "I finally found a job that can hold my interest. It's fun. Every day I'm doing something different. I can't get bored. They throw money at me and treat me like a god."

"Really." It was her turn to scoff.

"Well, they put up with me."

"They must be very tolerant."

He accepted her ribbing with a good-natured grin. "It's a great job. All these years, I finally found what I was meant to do."

"I knew you weren't meant to pump gas," she said, then bit her lip. She shouldn't have mentioned his old summer job. He might think she was condescending or contemptuous of the work he'd done. He might think back to that romantic summer after high school, and how it had ended, how they had ended.

If her comment bothered him, he didn't let on. "You're looking great, Erika," he said. He leaned toward her and an odd shiver of excitement seized her, but then she realized he was only reaching for his beer. His eyes never leaving her, he took a sip and lowered his glass. "It's obvious life is treating you well."

"I can't complain."

"Do you still ride?"

"Horses?" She sighed. "Not often. I just don't have the time to commit to it."

He opened his mouth and then shut it without speaking. What had he been about to say? Something about time, perhaps? Something about commitment?

She might have explained that she was a perfectionist, that to ride the way she'd ridden during her competitive days would entail more effort than she could devote to the sport. As a child and a teenager, she'd spent every spare minute she wasn't doing schoolwork at the stables, training. She'd been good. Better than good. Her parents still had all her ribbons and trophies stored in their house—enough ribbons and trophies to fill several shelves. She'd qualified for Nationals. She'd ridden in the Meadowlands and at Madison Square Garden. For her, riding hadn't been just a girlie thing. It had been her life, her one true passion . . . until she'd started dating Ted.

Now, she was doing other things, pursuing other passions . . . although, for the life of her, she wasn't sure what those passions might be. The job she'd just landed was a major score, but it wasn't her passion. How could high-stress paper-pushing at a financial company be anybody's passion?

"So," he said with disconcerting nonchalance, "are you seeing anyone?"

She imitated his casual tone when she replied, "I'm seeing lots of people." Which was both true and false. In Fanelli's alone, she could see several dozen people.

She knew what Ted was asking, of course. And sure, she was seeing people. No one for whom the word *passion* would be relevant. She'd pretty much given up on finding her soul mate; she no longer believed such a person existed. And she was all right with that.

Dating was fun. Sex could be, on occasion, even more fun. She'd like to have a child someday, and she supposed she'd need a man for that. Or a sperm bank. She could easily imagine herself feeling passionate about motherhood.

"No one serious, huh," Ted said.

She shook her head. "How about you?"

He hesitated, and she felt a sudden, painful spasm in the vicinity of her heart. It shouldn't bother her that Ted was involved with someone—just as she shouldn't have been nervous about seeing him at all. They were *old friends*, she reminded herself. Old friends rejoiced in one another's good fortune when one of them found true love.

The tiny pang of regret, or envy, or whatever it was she was experiencing was just a vestigial thing, a remnant of nostalgic memory of their long-dead romance.

"I'm sort of . . . well, yeah," he said.

Curiosity mixed with the regret, envy, and other unidentifiable emotions spinning through her. Who was he seeing? What was she like? Gorgeous? Blond? Blessed with big boobs?

She smothered her curiosity. Honestly, she'd rather not know. "Good," she said with what she hoped was a friendly smile. An *old friends* smile.

"I don't know where she and I are headed," he went on, then shrugged. "But we've been together a while, so . . ."

"You're a great catch," Erika said, meaning it. "She's a lucky woman."

He flashed her another bright smile. "Thanks."

"Girls always loved you. You were so adorable."

"Oh, yeah." He laughed. "That's me. Adorable." His smile faded and he took several long swallows of beer, draining his glass. "This has been great, Fred, but I'm afraid I've got to hit the road."

That he'd called her "Fred"—his old nickname for her, a play on her last name—touched her. That he so abruptly announced that he had to leave touched her in a different, colder way. She would have been happy to sit talking with him some more. Not about the lucky woman who'd snared him, but about other things. About how he'd spent the last sixteen years of his life. About whether he valued the same things now that he did then, whether he still listened to Phish and Fleetwood Mac, whether he still thought donkeys were cuter than horses.

Her glass was nearly half full, but this encounter was over. It was good-bye time. A few long swallows drained the last of the beer from the glass. "This has been great," she said as she lowered her glass. "Thanks so much for the drink."

"My pleasure."

"I'm glad you got in touch." *Shut up, Erika. It's good-bye time.*

"I'm glad I did, too." He caught the bartender's eye, and he hustled over and asked if they wanted to order another round. Ted declined, placed a few bills on the bar next to his empty glass, and stood. "Maybe we can do this again sometime," he said.

"That would be nice." Erika wondered if he would have stayed longer if they hadn't ventured onto the subject of seeing other people. She wondered if his sudden desire to leave had to do with his current lover. She wondered why she was wondering. She wondered why she even cared. She wondered if *old friends* no longer described what they were to each other. *Former* friends might be more accurate. *Former more-than-friends.*

"I'm glad you were free," he added once he'd escorted her through the crowd and out onto Prince Street. "Both of us working in Manhattan now . . . how could we not get together?"

"Absolutely." The rain was coming down a little harder now, cool drops dancing across her cheeks and settling into her hair.

"It was good seeing you."

"You, too," she said, convinced at that moment that she meant it. It was good seeing how he'd turned out. That long-ago summer they'd been together, he'd seemed so aimless, so unmotivated. No plans for college. No career goals. He'd wanted only one thing in life back then: her.

And he couldn't have her. As rhapsodic as their relationship had been, she couldn't stand to be the one single goal in an eighteen-year-old boy's life. She'd wanted so many other things: a college degree, travel, adventures, experience. To have given up all her dreams and ambitions because Ted loved her and wanted her to be his wife would have killed her.

Killed them both, probably. Or, like so many ill-prepared teenagers who'd married too young, they might well have wound up wanting to kill each other.

Prince Street was even more crowded than when she'd arrived at Fanelli's. Despite the summer rain, people filled the sidewalks, strolling, pub-crawling, flirting, on their way to a restaurant or an off-off Broadway performance or a gallery opening. Or they were just hanging out, gossiping, grabbing a smoke, gazing at one another with invitations in their eyes.

Erika was on her way nowhere and extending no invitations. She just wanted to leave, get away, go home. She felt a headache taking shape behind her eyes, blossoming in her temples.

"So," Ted said.

"Thanks again for the drink," she said. "And for getting in touch. This was lovely." She'd never been a good liar, and she worried that he'd be able to see right through her words to the truth, which was that it hadn't been lovely at all.

If he guessed she was lying, he didn't call her on it. He appeared pensive, lost in his own thoughts. "Yeah, well." He smiled, a crooked, tentative curve of his lips, then wrapped her in a quick hug. She caught a whiff of his scent—clean, spicy, irrefutably male—and felt the warmth of his embrace for a moment too brief to measure. And then he released her. "Take care, Erika," he said.

"You, too." She managed one more bright, cheery, utterly phony *old-friends* smile for him, then pivoted on her heel and strolled down the sidewalk, weaving among the milling pedestrians, picking her way around the puddles, refusing to look back.

She made it all the way around the corner with her head held high and that fake smile frozen on her lips. Then, in the shadow of a brownstone, her smile collapsed. The sky wept on her, big, cool raindrops. And she started to sob.

Two

SIXTEEN YEARS EARLIER

You think it's going to be just another day. It starts out normal: pounding on the bathroom door because your sister Nancy is in there and—hello!—she is not the only person in the family with a bladder that needs emptying, but she sees nothing wrong in tying up the room for what seems like hours while she fusses with her hair or curls her eyelashes or whatever the hell she does when she's beaten everyone else to the bathroom and locked herself inside. Then a hike across the yard to the barn to feed the animals, who live there in pairs like the creatures of Noah's Ark and who are fortunate enough not to have an obnoxious younger sister hogging the bathroom, but who instead use the barn as their bathroom, so there's inevitably a mess or two to clean up. Back to the house to make your bed, which is marginally easier now that a couple of your older brothers have left home and you're no longer fighting for access to your berth in one of the two bunk beds in the cramped bedroom all four of you have shared for most of your childhood—and is also marginally easier because said older brothers aren't thumping you on the head or hauling you out of their way so they can gain access to the closet. Then breakfast—invariably healthy, nutritious stuff, eggs or oatmeal, because when you're a wrestler you don't want to gain weight

15

consuming the empty calories provided by doughnuts or sugary cereal.

You check your watch, grab your jacket and your backpack, race outside for the bus and wish you were one of the rich kids with a car of your own, because riding the bus to school is dorky, especially when you're a senior. You don't even want to be in school, but hey, it's the law, and at least your friends are there, and no one dares to thump you or shove you because everyone knows that, thanks to your training as a wrestler, you can flip and pin them in no time flat. And you've got art to look forward to, if you can manage to survive trig and biology and health, which it's practically impossible to sit through without snickering because the teacher acts as if no one knows what a condom is and she's got to explain it to you four different ways. And after school, wrestling practice, and after that a detour to Country Coffee Shop for a cheese steak with some of the guys from the team.

And then, while you're leaving Country Coffee Shop with the taste of cheese and onions lingering on your tongue, and climbing into your teammate Will's car, your old friend Laura Maher drives across the parking lot, rolls down her window, and calls out to you, "Hey, Ted—I know the perfect girl for you," and then drives away before you can demand that she tell you who the perfect girl is.

And suddenly your day isn't just like any other day.

"Who?" Ted shouted after Laura, but she was long gone, leaving only the sour scent of her car's exhaust behind. "Who's this perfect girl?"

Will gave him a playful shove. Matt, who'd been about to get into the backseat, muttered the name of a really creepy girl who'd been in several of Ted's classes in elementary school and had the habit of eating her own boogers, which, Ted supposed, was better than eating someone else's boogers but not by much.

"It better not be her," Ted said. Not that he thought ill of any of his classmates, and she'd probably outgrown the whole booger thing long ago, but still. Whoever this perfect girl was, he wanted her to be . . . okay, call him shallow, but he wanted her to be beautiful. He wanted her to be sweet and smart and funny, too, but beautiful was pretty high up on his list. If he got to vote on particulars, he wanted her to have long, straight, light brown hair with golden highlights shimmering through it, and big brown eyes, and the kind of dimples that didn't look like someone had dented her face with an awl but were subtle and graceful and drew his eyes to her elegant cheeks.

Elegant. Yes. He wanted her to be elegant.

He wanted her to be a few inches shorter than him, and physically fit, and he wanted her to have perfect posture. He wanted her to walk with purpose, as if she knew where she was heading, and where she was heading was exactly where she wanted to be.

Not that he had a specific girl in mind or anything.

Will muttered, "I think we've lost him, doctor," while Matt cupped his hands over his mouth and did the whole "Earth to Skala" thing. Ted shook his head to clear it. Sometimes he thought of his brain as an Etch-a-Sketch; one sharp shake and whatever image he wanted to erase dissolved, leaving him with a flat gray emptiness.

But the image of Erika Fredell never really disappeared from his mind.

How long had he had a crush on her?

When was the first time he'd ever seen her? That long.

Not that she cared about him, one way or another. He could plant himself in front of her, douse himself in gasoline, and light a match, and she'd probably say, "I really should try to put this fire out, but I've got to go horseback riding."

That was what she did. He knew this because Mendham High was small enough for everyone to know everything, at least about the people in their own class, and because he and Erika traveled in overlapping social circles. He knew that Erika didn't just go horseback riding. She was into competitive riding, show jumping. Equestrianism. He'd first heard about that from a classmate who lived near her and told Ted she was an "Aquarian," as if her zodiac sign carried special significance. It took him a few days to find out she was an *equestrian*, not an *Aquarian*. But by now, everyone in the school knew how seriously she took her riding. Hell, she rode in national competitions. She won ribbons and trophies. When it came to horses, she was hot stuff.

As a jock in a family of jocks, Ted had a great deal of respect for winners.

He had even more respect for Erika Fredell's discipline. He was in awe of the fact that she went to a stable every day after school to train. Every single day. Weekends, she trained some more, or traveled to competitions. Unlike him and his friends, she didn't hang around the school after the final bell rang. She didn't loiter in the school's parking lot or down by the bleachers. She never showed up at Country Coffee Shop on early release days, when half the school wound up there to buy burgers or ice cream.

He didn't have a prayer with her, he knew that. She took honors classes. She dwelled a few rungs up the economic ladder from him and lived in a big house with, he was willing to bet, more than one bathroom.

Besides, one of the frustrating mysteries of love was that the girl you had a crush on was never the same person as the girl who had a crush on you. If Erika Fredell had a crush on anyone, it was probably one of the rich boys, someone sophisticated, someone as at home in the world of horse shows as she was. Ted had heard rumors back in sophomore year that she was seeing an older guy, although he had no idea how much older the guy was. Older than Ted, in any case. Then she'd dated someone on the lacrosse team for a while, and Ted had thought, *lacrosse?* Why date someone who needed a stick to play his game when you could date a wrestler who relied on nothing but his own body to excel in his sport? Maybe the stick had turned her on. Expensive equipment might have appealed to her.

Or might not. She wasn't with the lacrosse player anymore. She wasn't with anybody. Ted was friendly with her, but not friendly enough to ask why. He figured that either she thought mere high school boys were beneath her or she was too busy with her horses to be bothered with the whole social scene. Given her schedule—schoolwork, training, competing—she couldn't possibly have time to think about boys, let alone go out with one.

And anyway, he was dating Kate, and he shouldn't even be thinking about Erika. A two-year-old crush was a silly thing, kind of lame, kind of pointless. Kate was nice enough, she was cute, she was hot, and he should count his blessings.

For some reason, thinking about Kate gave him heartburn. Or maybe it was the cheese steak he'd just eaten. He tried not to consume junk food during wrestling season, because he had to make weight before each meet. Cheese steaks were a treat he indulged in no more than once a week. For the most part, he tried to stick to a diet of high-quality protein and veggies during the season. He might not have the kind of discipline a girl like Erika had, spending every freaking afternoon practicing her jumps and turns and figure eights, or whatever it was she did on her horse, but when it came to wrestling he knew how to focus. Better to eat smart than to have to sweat off pounds in a sauna hours before a meet.

He wondered if Erika Fredell ever attended a wrestling meet. It wasn't like wrestling attracted the kind of audience the football team did, or the basketball team. The wrestling team probably had more fans in attendance at its meets than the lacrosse team did, but that wasn't saying much.

If she did attend wrestling meets, he wouldn't know. He never looked at the audience when he was wrestling. Too distracting. If he knew she was there, he might start showing off for her, hot-dogging, trying high-risk maneuvers. He might lose his concentration. Just as he'd be going for a pin, he'd glimpse her in the stands and forget where he was, and next thing, he'd be shoulders against the mat, listening to the ref count him out.

Once he, Will, and Matt were in the car and tearing out of the parking lot, the other guys decided to devote themselves to figuring out who his perfect girl was. "Emily," Will guessed. "She's been with every guy in the school at least once. It's probably your turn, Skala."

"Yeah," Matt chimed in. "She's run out of other guys. You're the only one left."

"And she doesn't like Kate, so it makes sense that she'd try to steal you from her."

"Maybe she's not into you at all. Maybe she just wants to piss Kate off."

"Kate's pretty easy to piss off," Will noted. "You piss her off all the time, Skala, don't you?"

Ted laughed good-naturedly with his friends, and secretly suppressed the desire to throw a few punches. He didn't mind being teased; growing up with four older brothers, he'd developed a skin as thick as a rhino's. But being teased about girls rankled him, for some reason.

Probably because he knew the one girl he dreamed about, the one girl he believed was perfect, would never be interested in someone like him.

"Come on," Laura's voice spun through the wire. "It's just a small party. You should go."

Erika lounged on the bed, her head cushioned by her pillow and the phone receiver tucked against her ear. "I'll be riding all day Saturday," she said. "Then I'm supposed to go out to a party that night?"

"That's the general idea. I'm riding, too," Laura reminded her. "A day in the saddle has never kept me from a night of partying."

Erika sighed, although Laura's cheerful wheedling made her smile. "I'll be exhausted."

"Take a nap."

"And smelling like a horse."

"Take a shower."

"What's so special about this party?" she demanded to know.

"It's senior year, Erika. You need to go to at least one party before you graduate."

"Oh, good. I thought you were going to say I needed to go to at least one party before I die."

"That, too."

"I go to parties," Erika defended herself. In general, she went to parties only because Laura dragged her to them. Laura was one of her closest riding friends. They'd known each other for years, from back when Erika's family was still living in South Orange. The Fredells had moved to Mendham when Erika was about to start tenth grade—a horrible time to move to a new town and a new high school. Everyone else in the high school already knew one another. They'd grown up together. They had memories of one another dating back to preschool. They'd eaten cookies and milk at one another's houses, swum in one another's pools, played hoops and sung in the school choir together. Erika had been the odd one out, the new girl who had no history with these people.

But she'd survived. Most of her social circle had consisted of other riders when she'd lived in South Orange, and the same was true in Mendham. She was glad her family had moved, because Mendham was horse country. Her family's new house was much closer to the stable where she trained, much closer to Five Star, her favorite horse.

And much closer to Laura Maher, whom she'd known for years through riding and who attended a private school in Morristown, one town away. Even if they didn't see each other in school, they could get together afterward. And Laura could drag Erika to parties, which she did with frequency despite implying that the party she wanted Erika to accompany her to this Saturday would be the one and only party Erika went to before she died. Or graduated.

"You'll know a lot of the people there," Laura promised.

"Who?"

"The usual people. Kids from Mendham and Morristown. Allyson will be there."

The party suddenly became much more appealing to Erika. Allyson Rhatican was her closest friend at the high school. Allyson didn't ride, but like Erika, she'd lived in South Orange before moving to Mendham in middle school. By the time Erika's family had moved to Mendham a few years later, Allyson was one of the most popular girls in town. And she'd chosen to take a fellow South Orange refugee under her wing.

If Erika was stuck knowing only one person in the entire school, Allyson had been the right person to know. If not for her, Erika would probably still be a loner two years after her arrival in

Mendham, acquainted with no one, a weirdo pariah at Mendham High.

Which, as far as she was concerned, wouldn't have been the end of the world. But between Allyson's willingness to welcome Erika into her circle and Laura's insistence on dragging Erika to parties, Erika didn't have much chance to be a hermit.

"And there's tons of bedrooms," Laura cajoled. "If you play your cards right, you won't have to sleep on the living room floor."

Erika laughed. Most people thought of New Jersey as an industrial sprawl, the New Jersey Turnpike slashing through miles of factories and refineries that belched pollution into the air. But New Jersey was the Garden State, and the northwest corner, where Mendham was located, justified that nickname. The region was bucolic, its rolling hills dotted with small farms and stables and homes surrounded by vast, undeveloped acreage. When someone was hosting a party, the guests often wound up spending the night rather than facing a long drive home. The host's parents would collect kids' car keys as the kids arrived so no one would be tempted to cruise home, twenty or more miles over the winding, unlit country roads, after partying half the night.

Erika had slept on a few floors after parties. Couches were better than the floor. Beds were better than couches.

"All right," she conceded. "If I'm not too tired, I'll go to the party with you."

"Don't be too tired," Laura warned her. "I'll pick you up around eight."

On days when Erika was competing in a horse show, she often arose as early as three-thirty in the morning to allow herself the time she needed to dress, eat, drive to the stable with one of her parents, load Five Star into the trailer, and then travel to the venue. When she'd told Laura she might be too tired afterward to attend a party that evening, she hadn't meant that the riding itself would exhaust her. In fact, she found riding invigorating. She loved the way she felt perched in her saddle, the way she and Five Star read each other, felt each other, merged until they were like a single living creature gliding down the course and then leaping, levitating, soaring over the fences. After a good ride, she was invariably invigorated, drunk on her own adrenaline.

But the early mornings, the long drives, the brisk air, the noise and bustle and stress—all of that tired her out.

Still, she had promised to go to the party with Laura on Saturday night. She was hardly the most social girl in Mendham, yet she appreciated Laura's attempts to liberate her from her tidy, limited world of high school and riding. And Laura was right: she was a senior. She'd already received an early-decision acceptance into Colorado College's Summer Start program, which meant she'd be starting college over the summer rather than in the fall. Her plans were in place. She ought to cut loose a little.

So when she got back from her horse show on Saturday, with a new ribbon to add to the scores she already possessed, she napped, showered, and shampooed the heavy perfume of leather and sweat and hay and horse from her hair. When Laura pulled into her driveway at a few minutes past eight that evening, Erika climbed into her car, gave her friend a smile and said, "Here I am."

Laura drove out into the country. Erika was used to the hills and forests, meadows and split-log fences, but she still responded to the beauty of northwestern New Jersey's landscape. If only she had a modicum of artistic talent, she'd capture the pastoral scenery in a painting. She was in awe of people who could paint and draw and sculpt. All she seemed able to do was earn good grades and ride.

She assured herself that that was enough.

She wasn't one of those girls who got all insecure and self-conscious at parties. As a competitive rider, she'd developed a level of confidence that was probably disproportionately high, given that she was cursed with her fair share of flaws and short-comings. She'd learned that if you lacked confidence, you couldn't compete in show jumping. The horse would feel your fear, and you wouldn't be able to commit to the jump.

The lessons learned on the back of a horse stayed with a rider once her boots were planted on the ground. She saw no point in second-guessing herself. If she was filled with doubt, she'd fall, so she refused to admit to any doubt.

The party was already going strong by the time she and Laura descended the stairs to the rec room of the sprawling mansion. Music blasted from a pair of floor speakers—Pearl Jam—and at least thirty kids filled the room, a couple playing a SEGA game on the TV in the corner with a small audience surrounding them and shouting advice, a cluster of kids near the sliding glass doors that opened onto a backyard patio, another cluster crammed onto a pair of overstuffed couches, clutching cans of soda and beer and emptying a gigantic bowl of popcorn, which made the room smell like the lobby of a movie theater. Allyson sat on one of the couches, surrounded by her usual posse of cool friends. The minute she saw Erika, she shifted on the couch and patted the cushion. "Erika! Come eat some of this popcorn before I eat it all," she said.

Erika wiggled her butt into the narrow space on the couch between Allyson and Ted Skala. Fortunately, Ted was pretty skinny and she was able to squeeze in. Or maybe he was just happy to inch closer to his girlfriend Kate, who sat on his other side, a can of light beer clutched in her hand.

"Hey, Fred," Ted greeted her. "How's it going?"

"Great," she said, filled with a sudden rush of delight. Laura had been right to drag her to this party. She'd ridden well, she'd rested, and now she was surrounded by laughing, chattering, popcorn-devouring compatriots who welcomed her into their midst.

She spotted Laura near the cooler chest, wrestling a can of soda from the ice. As Laura straightened, her gaze met Erika's and she raised the can in a toast. Erika grinned as a scruffy guy wearing a sweatshirt that identified him as a student from Delbarton, a private all-boys academy just up the road from Mendham, moved in on Laura. From across the room, Erika could tell when Laura was connecting with her inner flirt. Laura's eyes grew wide, her smile turned mysterious, and the Delbarton boy didn't have a chance.

Someday Erika ought to consider taking flirting lessons from Laura. But her lack of flirting skills didn't bother her. She didn't want a boyfriend. She'd dated two boys since moving to Mendham—one wasn't exactly a boy, and as it had turned out, he wasn't exactly appropriate, either. The other had been a lacrosse player at the high school—and she found that life was a lot simpler without boys or love or sexual pressures or flirtations.

She had no time for love. But on a cold Saturday night after a good day's ride, she had friends and music and a handful of popcorn to stuff into her mouth. More than that she didn't want.

Three

AFTER A WHILE YOU START TO WONDER why every time you go to a party Laura Maher has told you about, Erika Fredell is there, too. Sure, Laura and Erika have been friends since before Erika moved to Mendham. But still, it's kind of funny how often Laura calls and says, "You've really, really got to come to this party, Ted," and you go, and Erika is there.

Maybe it's not funny. Maybe it's not worth noting at all. Maybe Laura calls up everyone she knows and tells them they really, really have to go to this or that party, and you and Erika are the only people who actually obey Laura when she starts spewing the really's.

Maybe you're just aware of the coincidence because you're so aware of Erika. Because she's the coolest girl you've ever known, and you love the fact that you and she are actually friends, however superficially. Because you want to be more than friends with her.

Which is nuts, because you've already got a girlfriend, and Erika obviously isn't interested in anything more than friendship with you. And why should she be? She's rich. She's smart. She's a champion rider. She's in a class by herself.

At least you can count her as a friend. At least she doesn't hesitate to plunk herself down on the sofa next to you when she arrives at a party and send you a gorgeous smile that makes your pulse rate accelerate.

With someone like Erika, you take what you can get. In your book, friendship is worth a lot. Especially her friendship. So if you can't have more than friendship with her, you accept what you can have, and you're grateful for it.

Ted felt like an asshole. There he was, his arm slung around Kate, whom he'd been dating for months, and all he could think of was that Erika Fredell was sitting next to him. The couch was so crowded that every time she moved, he felt her—her elbow poking his ribs, her shoulder bumping his, her thigh pressed against his. Her hair brushing his cheek like a whisper of silk when she turned her head.

He wished Kate would get up and go somewhere. Just to give them all a little more room on the sofa, he told himself, but this wasn't about comfort. Although sandwiched between the girl he was seeing and the girl he had a crush on was kind of an uncomfortable place to wind up.

As if he'd spoken his preference out loud, Kate abruptly pushed herself to her feet, one hand on the arm of the sofa and the other on Ted's knee. Ordinarily, having a pretty girl's hand on his knee would turn him on. But as he stared at Kate's fingers pressed into his leg, all he could think of was, *I wish Erika's hand was there.* Kate said something about someone who'd just arrived, and she leaned over and kissed his cheek—not the cheek Erika's hair had brushed against—and he nodded and grinned and pretended to be hugely interested in whatever the hell she was telling him. Then she spun away and crossed the room to where a couple of other girls were standing, and Ted was able to shift on the sofa, putting a sliver of space between himself and Erika.

Much as he missed the contact of her thigh against his, moving a couple of inches from her enabled him to turn so he could look at her. The smile she gave him was dazzling. But then, he was pretty much dazzled by anything she did.

"So, here we are again," she said cheerfully. "Every party I go to, I see you."

"I'm such a party animal," he joked, secretly thrilled that she'd also noticed how Laura was always inviting them both to the same parties. "How's it going?" he asked.

"I'm tired," she said, though she looked refreshed and downright sparkling to him.

"Yeah, life is boring, isn't it." *I'm Too Sexy* started playing and Ted sang along, doctoring the words to fit Erika: "I'm too sleepy for my shirt . . ."

She laughed. "Listen to you sing. You have well-hidden talents."

"Oh, yeah, I'm a really good singer," he bragged, then shrugged. "My mother made all us kids participate in choir from an early age. So I learned how to sing. I was even the lead singer in a rock band for a few minutes."

"No kidding?"

"We sucked," he added with a laugh. "We played at a school dance once, and managed to empty the room in no time flat." He took a swig from the bottle of beer he was holding, then extended it to her when he noticed she didn't have a drink.

To his great delight, she took the bottle, raised it to her lips and sipped. He liked knowing her lips closed around the glass where his had just been. "I took a nap but I'm still tired," she told him as she handed the bottle back. "I rode in a show today. I had to get up before dawn."

"Where do you find the energy?" he asked, genuinely impressed.

"I don't. That's why I took a nap." Because he'd given her a little more room on the couch, she was able to settle deeper into the cushions. Her hair swayed gently around her face, straight and glossy, and he was glad to see she wasn't wearing lipstick. Kate wore lipstick all the time, and it made her mouth taste funny when they kissed. "You probably slept 'til noon."

"I did not," he defended himself. "I was up at dawn, too."

"I was up *before* dawn," she reminded him.

Her competitive spirit amused him. "You got up before dawn and rode horses. I got up *at* dawn and fed sheep."

"You have sheep?"

"Two sheep. Ba Ba and Bunky."

Her eyebrows rose. "Ba Ba? That's its name?"

He launched into another song: "'Baa baa, black sheep . . .' Only our sheep aren't black."

"So, you fed the sheep," she said, her eyes glowing with amusement. "I didn't know you were a farm boy."

"Yeah, that's me. And then—in case you thought I went back to bed after feeding the sheep, and the ducks, and the rabbits—"

"My God, it's a whole menagerie," she said.

"We've got a big barn, and my mother likes to keep it filled. I'm lucky she doesn't make me live there."

"I suppose you're a little neater than the sheep and the ducks."

"A little. But the rabbits are so neat they're practically anal."

That she laughed at his stupid joke pleased him enormously.

"And then I spent the day helping my dad grout the bathroom."

"Wow. That must have been fun." Sarcasm filtered through her tone.

Sealing the bathroom tiles with fresh grout wasn't exactly fun, but Ted was used to helping his father with home repairs. When you lived in a nearly two-hundred-year-old house, things were always falling apart and demanding attention. Ted and his brothers and sister had grown up learning how to deal with dry rot, how to unclog pipes, how to change a fuse and rewire a light switch without electrocuting themselves. When his parents asked for assistance from their children, they received it. Sometimes eagerly, sometimes begrudgingly, but Ted's parents worked damned hard and they deserved whatever assistance they asked for.

He could have thought of a dozen things he'd rather be doing that day than smearing white paste around the tiles edging the bathtub. Sleeping until noon would have made his short list. Meeting his friends and driving somewhere. Taking in a movie, maybe, or heading down to the shore, even though it was off season. *Especially* because it was off season and the beach would be empty, the boardwalk shuttered and peaceful. Or just going to someone's house, listening to tunes, playing Ghouls 'N Ghosts. Or driving west into Pennsylvania and catching a wrestling meet at Lehigh University. That school was a wrestling powerhouse; Ted and his teammates could probably learn a hell of a lot just by watching the Lehigh boys do their thing on the mat.

But when his dad said he needed help, Ted helped. With his older brothers one foot into adulthood and independence, he helped even more. His parents were getting older, and the house was already too old.

"The problem with the grouting," he told Erika before drinking a little more beer, "is that the ghosts eat it."

"What ghosts?"

"The ghosts that live in my house."

"Oh. Right." She rolled her eyes and laughed.

"You think I'm kidding? The place is haunted."

"I'm sure it is." She wiggled her fingers in the air, as if conjuring a spirit from the beyond, and attempted a spooky moan, although it didn't sound the least bit scary. She was probably the kind of girl who used to dress as a fairy princess or a ballerina on Halloween, not realizing that the whole idea of the holiday was to frighten people. Fairy princesses and ballerinas were about as frightening as Ba Ba and Bunky.

"My house sits on what used to be a cemetery," he explained. "Pleasant Hill Road. You know the Pleasant Hill Cemetery?"

She nodded, still obviously amused and skeptical.

"The original location of the cemetery is where my house sits. The bodies were moved down the street to where the cemetery is now, and my house was built on the land where their graves used to be."

She took a minute to digest this. "So the bodies were moved down the street, but their souls remained behind?"

"I don't know if they remained behind or they just wander back down the street to visit their old home."

"Their old *haunt*, you mean?" Her eyes glinted with suppressed laughter.

Bad pun, but he appreciated it anyway. "Exactly. You should come to my house sometime, Erika. Just sit on the stairs and turn off the lights. You'll hear them moving around. You'll *feel* them."

"Just what I want to do," she said. "Sit on a stairway in the dark and listen for ghosts."

"You don't have to listen for them. You'll hear them."

"What do they sound like?"

He leaned toward her, hoping he looked somber and just a little bit spooky. "They sneak up behind you and whisper. You feel their icy breath on the back of your neck. They say, 'Eh-eh-eh-eh-rik-ah-ah-ah.'" He murmured her name long and low and realized he probably sounded more like a dog on the prowl than a ghost. When Spot, his golden retriever, the one animal allowed to live in the house rather than the barn, sensed a dog in heat within a three-mile radius, he made a deep, groaning sound like Ted's throaty wail.

"These ghosts would know my name?"

"Sure. They're from the beyond. They know everything." He reached behind her and ran his fingers lightly over the nape of her neck. "It feels like this," he whispered. "You feel their nearness right here."

She held her breath for a moment, then laughed and leaned away from him. "If this is supposed to be scary, it's not working."

"Of course it's not. I'm not a ghost." But he liked having his hand against her smooth, soft skin, with her hair spilling like rain over his fingers.

"Are you telling her about the ghosts?" Kate asked.

He hadn't even realized she had returned to the sofa. He withdrew his hand from Erika's neck and smiled up at his girlfriend. "She doesn't believe they exist," he told Kate. "Tell her I'm not making this up."

Kate eyed Erika and grinned. "He's not making this up," she recited, sounding not the least bit convincing. Then she extended her hand, wrapped her fingers around his wrist and tugged. "Matt thinks one of his tires is flat. He wants you to look at it."

Ted allowed himself to be hauled to his feet. He shot Erika a long-suffering look. "Not only can I grout a bathroom, but I can also change a tire," he said. "I'm the most handy guy in this room."

"And you can ward off ghosts, too," Erika said, then exchanged an amused look with Kate. "What a guy. You'd better hang onto him."

"'Yeah," Kate said. "Just in case I ever have a flat, or a ghost."

"Or a bathtub in need of grouting," Ted reminded them both before following Kate through the room to the back door, away from Erika.

Just as well, he thought as he stepped outside and the cold evening air slapped his face. He shouldn't be coming on to Erika when he was at a party with Kate. He shouldn't be caressing the nape of Erika's neck when he was sleeping with Kate. He shouldn't be thinking the things he always thought when Erika was in the vicinity.

Especially since she clearly had no interest in him. If she did, she wouldn't be advising Kate to hang onto him.

What was that song he sometimes heard when his parents had the radio tuned to oldies rock? *If you can't be with the one you love, love the one you're with.*

He supposed he could do that, he thought as he wove his fingers through Kate's and paused by the side of the garage to kiss her. But the lyrics that remained with him were from the song they'd been listening to in the rec room.

I'm too sexy for my love . . .

He wouldn't tell Kate she was too sexy, because she wasn't.

And he wouldn't tell Erika she was too sexy, because even though she was, that was something she didn't seem inclined to believe.

Four

ERIKA HAD NEVER GONE TO A WRESTLING MATCH at the high school. She never had the time. She was always racing off as soon as the final bell rang, hurrying to her car and driving down to the stable to squeeze in a riding lesson before the sun set. But that afternoon it was raining, and she didn't feel like practicing in the indoor corral. The indoor air tended to get musty, and the horses kicked up sawdust and sand that left her nose congested and her eyes watery. She put up with a lot in her training regimen—willingly, happily—but when Allyson mentioned that she and a few other girls were going to check out the wrestling meet after school, Erika decided to skip practice and join them.

Just out of curiosity. Just for a change of pace. Just because.

She met up with Allyson and the others after their last class and strolled down the hall to the gym. "You'll have to explain everything to me," she warned Allyson as they reached the gym's double doors. "All I know about wrestling is that goofy stuff on TV, with the guys on steroids breaking chairs over each other's heads."

"This is a little different," Allyson said dryly, then laughed. "I don't know too much about the sport, either. But it's fun to watch."

"It is?"

"Allyson likes to check out the guys," one of the other girls teased.

Allyson didn't argue. "They wear these skin-tight singlets that don't hide much. You'll see."

Erika shook her head and grinned. Allyson was so much more into guys than Erika was. Not that she was averse to admiring buff male bodies should the opportunity arise. That afternoon, apparently, the opportunity had arisen.

She followed Allyson and the others into the gym. The bleachers weren't exactly crowded; no more than a hundred students sat along the polished wooden benches that extended out from one cinderblock wall, and a fair number of them were unfamiliar to Erika. She surmised they were from the visiting team's school.

Allyson, Erika, and the others climbed halfway up the bleachers and settled in a row on an empty bench. Down below, the gym floor was covered by a large blue mat with a broad circle printed on it. "The wrestlers have to stay inside the circle," Allyson told her. "They lose points if they step outside the circle. See?" she added, turning to the other girls. "I know more about wrestling than just how cute the guys look with their rippling muscles on display."

Rippling muscles on display. That sounded like fun to Erika.

A few more students trickled into the gym and climbed onto the bleachers. The visiting team filed into the gym through a locker-room door and Erika gave them the once-over. She paid less attention to their physiques than to whether they looked mean and tough and capable of trouncing the Mendham High School boys.

Maybe. Maybe not.

Their fans in the stands greeted them with a cheer that sounded pretty anemic. A few dozen fans couldn't very well roar like a stadium full of crazed football lovers. Their cheers echoed off the hard walls, the high ceiling, and the steel rafters spanning the gym overhead, and then were swallowed by the much louder cheering of the Mendham fans welcoming their team as they marched proudly from the locker room into the gym.

Erika recognized a couple of them—that huge guy at the end of the line was in her English class, and he looked a lot more fit in his uniform than he did in the baggy, droopy clothes he wore to class, which seemed chosen to conceal his enormous bulk. Erika had always assumed he was fat. He wasn't exactly skinny, but he boasted more muscle than flab.

At the opposite end of the line, leading the team in, was a short, skinny boy, an underclassman, Erika was pretty sure. She couldn't think of any seniors as small as he was. Unlike the uniform of the heavyweight wrestler, which stretched as taut as an overinflated balloon on his hulking frame, the featherweight wrestler's uniform puckered slightly under his arms. The uniforms reminded her of pictures she'd seen of men's swimsuits in the Roaring Twenties. Narrow shoulder straps, a U-shaped neckline that revealed a serious lack of hair on the chests of the Mendham wrestlers, the form-fitting fabric ending at mid-thigh. The singlets were so snug on most of the wrestlers, they looked as if they'd been painted on.

Ted Skala looked damned good in a singlet, she noted.

She'd known he was a wrestler. One of the team stars, in fact. Unlike some of his teammates, he didn't have a compact, powerful build. His limbs were long and lean, his shoulders bony. Because he was thin, his muscles seemed more clearly defined. He stared straight ahead, refusing to acknowledge the cheers of the Mendham fans as he moved with his teammates to the home-team bench.

"They don't wear regular sneakers, huh," she whispered to Allyson.

"I think those shoes are more flexible."

The shoes the wrestlers wore resembled high-tops without the padding and the thick soles. Not very flattering, but Erika supposed that if she and Allyson were there to ogle, she could focus her ogling higher, on the wrestlers' sturdy legs and solid torsos. Or, in at least one wrestler's case, on his lean limbs and bony shoulders.

An announcer called the first wrestlers to the mat—the tiny featherweight boys. They scampered around inside the circle, grabbing each other, twisting each other, flopping, flipping. One was on top, then the other. Despite their diminutive size, they were obviously strong, using leverage and agility. When Allyson cheered, Erika cheered. When the other wrestler seemed ascendant, she scowled. The referee hovered over them, whistle in mouth, watching their moves almost voyeuristically.

"This is interesting," she said when the first bout was over, with a win for the Mendham featherweight.

"Not exactly like show jumping, huh," Allyson replied.

Indeed, it wasn't. It wasn't like any sport she'd ever watched. The wrestlers were a team, but they competed solo. There was a rawness to their bouts, something profoundly elemental. No equipment was used, no bats, no balls, no sticks or pads, and instead of helmets they wore what appeared to be glorified ear muffs strapped over their skulls and under their chins. Given the intimacy of the wrestlers' combat, she imagined that unprotected ears would be vulnerable to injury.

Another pair of wrestlers began their bout. The whistle blew. A buzzer sounded. They rounded each other, gripped each other's waists, bent and stretched and contorted. The visiting wrestler won that bout. His victory was greeted by a smattering of joyful hoots from the visiting school's fans.

"Our next bout will be at one thirty-five," the announcer said. Erika instinctively glanced toward the wall clock above the locker room door, then realized the announcer was referring to the weight class, not the time. Turning back to the mat, she saw Ted Skala rise from the bench, strap on his ear-protecting head gear, and stride to the mat.

He was wearing a game face, not the smile Erika was used to seeing whenever they crossed paths in school or at parties. His jaw was set, his gaze steel-hard. His opponent was a couple of inches shorter and much beefier, his neck as thick as Erika's thigh and his shoulders round with muscle.

"Go, Ted!" a voice a few benches below Erika cried. Craning her neck, she spotted Ted's girlfriend Kate, blond and beautiful and leaning forward, her arms wrapped around her knees and her head tilted to one side so her hair spilled delicately over her shoulder.

Ted ignored her.

Erika watched. There was something almost erotic about the way Ted and the other boy came together, their bodies so close, their arms wrapped around each other, their legs intertwined. Erotic yet ferocious. The other boy looked strong enough to pick Ted up and slam him to the mat, but Ted was sly. He was quick. He broke out of the other boy's embrace, stretched, reached, and suddenly the other boy was down. They tangled together at the center of the circle, Ted straddling the other boy, the other boy trying to writhe free, Ted scissoring his legs, winding his hand around the other boy's shoulder.

He was sweaty and supple and sinewy. And surprisingly strong for such a lanky guy.

The referee got down on his hands and knees next to the two wrestlers. He angled his head, he leaned in and out. He gauged the other boy's shoulders, measured with his eyes how close they were to the mat, and counted to three. He blew his whistle; the buzzer sounded. Ted released the boy, stood, and backed away, breathing hard.

"That was a pin," Allyson unnecessarily informed Erika.

"I figured that out."

"The earlier bouts were decided on points. It's cool when you get a real pin. Ted is so good."

Erika had figured that out, too.

The meet continued, but none of the other bouts held Erika's attention the way Ted's had. The bigger boys made louder thumps when they hit the mats. They grunted more, perspired more, shook the gym more. But they lacked Ted's grace. He'd looked like a dancer on the mat. A calculating dancer, one who seemed to rely on his brain as much as his arms and legs to best his opponent.

She could relate to that. Some sports were pure instinct, but she had always found riding as intellectual as it was physical. Riding was a dance between her and her mount. Whatever the horse did, she had to adjust, rethink, strategize.

She'd sensed Ted's mind churning the entire time he'd been wrestling. He'd been fierce, aggressive, but never out of control, never acting reflexively. At least that was how he'd appeared to her. He'd stepped onto the mat, appraised his opponent as if the guy were a problem he had to solve, and then he'd solved the problem.

Then he'd sat down, not even acknowledging the applause of the people in the stands. He'd removed his headgear and wrapped a towel around his neck. He'd rubbed the towel over his face and through his hair, then twisted to reach for a water bottle on the floor behind the team bench.

His face was still intense and unsmiling, she observed. Even after his match was finished and he'd vanquished his opponent, he still had some fight in his eyes. He shut them as he guzzled water from the bottle, the bone in his neck bobbing with each swallow. Finally rehydrated, he closed the bottle and his gaze met hers.

His eyebrows rose slightly, and the corners of his mouth twitched upward. And then, in less than an instant, his game face returned and he swiveled back to face the mat, shouting encouragement to his teammate who was currently out in the circle, grappling with a guy whose long arms reminded Erika of a gorilla's.

Maybe the reason she found the remaining bouts less interesting wasn't that the other wrestlers weren't as skilled or as clever as Ted. Maybe it was that a part of her mind had wrapped itself around him, the way he'd looked at her for that fraction of a second. She could no longer concentrate fully on the wrestlers on the mat, not when she was distracted by Ted's back, the ridge of his spine visible as he hunched forward and rested his forearms on his knees. The breadth of his shoulders. The tendrils of his hair curling at the nape of his neck as the sweat dried from them.

She'd always thought Ted was a fun, easygoing guy—and he was, most of the time. She gathered that he was a decent artist. She enjoyed being around him, talking to him, laughing with him.

But there was more to him, much more. There was determination. Calculation. Strength. Aggression. The hunger to win.

After watching him wrestle, she would never be able to think of him the same way.

And—even more unsettling—she *would* think of him. Ted Skala had lodged himself in her mind, and she wasn't sure he would ever leave.

Whoa. Erika Fredell had come to a wrestling meet.

Ted wasn't delusional enough to think she'd come specifically to see him wrestle. She'd probably come because she was suffering from an unexpected spasm of school spirit, or because her friends had dragged her with them. Or because she had nothing better to do.

Except he knew she did have something better to do. She had her horseback riding. She did that every afternoon after school. Why had she taken today off?

Not to see you, asshole.

He took another deep slug of water from his bottle, ran the towel over his still sweaty face, and watched the one-sixty-sevens go at it. The heavier the weight class, the less finesse. They didn't need finesse. They had brute strength. As one of the skinnier guys on the team, Ted was all about finesse.

He was used to being the smallest guy. The youngest boy in his family, he'd been an easy target for his three older brothers. He'd learned how to run fast, and when he couldn't run fast enough he'd fought back as best he could. But how could a squirt like him fight back against guys like his brothers, who were all so much larger than him?

His dad must have detected his talent for fighting, or else simply wanted to improve his odds of not getting flattened beneath George's or Adam's or Josh's big, fat fists, because when he was five, his father enrolled him in a wrestling program. His oldest brother, George, was already a wrestler, and Ted had always enjoyed watching the sport. It wasn't just self-defense; it wasn't just a puny kid trying to stay alive in a family of big, domineering older brothers. Wrestling was fighting with rules, fighting with dignity. And fighting someone your own size, which really appealed to Ted.

So he'd started working with a coach and taking lessons, and after a few years he'd gotten good. It no longer mattered that he was small and skinny. By the time he was eight, he could take down pretty much anyone. Well, not his brother George, but anyone who challenged him, the bullies and turds whose sole reason for existence was to make life hard for everyone in Ted's primary school.

When he was out on the mat, the universe was reduced to just the space within the circle. Him, his opponent, and the referee. There was something pure about it, something both profoundly physical and surprisingly intellectual. Wrestling was like playing chess, except your body was all the pieces rolled into one. You had to see three moves into the future, you had to know what your opponent was going to try before he tried it—and sometimes you had to resort to unadulterated force. Wrestling demanded unwavering concentration. Nothing distracted Ted when he was on the mat. Nothing existed but the moment.

If he'd known Erika was in the stands, would that have changed? Hell, he knew Kate was there. She was his girlfriend, and yet he hadn't given her a thought. If she'd been cheering for him, if she'd been fluffing her hair and smiling beguilingly at him, he hadn't known and he hadn't cared.

Now . . . now he was aware of Erika a good ten rows behind and above him. She was undoubtedly watching the one-hundred-sixty-seven-pound guys tussling. Ted's match was done and she'd probably deleted it from her memory bank. There were more interesting things for her to focus on.

But he could hardly focus on his own teammates. He drank some more water and told himself the heat in his body was a residue from his match, not a reaction to her. It *couldn't* be a reaction to her. She was just a girl, a classmate.

Forget about her, Skala. She is so out of your league.

He did his best to tune into the rest of the meet, slapping each teammate's hand as he came off the mat, regardless of whether he'd won or lost. Wrestling was individual combat, but it was also a team sport. Every member of the team had to be there for his teammates. And despite his knowledge that Erika was in the gym, an awareness that hummed inside his brain like white noise, Ted was a team guy. He was there for his wrestling brothers.

Mendham wound up winning the meet. After the battle of the heavyweights, his team shook hands with the other team—false courtesy, but the coaches made their wrestlers pretend that once they left the mat, they and their rivals were all one big, happy family—and then Ted and the rest of the Mendham team retired to the locker room. They listened as the coach lectured them on where they'd done well, where they'd fallen short, when their next meet would be, and what school they'd be wrestling. Ted took it all in as best he could, but his brain was still humming.

Once the coach was done with his speech, Ted headed for the shower room. As he stood beneath the shower's hot spray, he noticed a red welt on his upper arm and recalled the way his opponent had pulled at his skin. Ted had suffered his share of broken fingers and strained muscles from wrestling. A welt was nothing.

Kate would be waiting for him outside the locker room, and he tried to lock onto that thought as he dried off and got dressed. Maybe they could drive down to Village Pizza and buy a couple of slices. His mother would give him hell for eating pizza so close to dinnertime, but Ted was starving. A wedge of pizza wouldn't put a dent in his appetite. Whatever Mom placed before him at the dinner table, he'd wolf it down. She knew the only time he didn't eat was when he was upset about something, and he wasn't upset now. He was kind of jazzed, actually.

Erika Fredell had watched him wrestle. Yeah, definitely jazzed.

He rubbed a towel through his wet hair, then tossed the towel into the hamper outside the shower room, ran a comb through the tangled locks, grabbed his jacket and backpack and shouted a good-bye to the teammates who were still getting dressed. Then he stepped out into the hall.

Kate was there—but so was Erika. And Allyson, and a few other girls. They stood in a cozy little group, chattering, their voices blending and colliding and rippling over each other. How a bunch of girls could talk simultaneously—and manage to hear what everyone was saying, even as they were talking—was a mystery to him.

Another mystery was why, when Kate was practically in front of him, his gaze locked onto Erika like a laser sight on a rifle.

Kate immediately latched onto him, and he slung his arm around her. But his gaze met Erika's and he returned her smile. "That was really interesting," she said.

"Interesting?" Of all the words he could think of to describe wrestling—hard, aggressive, primitive, sweaty—*interesting* wouldn't make his top ten. For someone who'd never seen a meet before, though, he supposed it would work. "I hope you're impressed."

"He's so macho," Kate teased, giving his biceps a squeeze. "Ooh. All man," she said dryly.

"See? She's impressed," he said to Erika. "You should be impressed, too."

"I'm impressed." Her smile softened. "Really."

"Anyone up for pizza?" he asked.

His friend Will, who wrestled heavyweight, chose that moment to barrel out of the locker room. "I am!" he shouted.

Fifteen minutes later, six of them were crowded around a table at Village Pizza, divvying up a Sicilian pie. The girls amused Ted as they requested knives and carefully cut the gooey rectangular slabs into smaller pieces for themselves. It took them more time to figure out who would get which fraction of which slice than for him to devour an entire piece by himself.

"So," Kate said after taking a dainty bite of her sliver, "I think we should all share a limo for the prom."

Ted grimaced. The prom was a couple of months off. No one wanted to think about it. At least, *he* didn't want to. Every time he contemplated how much it would cost, he broke out in a cold sweat. He'd have to spend an awful lot of Saturday mornings caddying at the golf club to pay for the tickets, rent a tux, buy flowers, and—crap, cough up big bucks for a limousine. And all for what? To impress Kate? To give her a night she'd never forget?

For all that money, shouldn't he go to the prom with the girl who held center stage in his imagination?

That particular girl had no interest in going with him, though, he thought as he glanced across the table at Erika, who was plucking at a long, droopy string of melted mozzarella that had oozed off her portion of pizza. "Do you have to have a boyfriend to go to the prom?" she asked.

"You don't even have to have a date," Allyson assured her.

"Because right now, the only guy in my life is Five Star." She grinned in Ted's direction. "That's the horse I ride."

"Would he fit in a limo?" Will asked.

"We could hitch a trailer to the rear bumper," she said, still grinning. "I've dated a few horses' asses in my life. I don't see why I can't go to the prom with a horse."

"Kind of a Catherine the Great thing," Ted ventured.

Erika eyed him curiously.

Damn. She didn't know what they said about Catherine the Great? "The Tsarina of Russia. She was supposedly insatiable. Rumor had it she had sex with a horse."

"She was hot to trot, literally," Will punned as he reached for another slice of pizza.

"That's about all I remember from European history," Ted said, shrugging apologetically. "Not that it was part of the curriculum. I just heard about it when we were studying Russia."

"That's disgusting," Kate said, making a face. Erika was laughing, though. He hadn't offended her—and he realized belatedly that he could have, given how into horses she was. But she seemed to think the legend of Catherine the Great was hilarious, which only made him like her even more.

"I don't want to think about the prom," Allyson declared. "I'll probably have to go with a cousin or something."

"I'll take you," Will offered.

Allyson threw back her head and laughed. "I'll go with my cousin."

Will pretended to be deeply hurt, but he chuckled as he reached for a third slice of pizza. Guys who wrestled heavyweight tended to eat a lot. And Will had to know that Allyson Rhatican would never go to the prom with him. She was one of the most popular girls in the high school. For that matter, Ted was sure she wouldn't have to resign herself to attending the prom with her cousin.

Unless they had some sort of spectacular falling out, he would go with Kate. Theirs wasn't the love of the century. It wasn't even the love of the high school. But she was attractive and pleasant, and he had faith that they'd experience a natural parting of the ways when she left for college in the fall. He had no idea what he'd be doing, other than earning some money and trying to figure out what he wanted to be when he grew up. But he and Kate would go their separate ways, and no one would cry too hard when it was all over.

He'd better start lining up caddying gigs, though. No one

golfed in early March, at least not in northern Jersey. But if he was going to do the prom thing—complete with a freaking rented limo—he was going to need some money. The minute the golf club opened, he'd be there, hustling. He didn't want to miss the big senior-class event.

After all, if Erika showed up at the prom riding a horse, he sure as hell wanted to be there to see it.

Five

ERIKA WOUND UP GOING TO THE PROM with Peter, a boy she knew through Allyson. He was nice, he looked less dorky in a tux than most high school boys did, he bought her a delicate orchid corsage, and they traveled to the prom in a limo with Allyson and her date and a few other kids. If Ted and Kate were in another group limo, Erika didn't know.

It was just as well they weren't in Erika's limo. Ever since she'd attended that wrestling meet a couple of months ago, she'd been more aware of Ted Skala than she ought to be. Her memory was haunted not only by his grace on the mat but by the flinty intensity in his eyes when he'd faced his opponent, the pugnacious tilt to his chin, his entire bearing. His attitude. His body, his strength, his moves, his posture all seemed to be saying, *I will win this thing. I will emerge triumphant. I will find the route to success and take it.*

It was an aura of determination and purposefulness she wasn't used to associating with Ted. Most of the time he was funny and full of energy, the kind of guy who greeted life's shadows and dark places with a shrug and a smile. In a school as small as Mendham High, he couldn't hide his mediocre scholastic performance, and he didn't try. He couldn't evade his record of detentions—never for anything awful, but he got himself into minor scrapes fairly consistently and didn't seem to care. As far as Erika could tell, he didn't take anything seriously. He approached life with a carefree spirit, which, to someone like her, who was so serious about her riding, had a certain enviable appeal.

Except that he clearly *did* take his wrestling seriously. When he was wrestling, he became someone different. Someone deeper, more complex. Someone she'd been thinking about in ways a girl shouldn't think about a guy who was seeing someone else.

It was silly. He and Kate had been a couple for a long time. Besides, Erika didn't want a boyfriend. High school was winding down, and when she fantasized about her future, it included learning new things, living in new places, conquering new skills—but not falling in love. Who needed that? It would only get in the way.

What she felt when she thought about Ted wasn't love. Not even close. But it was . . . *something*.

She felt it as soon as she and Peter entered the hotel banquet room where the prom was taking place and she spotted Ted standing in a circle of friends near the bar. He didn't look silly in his tux, either. His hair was wild with curls and waves, but from the forehead down, he appeared remarkably presentable. His tux fit well on his lanky frame, emphasizing his long legs and horizontal shoulders. His tie sat like a symmetrical satin butterfly at the base of his throat. His eyes—the eyes that could harden into ice when he wrestled—were bright with laughter.

Kate stood beside him, looking gorgeous in a sleek, dark dress. Erika felt unfashionably boring in her pastel-hued gown. It was pretty enough, and her mother and sister had assured her that it made her look slim and willowy. But it wasn't sleek.

Erika had never compared herself to other girls before, unless they were riders and she was comparing her form to theirs when they jumped. She saw no reason to start comparing now.

As soon as her group had found an empty table where they could leave their purses and favors, Erika decided she was terribly thirsty. "I'm going to get something to drink."

"I'll come with you," Peter offered. She smiled and hooked her hand through the bend in his elbow, feeling just the slightest bit debutante-ish as they promenaded across the room to the bar. Its mahogany counter was lined with bottles of water, fruit juice, and assorted sodas.

She would have felt a lot more sophisticated if she'd been able to ask the bartender for a glass of wine, but obviously that wasn't going to happen at a high school–sponsored event. "I'll have a diet Coke," she requested.

Peter asked for a ginger ale. Once they had their drinks, they turned from the bar. Ted's eyes met hers, and his smile widened. He raised his glass in a silent toast.

God, he looked adorable. Something about the contrast between his scruffy hair and his suave tuxedo ignited a warm, tingly sensation in Erika's gut.

"I've got to say hello to Ted," she said, steering Peter toward the group where Ted was standing. "And Kate," she added, as if acknowledging Ted's girlfriend would make him seem less attractive to her.

"Hey, Fred," Ted greeted her as she neared him. "Wow, you look great!"

"You clean up pretty well, too."

"Rumor has it he even showered," Kate teased, although there was a caustic edge to her voice. Did she mean to imply that he didn't shower often?

Of course he showered. And Erika was probably just imagining the brittle, slightly bitchy undertone in Kate's voice. "Well," she said amiably. "Here we all are."

"Adam smuggled in a flask if you want to spike your soda," Ted murmured.

Peter looked intrigued, but Erika shook her head. "Walking around in these high heels is difficult enough when I'm sober."

"High heels, huh? Let's see," Ted demanded.

Erika dutifully inched the hem of her dress up to mid-shin and showed off her strappy metallic-leather sandals with their three-inch heels. Her mother had treated her to a manicure and pedicure that afternoon, and her toes looked daintier and more feminine than they'd ever been before.

Peter clearly appreciated her feet. "This is like Victorian times," he said. "Ah, for a glimpse of ankle."

Erika had assumed that, given her gown's spaghetti straps and the daring swoop of its neckline, plenty enough of her skin was exposed, even if the floor-length hem concealed her feet. Victorian the dress was not.

Across the room, a deejay began spinning tunes. The air smelled of perfume and cologne and the faintly ozone-y scent of industrial air conditioning. The carpet below Erika's polished toenails bore an ugly pattern, mustard and maroon interlocking rectangles.

"Let's dance," she said to Peter. Near the deejay, the carpet gave way to a parquet dance floor. She'd rather have her pretty feet on that than on the carpet.

Peter emitted a long-suffering sigh and mumbled, "Okay." Only when they'd reached the dance floor, after stopping en route at their table to stash their drinks, and merged with the dozens of other classmates dancing and singing along with Bon Jovi did she realize the carpet had nothing to do with her desire to cross the room. She'd needed to dance so she wouldn't be standing so close to Ted. She was too conscious of him. Too drawn to him. When she'd shown him her feet, his eyes had narrowed with the same intensity she'd perceived when she'd seen him wrestle, the intensity that seemed to trip a switch inside her.

Had he been planning to wrestle her to the ground? Pin her? Wrap his legs around hers the way he'd wrapped them around his opponent?

The idea of Ted Skala pinning her, pressing her shoulders to the floor, straddling her, and gazing down into her face with his dazzling green eyes reignited that tingling sensation low in her belly.

The crowd swallowed her and Peter up and the music washed over them, twanging guitars, thumping drums, and Jon Bon Jovi's harrowing wail. At the song's chorus, everyone belted out the words—*You were born to be my baby.*

We're not babies anymore, Erika thought. They were mere days away from being high school graduates.

Someone jostled her and she opened her eyes. The dance floor had grown much more crowded, which she kind of liked, actually. She had always felt somewhat like an outsider at Mendham High School, having moved to the town barely two and a half years ago. But right now, surrounded by her classmates, she didn't feel like an outsider. She danced with them, was a part of them, moved in sync with them. Sang Bon Jovi lyrics with them.

As long as no one stomped on her pedicured feet she'd be fine.

The song ended and another one began: Bruce Springsteen, *Human Touch.* Erika briefly wondered whether the deejay intended to play only songs by New Jersey rockers for the entire prom. She started to laugh, and then stopped when she saw Ted out on the floor, separated from her by only a couple of people.

His gaze met hers and he smiled.

She smiled back.

This wasn't good, she thought. She shouldn't take such delight in his smile, in his appreciative gaze. She shouldn't be thinking about whether there was a discreet way to maneuver past the two people who stood between her and Ted, dancing their hearts out. It shouldn't matter to her that he looked cute in a tux. After tonight, she would never see him in formal apparel again, unless they both got invited to a classmate's wedding sometime down the road and he happened to be one of the ushers.

Ted Skala shouldn't matter to her. But he did.

Was there some law that said you had to do the prom thing? Had to spend tons of money, dress in a stupid penguin suit with adjustable waistband trousers that didn't quite adjust snugly enough, so you kept feeling as if your pants were going to slide down over your butt? Had to act like you wanted to preserve every precious moment of the night in your mental memory scrapbook? Did they withhold your diploma if you used the wrong fork to eat your salad, assuming you could call a few limp green weeds and a single cherry tomato drowning in oil and vinegar a salad?

Hell. The prom was fine. Nothing really wrong with it. Nothing wrong with posing for a bunch of photos and chatting politely with Kate's parents—and a few hundred of her closest neighbors, who'd all trooped over to her house to ooh and ahh over how nice the young couple looked. Nothing wrong with sneaking just a few drops of Adam's vodka into your Coke. You weren't driving. You'd paid all that freaking money for the limo, after all.

No, the problem wasn't the prom. The problem was that you were standing at a doorway, about to open it and cross the threshold into the next stage of your life, and all you could think of was missed opportunities, things left undone, and the cruel truth that once you exited this room you would never be allowed back into it.

There were so many things in the room you were leaving that you had never bothered to appreciate. So many knickknacks you'd never stopped to admire, so many leaks around the window you should have taken the time to seal. Maybe you could have learned to sit still more often, and pay attention, and you could have taken proper notes in English instead of drawing caricatures of the teacher. Damned good caricatures, but maybe you could have learned something more important than how to draw a nose so the nostrils didn't look like bullet holes.

There were people in the room you could have gotten to know better. Friendships that might have gone deeper than the sock-in-the-arm how's-it-going? level. Teachers you ignored when they insisted you were smart and ought to apply yourself more.

Girls you could have dated.

One girl in particular. One girl with long, honey-brown hair and a smile that was both shy and mischievous, and a fantastic figure and, as it turned out, beautiful feet.

Maybe, when all was said and done, you never could have dated her. But you could have tried. You could have made a move. You could have taken the risk. You'd never been afraid to make a fool of yourself—except with her.

The prom reminded you that in a few days you were going to walk through that door and leave the first eighteen years of your life behind. And although you would journey forward, see new places, try new things, live your life, and have a damned good time while you were at it, you'd always wonder what might have happened if you'd dared to make a fool of yourself with Erika Fredell.

Prom night had been fine, Erika supposed. Bland food, too-loud music, a few maudlin speeches that provoked both nostalgic sniffles and raucous jeers, everyone looking just a bit too shiny and only a few girls dissolving into tears in the bathroom. Erika's pedicure had survived a lot of boogying on that crowded dance floor, and her head ached only a little bit from the constant din of rock and hip-hop thumping through the deejay's speakers and people shouting to be heard above the music.

She hoped with all her heart that prom night wouldn't turn out to have been the best night of her life, however. Because honestly, it wasn't that great.

The truth was, she was looking forward to the party at Jennifer's house that Laura had told her about much more than she'd looked forward to the prom. Khaki shorts and a camisole top were much more her style than a formal gown, and Teva sandals were a lot kinder to her feet than three-inch heels. Peter would be at the party, but they'd never really been a couple, so he wouldn't expect her to hang out with him. And if the music was too loud, she'd ask Jennifer to turn it down, or go into another room.

"You're so quiet," Laura said as she drove down a winding road dense with evening shadows. "What's up?"

"Nothing." Erika sighed. She hated lying to her friend.

"It's going to be a good party," Laura remarked. "Everyone'll be there. And we're all free now! We've been sprung."

"I know," Erika said, trying not to sound melancholy.

Laura shot her a quick glance. "You're not worried about seeing Peter, are you?"

"No. Everything's cool between us." She sighed again. "The thing is . . . I've kind of got this crush on someone else."

"Who?"

MEET ME IN MANHATTAN

"Promise you won't laugh?"

Laura looked offended by the question, then grinned. "I'll laugh only if it's funny."

"It's funny," Erika warned her. One final sigh, and she confessed. "Ted Skala."

"Ted!" Laura didn't laugh. In fact, she swerved halfway over the double yellow line bisecting the road, then steered back into the lane and hooted. "Of course Ted."

"What do you mean, *of course Ted*?"

"He's perfect for you. I've known this for months."

"You have?"

"Why do you think I keep dragging you to parties where I know he'll be? Same with him. If I know you're coming to a party, I'll call him and tell him to come."

"But he's already got a girlfriend."

"Eh." Laura steered with her left hand and waved her right through the air, as if brushing away a mosquito. "He is so perfect for you. It's about time you realized it."

"First of all, he's not perfect," Erika debated calmly. Ted Skala might be handsome, he might be intriguing, he might have amazing green eyes that expressed so much. But he was a little wild and a little rough-hewn, and he wasn't going to college, and . . . and she was sure she could come up with a long list of his shortcomings if given the time.

Not that it mattered. She wasn't looking for perfect. She wasn't even looking for *him*. It just happened that she had a crush on him, that was all.

"Okay, that's first of all," Laura said. "What's second of all?"

"Second of all, he's got a girlfriend—"

"—Who is absolutely not perfect for him. I'm going to get you two together," Laura resolved.

Erika felt her cheeks warm with a blush. "How? What are you going to do? Will I die of embarrassment?"

"The only way you'll die is if I kill you for being stubborn and uncooperative. Trust me, Erika. I'm going to make this happen."

Erika snorted. Laura might be one of her closest friends, but at that moment, Erika didn't trust her at all.

Ted had gotten a ride to Jennifer's house with Will. A week ago, he would have driven over with Kate, but a lot could happen in a week. Kate could throw a hissy fit to end all hissy fits, tell him she thought he was an asshole because he'd wanted to spend the night before graduation with his buddies instead of with her, tell him he would never amount to anything because he was a jerk and jerks never amounted to anything, and in a fairly anticlimactic conclusion to her tirade, tell him that if he was planning to go to Jennifer's graduation party Friday night she wouldn't go, because she didn't want to be at a party with him.

After Kate had called him an asshole and a jerk and informed him he'd never amount to anything, he couldn't really get all worked up about how she planned to spend her Friday night. She was gone. Good-bye. Good riddance. Too bad she hadn't decided he was an asshole and a jerk before he'd spent all that money on the prom.

So he'd gone to the party with Will, and plenty of people were there, and he was free. Free from school, free from Kate, free from any expectations other than to show up at the golf course tomorrow for a day of caddying gigs. A beer and his friends tonight; lots of big tips tomorrow. No complaints.

He sat on a lawn chair on the slate patio that sprawled shapelessly out from the rear of Jennifer's house, sipping his beer and inhaling the beefy smoke rising from the gas grill, where burgers and hot dogs were sizzling. Placed on one end of a long table draped with a fluttering paper tablecloth reading, "Congratulations, Graduates!" in screaming red letters, a boom box blasted Nirvana into the warm evening air. The rest of the table held bowls of chips, pretzels, and other snacks. After a few more sips of beer, Ted might bestir himself to get a burger. But right now, it felt good just to sit and empty his mind of everything except Kurt Cobain's howling voice.

He closed his eyes, rolled his head back, and savored the peaceful emptiness of his mind. He was almost annoyed when someone poked him in the arm. Opening his eyes, he saw Laura plopping herself into the chair beside him and he decided not to be annoyed anymore. "Hey," he greeted her.

"I know the perfect girl for you," she said, unable to suppress a giggle.

"So you told me once before. I've been waiting ever since to find out who Miss Perfect is."

"Sometimes these things take time," Laura said. "Especially when everyone's being stubborn and foolish."

"You can't possibly be talking about me," he said with a grin.

"Well the thing is, this perfect girl has a crush on you."

As long as the allegedly perfect girl wasn't Kate, Ted was okay with it. "Yeah? So who is she?"

Laura gazed around the backyard. At least twenty-five kids were there, talking, eating, cutting up. Which one had a crush on him? Someone in the yard? Someone inside the house? Someone who hadn't arrived yet or hadn't been invited?

Laura turned back to him. "Erika," she whispered.

He bolted upright in his chair. "Fredell?"

"How many Erikas do you know?" Laura gave him another poke and stood. "Go get her," she said before waltzing off.

He recalled that day, months ago, when Laura had accosted him in the parking lot outside Country Coffee Shop with the news that she knew the perfect girl for him, and then driven away before he could ask her who. He'd stood in the lot, feeling—all right, foolish—and thinking of Erika. No wonder Kate thought he was an asshole and a jerk. She probably knew that when he thought of the perfect girl for him, the girl he was thinking of was Erika.

The perfect girl was Erika, and she had a crush on him.

Maybe that door hasn't slammed on you yet, Skala. Maybe it's time for you to do what you've wanted to do for years. Time for you to get this right. Time to go for the pin.

Six

ERIKA HOVERED NEAR THE GRILL. She wasn't particularly hungry, and the heavy scent of broiling meat made her even less hungry. But she'd promised she'd grab a hamburger for Laura once they were cooked, and she figured she ought to take one for herself, too. The backyard was filled with a lot of famished teenagers. If she didn't grab a burger now, she might not get one for a long time.

She didn't know why Laura couldn't get her own food. Laura had scampered away as soon as they'd reached the backyard, barely pausing to ask Erika to grab her a burger before she disappeared into the crowd.

Erika picked up a paper plate from the stack on the table, flipped it back and forth and exhaled, trying to blow away her irritation. Just because Laura had driven to the party didn't mean Erika had to be her slave, did it?

Someone tapped her on the shoulder and she spun around, expecting to see her slave mistress. Instead she saw Ted Skala. He was wearing a funny, quizzical smile, and his eyes glowed. He curled his fingers around her wrist and eased her away from the grill.

"I'm supposed to get a burger for Laura," she protested.

"Laura can get her own damned burger," he said.

That he shared her sentiments regarding Laura and the burger pleased Erika. That he continued to hold her, his fingers warm and strong as they circled her wrist, pleased her even more. He led her around to the side of the house, away from the crowd and the music and the hiss of the grill, and then loosened his grip on her slightly. He didn't completely let go of her, though.

"Is it true, what Laura told me?" he asked.

Erika's first thought was, *What did Laura tell him?* Her second was, *If she told him what I told her in the car, I'm going to kill her.* Her third was, *If she told him what I told her in the car, he doesn't seem too upset about it. And he's still holding my wrist.*

Her fourth and final thought was that if she was brave enough to fly over fences on the back of a horse, she was brave enough to tell Ted the truth. And if he laughed at her, well, high school was over. After tonight, she'd never have to see him again.

She drew in her breath, ordered herself not to fidget with the paper plate she still held, steeled her nerves as if preparing to fly over one of those fences, and said, "If she told you I have a crush on you, that's true."

He let his head fall back so he was staring straight up into the deepening night sky. Then he laughed. Then he straightened and stared straight into her eyes. "I've had a crush on you since the first moment I saw you."

"Oh." The first time he'd seen her had been, what, two and a half years ago? Her family had moved to Mendham in time for her to start her sophomore year at the high school, and soon after she'd arrived Allyson had taken Erika under her wing and introduced her to the kids she was friendly with, and so had Laura, and Ted had been one of those kids.

So, yes, sophomore year. He'd had a crush on her that long.

And he'd never done anything about it. Never said a word.

Never even hinted. He'd spent the past two years seeing other girls. What an idiot!

Except what would she have done if he'd confronted her two years ago? Back then, she'd been obsessed with her riding, and with doing well at her new school, and not making an ass of herself in front of her new classmates. She'd known Ted but hadn't thought of him as boyfriend material. She hadn't thought of *anyone* as boyfriend material, really. She'd dated that older boy Allyson had introduced her to, and the guy who played lacrosse, but for the most part she'd been just as happy to be accepted into a group of friends, one of the gang, no complications, no emotional entanglements, no risk of heartbreak. She'd found greater satisfaction riding Five Star than fending off her first boyfriend's pressure for sex, and she'd derived more pleasure talking to Five Star than listening to her second boyfriend recount every play of every lacrosse game, making sure to emphasize just how indispensable he'd been to the team.

She hadn't had a crush on Ted then. She hadn't seen him wrestle yet.

Why he would have had a crush on her was a mystery. She wasn't cute or flirty. She didn't hang out with everyone after school. All told, she was kind of a nerd. A horse nerd.

But he'd had a crush on her anyway. And all she could say was *Oh*.

"You want something to drink?" he asked, which was almost as prosaic as *Oh*. She assured herself that if he'd truly had a crush on her for all those years, she probably didn't have to knock herself out to impress him with her wit and charm.

"Okay," she said.

Ten minutes later, armed with two bottles of beer, they were seated on the grass under the arching, densely leafed branches of a maple tree, apart from the crowd. Ted leaned back on his elbows, his legs stretched out. His shorts ended at his knees and she found herself gazing at the lacy film of hair covering his calves.

"So what are you doing this summer?" he asked.

"Riding. And heading out to Colorado. How about you?"

"I've got a job at a gas station. And caddying up at Sommerset Country Club. I've got a caddy gig tomorrow morning. No rest for the weary."

"You're not weary," she teased. Just because they had crushes on each other didn't mean they couldn't still joke with each other the way they used to.

"Not now. Tomorrow morning I will be." He slapped at a mosquito on his arm, then took a sip of beer. She'd seen him at enough parties to know he wasn't the kind of guy who chugged down brew after brew and got drunk and acted like a jerk. "Your toes still look great," he noted.

She stared down the length of her legs to her feet. Her manicure from the prom had long ago chipped, but her pedicure still looked fresh. "You shouldn't have been checking out my feet while you were with Kate," she chided.

"I wasn't with Kate by then. Not really."

"You took her to the prom."

"Because what was I going to do, break up with her a week before graduation? You were at the prom with someone else, too."

"Because you were with Kate. And Peter asked me." She shot Ted a sly look. "And you *didn't* ask me."

"Well, that's history now," he said, refusing to let her needling get to him. "So what's in Colorado?"

"Colorado College, in Colorado Springs."

"Wow, couldn't you get any farther away?" He laughed. "No school in California would take you?"

She gave him a playful nudge. "I want to experience living in the mountains."

"We've got mountains here," he said, sweeping his hand through the air as if they were surrounded by alpine peaks.

"Hills," Erika argued. "We're a lot closer to the ocean than anything that could be considered a mountain." She shrugged. "It wasn't that I wanted to go far away. I just want to try something new. I love traveling."

"Yeah? Where do you travel?"

"My mother's from Colombia."

"Columbia? Like the university?"

"No, like the country in South America. She was born and grew up there. She still has lots of family there. Three sisters and a brother. I've got about a million cousins down there."

"No kidding. I never knew that."

"*Sí, es cierto!* That means, yes, it's true."

"Wow. So you, like, speak Spanish and everything?"

"It's funny—I sort of don't understand much Spanish when I'm here in New Jersey. But we used to go down to Colombia a lot when I was a kid, and after a day or two, I'd be speaking Spanish like a native. Well, not quite," she added modestly. "But enough to get around. People understood me. Then I would come back here and forget it all. Now I sit in Spanish class and knock myself out trying to keep up with the teacher."

"Not anymore," Ted reminded her, then chanted, "No more teachers, no more books."

"Not until I get to college." She plucked a long strand of grass that had sprouted between the bulging roots of the tree, where a lawn mower couldn't get to it. "You're not going to college, are you?"

"Not right away. I will eventually. I just need some time off." He grinned at her. "We can't all be straight-A honors students, you know."

"No, we can't," she said, meaning herself. She studied hard and did well in school, but she didn't think of herself as some sort of exalted scholar, destined for Phi Beta Kappa. "Colorado Springs is supposed to be gorgeous. Right at the base of Pike's Peak."

"Zebulon Pike," Ted murmured. "I couldn't remember a thing all through that boring American History class, but now I remember his name."

"Zebulon is a hard name to forget."

"His parents must've been tripping on something when they named him."

"That would be my guess," she agreed.

They eyed each other and exchanged a smile. And she felt that shimmery, quivery warmth in her belly again, that trill of sensation she'd never felt with anyone before. When Ted gazed at her with his soulful green eyes, she felt it.

She was hungry for new experiences—and she acknowledged that Ted Skala was going to be an amazing new experience for her.

Sometime well past midnight, she and Ted made their way indoors to find places to sleep. She was exhausted. He seemed far too energetic, given the late hour, but he insisted he needed to catch some z's because of his early morning caddying job. He sacked out on the plush carpeted floor in the den, and Erika folded herself up on an upholstered loveseat that would have been a lot more comfortable if it were about two feet longer. The room had a sofa, but someone else had already claimed it and was snoring softly.

As pumped as Ted had seemed, he fell asleep almost at once.

Erika lay curled up on the loveseat, her mind yearning to fall asleep but her heart fluttering, her emotions clamoring, refusing to let her shut down for a few hours of critically necessary rest. That Ted Skala liked her—that he'd liked her for *years*—was too astonishing. Too bizarre. Too utterly cool.

This isn't love, she told herself. It couldn't be. She wouldn't allow such a thing. She couldn't fall in love with someone when in a matter of weeks she would be traveling two thousand miles away to attend college. She couldn't fall in love when she had so many exciting adventures ahead of her, waiting for her. She wanted to live in the mountains. She wanted to learn to ski, and to sail, and to climb. She wanted to get a degree and make money. She wanted to have lots of affairs with gorgeous men. She wanted to see the world, eat exotic cuisine, learn how to tell a good wine from a bad one. She wanted to *live.*

She wanted to fall in love, too. But not yet.

However, her heart would not stop sending ripples of heat through her chest, as if its frenzied beat was Morse code spelling out the letters L-O-V-E. She thought of Ted slumbering on the carpet just a few feet away from her and her face exploded in a smile. She couldn't help herself. Thinking about him did that.

She must have drifted off eventually, because when she next opened her eyes, a milky dawn light was seeping through the slats in the wooden blinds covering the windows. Laura was shaking her gently. She glanced at the floor and saw that Ted was gone.

"Wake up," Laura whispered. The snores of the guy sleeping on the couch were louder than Laura's voice. "We've got to leave."

Erika wanted to ask where Ted was, but if the first words out of her mouth were about him, Laura would never let her forget it. "What time is it?" she asked instead, keeping her voice as low as Laura's.

"Seven-thirty. I told Ted we'd drive him to the golf club. He's got to caddy this morning."

"Oh. Okay." So he hadn't left. He was planning to leave with her and Laura. She hadn't imagined last night. The smile that had cradled her dreams through the night reclaimed her lips.

"You'll never guess who he's caddying for," Laura continued, still whispering as Erika pushed herself to sit and tried to unkink her joints. Sleeping in fetal position might be comfortable for a fetus, but not for a full-grown eighteen-year-old. Her neck was stiff, her legs cramped. She wiggled and stretched and heard dire clicks in her knees as she straightened them.

"Who?" she asked.

Laura grinned. "My dad."

A muted laugh escaped Erika. *Small world*, she thought, but she couldn't help believing that Ted's caddying for the father of her good friend—the friend who had manipulated Ted and Erika into revealing their feelings last night—was more than a coincidence. It was a sign. A sign that she and Ted belonged together.

Of course, in her drowsy, rapturously romantic mind, *anything* would have been a sign. The built-in bookshelves along the far wall were a sign. The sound of someone clattering around in the kitchen down the hall was a sign. The fact that Erika had spent the night on a *love*seat was definitely a sign.

She rubbed the sleep out of her eyes with the heels of her hands, then stood and tiptoed out of the room behind Laura. The guy on the couch was sleeping so soundly, they probably could have stomped out of the room, clapping their hands and bellowing the Mendham High School song, and he would have slept through it.

After a quick stop in the bathroom, Erika followed Laura into the kitchen. Ted was there, along with an older woman in a camp shirt and matching shorts in such a bright turquoise they hurt Erika's eyes. Jennifer's mom, Erika recalled. She'd met the woman briefly last night. Unlike Ted, who looked as sleepy as Erika felt, Jennifer's mother appeared sharp and energetic and ready to embrace the day.

She'd fixed a pot of coffee. A couple of large pink-and-white boxes from Dunkin Donuts stood open on the counter, displaying an assortment of doughnuts. "Good morning, girls!" she greeted Erika and Laura cheerfully.

Erika managed to return her greeting, but her attention was on Ted. His hair was even more tousled than usual, but he wore a collared polo shirt and khaki slacks, proper apparel for a caddy at Sommerset Country Club. He was holding a mug in both hands, lifting it to his mouth as if it were filled with precious nectar. Given the hour and the job awaiting him, the caffeinated drink was clearly essential to him.

Yet he apparently believed Erika was even more essential than coffee. He paused before sipping as his gaze zeroed in on her, and he smiled. "Hey," he said in a dark, husky voice.

That sexy hoarseness probably resulted from too little sleep, but Erika decided to believe it was a reaction to her. "Hey," she said back.

He smiled.

Evidently unaware of the current spinning between Erika and Ted, Jennifer's mother said, "I've got plenty of doughnuts. There's fruit and orange juice in the fridge, and we've got cornflakes—"

"Thanks anyway," Laura said, covering for Erika and Ted, who were gazing at each other like lovesick fools. "Coffee is fine."

"Well, help yourselves. Here's milk and sugar—" Jennifer's mother waved toward a small ceramic pitcher and a matching ceramic bowl situated near the coffee maker "—and there are cups in the cabinet." She gestured toward the polished cherry cabinet above the coffee maker. Her hostess responsibilities complete, she smiled and bounced out of the room, her sandals making quiet slapping noises against the soles of her feet.

"Coffee," Laura said, giving Erika a nudge to snap her out of her spell.

"Right." She eyed Ted and laughed helplessly. He smiled, leaned against the counter and sipped his coffee.

"You really should eat something," Laura advised Ted. "My father's going to run you ragged."

"Is he a good tipper?" Ted asked as he helped himself to a cinnamon cruller.

"Are you a good caddy?" Laura shot back. She pulled two mugs from the cabinet and filled them with coffee. "You want a doughnut?" she asked Erika.

Erika shook her head. She had no appetite. She was too sleep-deprived, too giddy. Ted looked as good to her this morning as he had last night. As he had at the prom last week. As he had when she'd seen him wrestling.

Correction: he looked even better today than he had ever before. Today she knew he liked her. He *liked* her.

She should have spent a little more time in the bathroom, working on her appearance before she let him see her. She'd brushed the tangles from her hair with her fingers and washed her face, but she'd looked bedraggled in the mirror above the vanity. A few minutes of fussing wouldn't have improved things much, and more than a few minutes might have resulted in Ted's arriving late for his caddying job. So she'd given up and figured that if Ted really had that much of a crush on her, he would just have to accept her with her eyes a little bloodshot and a faint impression from the loveseat's textured upholstery branded on her cheek.

Either he was staring at the little red dents in her cheek or he was just staring at her, taking her in, thinking—as she was—that last night had been some kind of miracle.

"Okay," he said abruptly as he slugged down the last of his coffee. "We'd better go."

He snatched another cruller from the box and they trooped out of the kitchen, out the back door and around the house to the front, where Laura's car was parked. The early morning sun was gentle, the grass wet with dew. Laura led the way, and Ted took Erika's hand.

Oh, God, she liked holding his hand. His palm was warm and smooth and his gait matched hers, and . . . man, she had it bad.

Laura didn't object when Ted and Erika both got into the backseat. If she felt like their chauffeur, well, it was her fault for bringing them together, putting this whole thing in motion. Erika glimpsed the reflection of her friend's face in the rear-view mirror and saw that Laura was grinning. Obviously she was too pleased with herself to mind the seating arrangement.

"How's your father's game?" Ted asked Laura as she eased her car past the other cars lining the driveway and steered out onto the empty road.

"He's pretty decent. And he won't bite your head off if you give him the wrong club."

"I would never give him the wrong club," Ted swore. "I'm the perfect caddy. Even when I'm half asleep," he murmured, giving Erika a sly smile.

She made a face. "You slept like a log."

"I felt like a log. That floor was hard."

"It had a thick carpet."

"Easy for you to say. You were on the couch."

"The loveseat, and it was much too short."

"Is this our first fight?" he asked, still smiling as he gave her hand a squeeze.

"Our first and last," she said solemnly.

He laughed. She did, too.

Too soon, Laura was cruising up the driveway of the Sommerset Country Club. "How are you going to get home?" she asked Ted as she slowed to a halt in front of the sprawling brown clubhouse at its end.

"I'm caddying all day," he said. "One of the other caddies will give me a lift." He turned to Erika. "Are you free this evening?"

She was pretty sure she was—and if she wasn't, she would change her plans, whatever they might be. She couldn't think of anything she'd rather do than spend the evening with Ted. "Call me," she said.

He pushed open his door, then turned back to her and touched his lips to hers. Very lightly, very tenderly. There was nothing hot or demanding in his kiss, nothing pushy or mushy. Just the loveliest kiss she'd ever experienced.

Somewhere through the haze of warmth that had engulfed her, she heard him thanking Laura for the lift. Then he jogged toward the clubhouse, tucking the tails of his polo shirt into the waistband of his khakis. He swung open a door, stepped inside, and disappeared.

Erika fell back against the seat, her eyes closed and her mind replaying the sweetness of his mouth on hers as she waited for her heart to stop galloping like a runaway horse. A long moment passed, and then she opened her eyes.

"Oh, my God," Laura said, then giggled.

"Oh, my God."

"Are you in love?"

"Of course not," Erika said indignantly, trying her best to act normal despite the fact that her heart was still beating crazily. She got out of the car, slammed the door and climbed into the passenger seat next to Laura, who was scrutinizing her like a scientist examining a lab specimen.

"Say thank you, Laura."

"Thank you, Laura," Erika said briskly. "Let's go home."

"Thank you, Laura, for getting me together with Ted," Laura coached her.

"If you gloat, I'll never speak to you again."

"I'm entitled to gloat," Laura declared as she started the engine. "I'm your fairy godmother. One wave of my magic wand, and *voila!*"

"Yeah," Erika said begrudgingly. "But I'll still never speak to you again. And don't stare at me like that. I'm not in love."

Laura only grinned and pulled away from the clubhouse. Erika gazed out the window at the expanse of manicured lawn, glittering with dewdrops beneath the morning sun as if someone had strewn tiny diamonds among the blades of grass. Beyond the lawn, pine trees stood like living spires poking into the cloudless sky. It was a beautiful morning for golf.

It was a beautiful morning for being in love.

Which she wasn't, she swore to herself.

She flicked her tongue over her lips and tasted cinnamon. She tasted heat. She tasted Ted.

Really. She couldn't possibly be in love with him.

Seven

TED HAD EIGHTY DOLLARS IN HIS WALLET when he got home from the golf course late that afternoon. Gotta love those generous tippers, he thought with a smile. He'd worked damned hard today. He'd lugged heavy golf bags around as the day grew progressively warmer and muggier, made a few discreet suggestions when a duffer he was caddying for asked for the wrong club, and said, "Yes sir," and "Thank you, sir," at all the right times. He'd earned those tips, although you never knew if the "sir" you were yessing and thanking would see things the same way you did.

But he had four reasonably crisp twenty-dollar bills stashed in his wallet now. Eighty dollars he could spend on Erika Fredell. Who liked him. Who had let him kiss her. Who was without a doubt the coolest, hottest girl he'd ever known.

His father was outside the house as Ted walked up the driveway. He took in the scene—the bucket, the hose, the old, threadbare towels, the can of Turtle Wax. The car shining as brightly as the late afternoon sun that was mirrored in its polished surfaces. His father stooped over, wiping the sidewall of one of the tires with a damp rag.

"Looks great," Ted said.

His father straightened and gave him a stern look. "It's a lot of work, washing a car all by yourself."

Ted suffered a sharp pang of guilt. "I was caddying all day," he said, apologizing even though he hadn't done anything wrong. "If you waited until tomorrow, I could've helped you." His voice drifted off. He was sure he'd told his parents he would be at the golf course all day.

"Well." His father dried off his hands. "It got done."

"Weren't any of the others around? Adam or Josh?"

His father shrugged. Back when Ted and his brothers and sister were young, they used to draw chores out of a bowl every Friday. You'd pick a room—if you were lucky, the living room, if you were unlucky the bathroom or the kitchen—and Saturday morning, you'd clean that room, top to bottom. Or you'd win some other chore: mowing the grass, raking the leaves, washing the car. Ted's father worked damned hard at AT&T, and his mother had her hands full fixing meals, getting everyone to a team practice or a dentist appointment or a million other places. A household with five kids, to say nothing of a barn full of animals, was chaotic. It took a lot of organizing on his parents' part to keep the family unit functioning.

But now Ted's brothers were older, halfway out of the house. This meant less chaos, but also fewer people to help when a car needed washing.

His younger sister could have helped wash the car, though, couldn't she?

His father must have read his mind. "Nancy took care of the animals today," he said, gesturing toward the barn. "You never came home."

All right. Feeding the animals in the morning was usually Ted's job. But come on. For once, couldn't he get a day off? He'd just received his high school diploma, after all. He deserved a break.

"There was a graduation party at Jennifer's," he reminded his father, giving the word *graduation* some extra emphasis, just in case that important fact about Ted might have slipped the old man's mind and left him thinking Ted was still the same little boy he'd been a week ago. He was annoyed, resentful. He wanted to yell, snap back at his father, abandon the "Yes, sir" obsequiousness he'd engaged in all day.

He would never talk back to his father, even if he was a newly minted graduate, a *man*, who ought to be allowed to party a little and to make some money so he could take out the girl he was crazy about. He deserved a little slack—but his father deserved his respect. Ted swallowed his indignation, even if it was big enough to choke him.

The old man regarded him for a long minute as he dried off his hands. "So, what are you going to do, caddy for the rest of your life?"

Ted sensed his father was talking about something other than caddying, something beyond not doing his chores. Wary, he attempted a joke. "It's a little hard to caddy in the winter."

"You're not going to college, Ted. You'll need to find a more substantial job than toting around other people's golf clubs."

"I've got that gas station job."

"Gas station." His father shook his head. "You're a smart kid. You're talented. You should be doing something better than pumping gas."

"I'm just putting college off for a year," Ted said, his anger rising back up into his throat. He tried desperately to keep it out of his voice.

He'd already had this argument with his father, several times. His parents wanted him to go to college, and he figured he would, eventually. But he'd spent the past twelve years of his life—thirteen, if you counted kindergarten—trying to sit still in classroom after classroom, at desk after desk, studying stuff he didn't care about when all he'd wanted to do was draw and daydream and wrestle.

He needed some time off. Lots of kids did. Taking a year off between high school and college was so common now, it had its own name. "I'm taking a gap year."

"Right. And during this gap year, you'll do what? Caddy until it starts snowing?"

"And work at the gas station. Or I'll find other work," he said. "You know I will."

Another long, measuring, vaguely disappointed look from his father. "Well," he finally said, drying his hands one final time and then tossing the rag into an empty bucket. "The car's done, anyway."

Ted nodded and strode into the house, trying to tamp down his fury. By the time he'd made it upstairs and into his bedroom, the rage burning inside him had cooled to a simmer. He sprawled out on his bed, an upper bunk just inches from the ceiling, and groaned.

His father hadn't been that hard on him, really. Ted should have made arrangements for the animals before he'd left for Jennifer's party last night. As his parents liked to remind their children, mopping and scrubbing could wait, but the animals couldn't. They needed to be fed every day, no matter what.

He'd have to remember to thank his sister for covering for him.

He gazed at the pine frame of the bunk bed. Over the years, he'd carved patterns of lines into the soft wood with his thumbnail. At first they'd been random, abstract indentations, but over time he'd begun to see patterns in the scratches. He'd turned them into pictures. Cartoons. A timeline of his life.

Now they were a touchstone, a reminder that even though he was a high school graduate he was also the kid who'd etched those designs into the wood. He stared at the lines and tried to define what he was feeling. His anger was fading, leaving behind a vacuum. Uneasiness rushed in to fill it.

It wasn't his father he worried about. It was Erika. She was going to college. No gap year for her.

She was smart. Scholarly. Academic. All the things he wasn't.

You are smart, Skala, he assured himself. But he didn't have the grades to prove it or the college acceptance letter or the scholarship money. Someday, that truth was going to smack Erika between the eyes. She was going to look at him and think, *Why am I with this loser who won't even be going to college?*

You're a long way from that moment, he told himself. She wouldn't be leaving for college for a couple of months. He had the whole summer to prove to her that he was smart, even if he wasn't following the expected route. He had until late August to demonstrate that college wasn't the only path to success, or that if it was he'd take that path next year.

Or else he had until late August to discover that Erika wasn't the girl for him, after all. Just because he'd been smitten with her for more than two years didn't mean she was going to live up to his fantasies. Maybe they'd go out a few times and he'd learn that all she cared about was horses. Or that she was mean, or selfish, or bitchy. He couldn't believe those things of her; after the more than two years he'd known her, he would have heard all the bad shit about her by now. She wouldn't be friends with girls like Laura and Allyson if she was a bitch. They wouldn't put up with that.

She was a good person. A class act. An old soul. She would accept him for who and what he was. His father's harping about his lack of college plans couldn't undermine his confidence in himself, and in Erika. He couldn't let it.

She'd kissed him. She knew he wasn't going to college, and she'd gone ahead and kissed him anyway. He closed his eyes, relived that moment in the backseat of Laura's car, the feel of Erika's lips touching his, and he knew that no matter what happened, no matter how they both felt about each other after they'd spent more time together, he was going to kiss her again.

And again.

It wasn't just the college thing. It was that she had a car and he didn't, and if he couldn't get access to his parents' car, going out with Erika meant she would do the driving.

He knew she was more privileged than he was. His family's vacations might entail a weekend at the shore, and hers entailed flying to Colombia, South America. He caddied at the golf club; her family probably belonged to the golf club.

But he'd phoned her between his third and fourth golf party that afternoon and asked to see her tonight and she'd said yes, so obviously none of that bothered her. And he had all that tip money burning a hole in his wallet.

She might drive, but he would impress her. He would take her someplace classy. He'd even tuck his shirt in. If he could do that for his caddying job, he could do it for Erika Fredell.

"The Black Horse Tavern?" She stared at him. "You really want to go there?"

He had just climbed into her Jeep Wagoneer, after first circling it and inspecting all the stickers her father had glued onto its windows and bumpers: a Trinity College decal denoting her sister's college and dozens of USET stickers. "What's USET?" he had asked as he'd swung open the door.

"The United States Equestrian Team," she'd told him. "My father gets a sticker at practically every horse show."

"He must be very proud of you."

Erika shrugged. Her father was very proud, period. He was proud of his daughters, but also proud of how far he'd come in the world, from his working-class childhood in the Bronx to a successful career as a stockbroker on Wall Street. And he was proud of how much he did for his daughters—sending them to prestigious private colleges, paying for the riding lessons and coaching that had turned Erika into a champion. The Wagoneer was actually pretty old, dinged, and mud-spattered, with unfashionable wood siding. But it got her where she wanted to go, and she wasn't about to complain.

Where Ted wanted to go was the Black Horse Tavern, which was one of the fanciest restaurants in town. It was the kind of place one's parents went to on their anniversary or took the family to when grandparents were visiting. When Ted had phoned and she'd told him that she was indeed free for dinner, she'd assumed they would go someplace normal, one of the chain restaurants, like Olive Garden or TGI Friday's, or a local place. Country Coffee Shop or Village Pizza would have suited her fine.

She wasn't even wearing a dress. Just some nice cotton slacks and an airy linen blouse.

"You really want to have dinner at the Black Horse Tavern?" she asked him.

"It's a nice place," he said.

"I know it's nice. What I asked was if that was really where you want to eat."

"I can afford it."

She refused to twist the ignition key until they'd worked this out. "I didn't think you'd want to go someplace you couldn't afford," she said. "I just . . ."

"What?"

She struggled to come up with a tactful phrasing, then gave up. "I don't want you to think you have to go out of your way to impress me, Ted. I mean, you impress me just by being yourself."

He gazed across the console at her. In the lavender twilight, she was acutely aware of the shadows playing across his angular face. Her gaze dropped to his neck and the vee of chest exposed where his shirt collar was unbuttoned, and she realized she wanted to kiss him there, right in the hollow at the base of his throat.

She'd never felt drawn to a boy the way she was drawn to Ted. Never felt that shimmering warmth with anyone else. It scared her a little and excited her a lot.

Yet there she was, challenging him. Arguing with him not only about where they should go for dinner but *why* they should go wherever they went. They'd barely gotten together, and they were already having a real fight.

Only it wasn't a fight. Ted's face relaxed into a smile. "I don't think I'm that impressive," he said. "But if you're impressed, we can go wherever you want."

They wound up at a pub on Route 510, ordering thick, juicy burgers and lemonade. The front of the tavern was the bar, which was crowded with adults who talked too loudly and laughed even more loudly. But in the back, where the tables were located and food rather than booze was the focus, the place was actually pretty pleasant. Old rock music spilled softly through the ceiling speakers and the lighting was dim, augmented by glass-enclosed candles on the scarred wooden tables. It was the kind of eatery that featured paper placemats and salt shakers with rice inside them to keep the salt from caking. The order of fries she and Ted decided to share came in a plastic basket lined with a paper napkin, and the portion was so big, fries kept spilling out of the basket and leaving greasy spots on the placemats.

It wasn't the Black Horse Tavern, for which Erika was grateful.

"So what should we do about Laura?" Ted asked after taking a lusty bite of his burger.

"Do we have to do anything about her?"

"She set us up. She manipulated us into this."

"Ah." Erika saw the laughter in his eyes and grinned.

"All year, she's been calling me and nagging me to go to this party and that party," he said. "You were at all those parties. I'm thinking maybe she was trying to play matchmaker."

"Maybe." Erika set down her burger. She'd eaten a little over half of it and was full. "Maybe it was just coincidence. I mean, you were dating Kate and all."

"That didn't keep Laura from plotting to get us together. Why would she care about whether I went to this or that party? She only twisted my arm about parties you were going to be at."

"Twisted your arm," Erika scoffed. "Like you had to be forced to go to all those parties." She ran a quick survey of her own memories and laughed. "She had to twist *my* arm, though. I'm not that into parties."

"You're kind of shy," Ted said. That he would describe her so bluntly intrigued her, especially since he was right. People who saw her—particularly at parties—wouldn't guess that she was reserved. But Ted had figured that out about her.

"The thing is, I would never have even thought of you, well, *this* way—" she motioned with her hand across the table to indicate that by *this way* she meant a couple, dating "—because you were with Kate."

"I'm not with Kate anymore."

She recalled him telling her last night that he'd had a crush on her from the first time he'd seen her. That meant he'd had a crush on her before he started dating Kate, and during his time with her. "Why didn't you ask me out?"

"I did." It was his turn to gesture toward their surroundings. "*Hello?* I asked you out."

"I mean before. If you had a crush on me for all that time."

"You were busy," he said, as if that explained everything. "You were into your horses. And you were kind of exotic. Maybe it's your Central American blood."

"South American," she corrected him. "There's a difference."

"Yeah. I didn't do so well in world history."

"I don't know why they called that class world history. We studied Europe, Asia, and a little bit of Africa. We hardly spent any time on South America at all." She sipped her lemonade and sighed. "You can't really learn about places by reading about them in textbooks. I want to visit all those places we read about. Europe, Asia, Africa. I want to travel around the world."

"I wouldn't mind seeing the world," Ted said. "But I'd kind of like to see America, too. I've hardly traveled at all."

Erika flashed on a fantasy of the two of them traveling together. Driving across the continent in the trusty old Wagoneer. Sailing across the ocean to Europe. Riding a mysterious train to the Middle East and roaming through northern Africa. Galloping on horses across the Sahara, kicking up sand beneath a relentless sun. Then moving on to Asia, hopping from India to China to Japan to Australia. Winding up on a South Sea island, lying on a white beach, surrounded by turquoise water and swaying palm trees.

It was a lovely fantasy, and a silly one. First she had to go to college. Then she had to figure out a way to pay for this around-the-world adventure. And if Ted started college next year, he'd be a year behind her and it would take a couple of years for him to earn enough money to help pay for their trip . . . and why was she thinking about him years into the future? This was their first date, for God's sake.

"Here," she said, pushing her plate with her half-consumed burger around the fries basket to his placemat. "I'm full. You can finish this."

"Thanks," he said. Obviously he wasn't full. And obviously he saw nothing wrong with eating her leftovers, as if they were already a steady couple. As if they'd been together long enough and knew each other well enough to share their entrees. As if he understood that finishing her burger was an intimate thing to do, and he was okay with that intimacy.

Maybe they *would* take that trip around the world someday. Today, her burger. Tomorrow, Europe.

For the first time in her life, Erika's dream of the future wasn't about winning another event at a horse show and bringing home another trophy. It was about Ted.

READER RESPONSE CARD

We care about your opinions! Please take a moment to fill out our Reader Survey online at **http://survey.hcibooks.com**. To show our appreciation, we'll give you an **instant discount coupon** for future book purchases, as well as a special gift available only online.

If you prefer, you may mail this survey card back to us and receive a discount coupon by mail. All answers are confidential.

(PLEASE PRINT IN ALL CAPS)

First Name		Last Name	
Address			
City	State	Zip	Email

1. Gender
- ❑ Female ❑ Male

2. Age
- ❑ Under 20
- ❑ 21-30 ❑ 31-40
- ❑ 41-50 ❑ 51-60
- ❑ Over 60

3. Marital Status
- ❑ Married ❑ Single

4. How you did get this book?
- ❑ Received as gift
- ❑ Bought for myself
- ❑ Borrowed from a friend
- ❑ Borrowed from my library

5. If bought for yourself, how did you find out about it?
- ❑ Recommendation
- ❑ Store Display
- ❑ Read about it on a Website
- ❑ Email message or e-newsletter
- ❑ Book review or author interview

6. How many books do you read a year, excluding educational material?
- ❑ 4 or less
- ❑ 9-12 ❑ 5-8
- ❑ 12 or more

7. Do you have children under the age of 18 at home?
- ❑ Yes ❑ No

8. What type of romance do you enjoy most?
- ❑ Contemporary
- ❑ Historical
- ❑ Paranormal
- ❑ Erotic
- ❑ All types

9. What are your sensuality preferences?
- ❑ Wild and erotic
- ❑ Steamy but moderate
- ❑ Sweet and sensual
- ❑ Doesn't matter as long as it fits the story

10. Where do you usually buy books?
- ❑ Online (amazon.com, etc.)
- ❑ Bookstore chain (Borders, B&N...)
- ❑ Independent/local bookstore
- ❑ Big Box store (Target, Wal-Mart...)
- ❑ Drug Store or Supermarket

11. How often do you read romance novels?
- ❑ Every now and then
- ❑ Several times a year
- ❑ Constantly

FOLD HERE

12. What influences you most when purchasing a book?
(Rank each from 1 to 5 with 1 being the top)

	1	2	3	4	5
Author	1	2	3	4	5
Price	1	2	3	4	5
Title	1	2	3	4	5
Reviews	1	2	3	4	5
Cover Design	1	2	3	4	5
Series/Publisher	1	2	3	4	5
Recommendation	1	2	3	4	5

13. Annual household income
☐ Under $25,000
☐ $25,000–$40,000
☐ $41,000–$50,000
☐ $51,000–$75,000
☐ Over $75,000

14. How long have you been reading romance novels?
☐ 1–2 years   ☐ 3–5 years
☐ More than 5 years

15. What other topics do you enjoy reading?
Non-Fiction
☐ Family/parenting
☐ Relationships
☐ Addictions/Recovery
☐ Health/nutrition
☐ Cooking
☐ Religious
☐ Spirituality
☐ Inspiration/affirmations
☐ Self-improvement
☐ Sports
☐ Pets
☐ Memoirs
☐ True Crime
Fiction
☐ Mystery
☐ Chick-lit
☐ Historical
☐ Paranormal

Comments _____

Eight

YOU KNOW THAT EXPRESSION, *"poetry in motion," but you never really understood what it meant until you watched Erika ride.*

Ted stood by a painted white fence, resting his arms on the top rail, one sneakered foot propped on a lower rail and his eyes squinting in the late-afternoon sunlight. On the other side of the fence was a long oval track of sand and sawdust framing a grass field interspersed with wooden structures that looked like high-jumper's bars at a track meet. They were painted white and red, and he could tell from the structure that if Erika's horse caught one of its hooves on the bar, the entire barrier would simply fall over and not tangle the horse up or endanger the beast or the rider.

Erika's horse didn't catch its hooves on any of the horizontal bars. She spurred it to gather speed as it approached each fence, and then, with ballet-like grace, the horse sprang into the air, leaping over the fence and landing on the other side without a thump or a jerk or a missed step.

The horse was beautiful, but Erika was even more beautiful. Despite the speed and power of the animal, her upper body seemed perfectly still, posture straight, arms bent symmetrically at her elbows, eyes and chin pointing forward. A form-fitting black helmet with a little visor covered her skull, but her hair, pulled back into a pony-tail, streamed behind her like a rippling gold-brown flag.

He wanted to draw her.

He had already drawn plenty of pictures for her. He'd drawn some before they'd become a couple, when he'd been secretly nursing his crush. But now that they'd been together for a few weeks, he'd started giving her his drawings. Not drawings of her; they came nowhere close to capturing everything he loved about her. But drawings of Greta and Garfield, the geese who shared the barn with Ba Ba and Bunky. And the ducks, Donald and Donna. He'd drawn a great caricature of Spot, his randy golden retriever, with his tongue drooling out the side of his mouth and his eyes glazed with lust. Ted had been a bit leery about introducing Erika to Spot, afraid the dog would try to hump her leg or something. But Spot had behaved well, nuzzling her knees and using his snout to direct her hand wherever he wanted scratching. Spot could be bossy, but Erika hadn't seemed to mind.

Today it was Ted's turn to meet her animal, Five Star. "He isn't actually my horse, but his owner loves to let me ride him," she had explained when she'd escorted Ted into the stable and over to Five Star's stall. "It's good for the horse—he's a jumper, he needs the exercise. And good for the owner, because every time I win a ribbon it increase's Five Star's value."

"So you don't own your own horse?"

"I wish I did," she'd admitted, "but it makes more sense this way. Owning a horse is so expensive. You have to pay to board him, pay for feed and grooming services and shoes . . . and the vet bills can be staggering. Anyway, I don't have to own Five Star to feel like he's mine. I depend on him, and he depends on me. We love each other, don't we?" she'd cooed to the horse, stroking the creature's nose and the flat expanse of his cheek before she'd fitted a bit between his teeth.

She'd let Ted hold Five Star's reins as she'd strapped a saddle onto him. The horse was huge. Not *huge* huge like those Clydesdales pulling the beer wagon in the Budweiser commercials, but when Ted thought of Erika seated on Five Star's back, so many feet above the ground, he felt queasy. He knew she was a champion rider, but if something went wrong, she'd be falling a long way before she finally hit the ground.

He was still wearing his caddying clothes from a gig earlier that day. He'd untucked his shirt as soon as Erika had picked him up in her Wagoneer, but he'd kept on his Sommerset Country Club cap because the brim cut the glare of the sloping late-day sun. Even with the hat, he had to shield his eyes as Erika galloped to the far end of the fenced-in enclosure. She had on tight-fitting gray pants and a tank top, the velvety black helmet, and a pair of knee-high black leather boots that he found incredibly sexy, even though they were styled for business, not pleasure.

Everything about her was sexy when she rode: the speed, the inherent risk, the fluidity of her body. The way she leaned forward with each jump, her torso parallel with the horse's neck and her sweet little behind rising out of the saddle. He was unable to see her face when she'd ridden to the far end of the enclosure, but when she rode back toward him he couldn't miss her expression, which was a complicated blend of intense concentration and otherworldly bliss.

That was what he wanted to draw: her face when she rode.

She cantered toward the fence where he stood watching her. The horse's hooves thundered against the track and he found himself thinking again of how high off the ground she was, and how big those hooves were, how much the horse weighed, and what would happen if she slid out of the saddle and got trampled. But of course she didn't. She was perfectly balanced and secure. Confidence— that was another element in her expression. Confidence, concentration, and sheer joy.

She'd told him she loved Five Star and depended on him. Ted wanted her to love and depend on *him*. As much as she loved and depended on her horse. More.

"I hope that didn't bore you," Erika said once they were back in the Wagoneer, coasting out of the stable's dirt lot and onto the road.

"Bore me? Are you kidding?"

She was driving, so she couldn't look at Ted. But she could feel his gaze on her. He didn't seem bored now—in fact he seemed more wired than usual, one leg jiggling and his voice bright with energy. But that was now. Watching her do some jumping runs couldn't have been *that* exciting. The excitement was in the riding. She herself got restless when she watched other people ride. She'd evaluate their form, rate them in her mind—but all the while, she'd be wishing she was on the horse, not standing on the side, watching.

"You were awesome," he said. "At first I thought, shit, what if you fall? But then I watched you and realized you weren't going to fall."

"I've fallen a few times," she told him. She could feel him start beside her, and she laughed. "Nothing serious. I'm still here. But sometimes, you get an ornery horse and he just doesn't want someone on his back, so he throws you. Five Star would never do that," she added. "He's my sweetheart."

"I thought *I* was your sweetheart," Ted grumbled, although she could hear laughter in his voice.

"You're my other sweetheart," she assured him, then taunted him by adding, "Don't forget, I've been with Five Star a lot longer than I've been with you." She cruised down the road in the waning light. The Wagoneer's windows were open, letting in a hot, dry breeze that carried the scent of pine and fresh-cut grass and summer. "I'm going to miss him so much when I leave for college."

Again she sensed Ted shifting next to her. She glanced his way and saw him staring out the side window.

"I'll miss you, too," she said, realizing that maybe she shouldn't have teased him. Maybe she should have told him that once they'd started dating, she'd reapplied to Colorado College with the request that she forego the Summer Start program and begin college in the fall, so she could spend the summer with him. If she told him that, however, he'd probably hear only the part about her beginning college in the fall, not the part about her asking the school to reprocess her application because she wanted to be with him all summer.

The subject of her leaving for college rarely came up, but when it did Ted grew quiet, melancholy. She *would* miss him. They'd been together nearly every day since the graduation party at Jennifer's house, and they'd talked on the phone when they couldn't see each other. She'd grown so comfortable around Ted, as comfortable as she was with Five Star. She could sense his moves, his moods. She could trust him.

Yet they'd been together for only a few weeks. And she'd known that even if the college agreed to accept her into the freshman class that would matriculate in the fall—which, thank goodness, the school did—she would eventually be leaving Mendham. She regularly reminded herself of that fact. She would be leaving Ted. If they were meant to last, they'd manage to keep things going while she was away. But her idea of a college experience didn't include sitting alone on Saturday nights, pining for her boyfriend back in New Jersey.

"Let's not think about it," she said.

Ted knew what *it* was. "Yeah, right."

"You could go to college, too," she suggested.

Not the best thing to say. She felt him bristling. "The only reason I'd go to college would be if it was Colorado College and I could be with you. And I don't think that would play real well on my application. 'Dear Colorado College, Please accept me despite my lousy transcript because I want to be with Erika Fredell. Oh, and make sure you toss in a full scholarship. Thanks.'"

Even though the subject was touchy and kind of depressing, she found herself laughing. Ted laughed, too.

She didn't love him. She kept telling herself that. She enjoyed his company, enjoyed his wit, enjoyed gazing at his beautiful face, his mesmerizing eyes. She enjoyed kissing him, steaming up the windows of the Wagoneer with him. She liked him more than any other guy she'd ever known, and then some. And when they were both descending into a funk about something—in general, the only thing that sent them both into a funk was discussions about her impending departure for college—she loved the way he could make them both laugh.

But she didn't love him. She couldn't. If she loved him, she would never be able to leave him at the end of the summer.

And she was determined to leave.

"I still don't believe your house is haunted," she said.

They were parked outside his house. It was after midnight, and the windows were all dark. His parents had left the porch light on for him, but they'd probably gone to bed hours ago.

Erika had driven back to her house after they'd left the stable, and she'd changed from her riding pants and boots into a pair of cut-offs and a sexy little sleeveless top that let her bra straps peek through. Her *black* bra straps. A guy couldn't help noticing.

From there, she'd driven to his house so he could change out of his caddying outfit into regular clothes. They'd tossed swimsuits and towels into the backseat and driven to Will's house, where they and a few other friends had swum in his pool and sent out for pizza. Things had finally wound down there, and Erika had driven Ted back to his house.

"How can a house not be haunted if it was built where a cemetery used to be?"

"Assuming you're right about that—"

"I'm right," he argued.

"Your house was built, what, two hundred years ago?"

"Not quite."

"And yet you're positive it was built on a cemetery."

"They moved the cemetery," he reminded her. "They reburied all the bodies up the road at Pleasant Hill Cemetery."

"Well, it makes more sense to me that the ghosts would have moved when the bodies moved. I mean, wouldn't the ghosts want to stay with their bodies?"

He loved when she got all logical. How could you be logical about something as ridiculous as ghosts? "I'm telling you, Erika, I know this stuff. I was born on Halloween."

"And that makes you an expert on ghosts?"

"It makes me an expert on getting Fun Size candy for my birthday," he said with a laugh, then feigned seriousness. "I've heard ghosts thump around the house all my life. I'll be lying in bed and I'll hear them moving around in the attic." Her skeptical frown only inspired him to greater heights of imagination. "I hear them whispering."

"That's the wind blowing through the cracks around your windows. I bet an old house like that must be pretty drafty."

"It's not drafty. What some people think is a draft is actually the hands of a ghost brushing against you. Ghosts' hands are very cold." He gave his voice a little shiver as he said this. "Very, very cold." He reached across the console and ran his hand lightly over her bare leg.

His hand wasn't cold. Her leg wasn't cold.

She didn't pull away. "So what do these ghosts say when they're whispering?" she asked, her voice sounding a little huskier than usual.

"They say, 'Make Erika believe.'" He whispered, too, because the air inside the Wagoneer was getting warmer and closer and he was getting warmer and closer to her.

She leaned toward him as he leaned toward her. He hooked his free hand around the back of her neck, drew her to him and kissed her.

They'd done a lot of kissing in the past few weeks. Light, easy kissing. Deep, hard kissing. Yet every kiss seemed like something new to him, some amazing discovery of just how good he could feel. Every time Erika's lips touched his, his entire body experienced a jolt of sensation. Not horniness, not lust but something more, something that felt like life itself.

If pressed, he wouldn't have been able to describe it. Words weren't his thing. Pictures were, and each time he kissed her it was like discovering a new color, one he'd never known the existence of before. Some of her kisses were a cool, fresh green, not quite mint and not quite emerald but a shade in between. Some of her kisses were a variation on hot pink, some a metallic bronze.

Tonight her kiss was dark blue, midnight blue, a blue that bled into black. Her kiss was shadow, smooth and round and dark. His fingers clenched reflexively against her thigh as her tongue met his and lured it into her mouth.

Oh, God. This was love. It had to be love. He'd kissed other girls. He'd had sex before. But nothing, nothing had ever felt as good as this.

Erika didn't remember moving from the front seat to the back, but somehow, there they were, stretched out along the leather upholstery, Ted on top of her, considerately distributing his weight so he wouldn't crush her.

She didn't care. If he wanted to crush her, she would die smiling.

She was a good girl. She'd never gone much beyond kissing with a boy before, but with Ted she wanted everything, welcomed everything. When he kissed her throat she wanted to purr like a cat. When he stroked her breast through her shirt, she wanted to arch into his hand. When he pressed his groin to hers, and she felt him through the layers of clothing separating their bodies, she wanted to strip naked, to see his body, to touch it.

She didn't dare.

Maybe, someday. Eventually. After she'd thought about it, analyzed it, made sure that this was the right thing to do, the right time. The right boy. Actually, she was already pretty sure about that.

She was by nature a cautious person. She made plans. She thought about the future. She wore a helmet when she rode, and she wanted the same protection for her heart. Ted had been right to worry about what might happen if she fell; a rider could get seriously injured, permanently damaged, even killed. A cracked heart could be as painful as a cracked skull.

And she didn't love Ted. She couldn't. Not when she knew she would be leaving him soon.

Still, when he kissed her like this, when he blanketed her body with his warmth, and she inhaled his clean sunshine scent, and the world beyond the fogged windows of her car fell away, she trusted him. She might not trust herself, but she trusted Ted to her very soul.

"I still don't think your house is haunted," she murmured when he lifted his head after a very long, probing kiss.

"There's this one ghost," he said, then dropped a light kiss on the bridge of her nose. "The ghost of a young guy who died when he was maybe twenty." He touched his mouth to her forehead. "He died a virgin. He sneaks into my room and whispers, 'Don't do what I did.'"

She laughed. "I'm glad to hear you're not going to die when you're twenty."

"He whispers, 'Have sex every chance you get. You never know what tomorrow may bring.'"

"That is the dumbest line I've ever heard," she said, even as her hips gave an involuntary wiggle against him.

He groaned softly. "I think he's making a lot of sense."

"I think he's about as real as all the other ghosts. It's your head that's haunted."

"You haunt me," he murmured, then dove in for another long, deep kiss.

"I can't," she moaned when he finally broke the kiss. "I want to, Ted, but . . . I'm not ready."

He was breathing hard, pressing himself into the valley between her legs. He moaned, too. "Okay," he said, closing his eyes, although she could tell pulling back was a struggle for him.

She was struggling, too. Struggling because she wanted him.

Struggling because the minute she said no, he said okay. Ghosts or no ghosts, he would never force her, never pressure her.

Which made her want him more. Which made her wonder if she *did* love him.

Which scared the hell out of her.

Nine

WORKING AT A GAS STATION IS SERIOUSLY BORING. *You sit behind the counter in the store, which thank God is air-conditioned, and wait for people to drive up to the pump. Then you go outside into the steamy summer heat and fill their tanks. Sometimes they'll pay you outside, and sometimes they'll follow you inside because, along with their gas, they want to buy a candy bar or a bag of pork rinds. Maybe something for their car—a bottle of motor oil or an air freshener shaped like a pine tree that they can hook over the rear-view mirror. Occasionally someone will ask you for directions, and you have to be friendly and helpful. If the customer is an old lady, you might exert yourself a bit and wash the dead bugs from her windshield—especially if the boss is around. And if the gas station is really dead, you might help out in the garage bay, patching punctured tires or carrying the sludge from oil changes to the drum in the back.*

Oh, and sometimes you get to refill the toilet paper dispensers in the rest room.

There are promises about giving you some training and letting you tackle greater challenges—having proven your skill at changing wiper blades and fuses, the mechanics have hinted that you might want to learn how to do state inspections. But this isn't what you want out of life. This isn't what you were born for. It isn't your calling.

Sometimes, however, if you're lucky, a beautiful girl drives up to the pump. Before she can get out of her vehicle, you're out the door, racing across the hot asphalt to the driver's side as she rolls down the window. "Can I fill you up?" you ask, and she gives you a sly, sexy smile and says something about how she'd really like it if you did just that. And you pump her Jeep Wagoneer with the Trinity College sticker and the horse decals all over it full of gas, and when the pump clicks off you return to her window, and she's smiling even more, and looking sexier than before, and you want to jump into the car with her and drive away. You don't care where. You don't care about paying for the gas, or keeping your spirit-killing job, or saying good-bye to your parents or even your dog. You just want to go. With her. Wherever she'll take you, that's where you want to be.

It was too soon to start packing for college, but Erika liked to be organized and on top of things. She didn't want to wait until the end of August, frantic and frenzied as she tried to figure out what to ship, what to bring with her, what to leave behind. Some things—her computer, her CDs—couldn't be packed yet. But her winter clothes could. She wouldn't need sweaters in New Jersey in July, but she sure as hell would need them in Colorado in December.

So she'd methodically packed most of her sweaters into a carton for shipping. They were too bulky to make the trip in a suitcase. She'd also packed the books she would need at college: dictionary, thesaurus, a few classic novels, her calculus textbook, although God knew she wasn't planning to take a lot of math courses.

Even though most of her bedroom remained untouched, it felt

different to her. She knew that several inches of the hanger rod in her closet were now exposed because she'd packed the flannel shirts and cardigans that used to hang there. She knew the desk drawer where she used to store printer paper and ink cartridges was empty.

She knew that in the not too distant future, she would be leaving. And her bedroom seemed to know it, too. Her bedspread, the matching curtains framing the window, the cordless phone on her night table, the alarm clock that used to rouse her for school and riding lessons and trips to horse shows, the shelves of trophies and ribbons—all these familiar things seemed to radiate a chill, as if they resented her decision to abandon them.

"I'll be back," she whispered, feeling like an idiot for talking to inanimate objects. "There'll be trips home for school breaks. It's not like I'm leaving forever."

Yet a part of her knew she *was* leaving forever. She was leaving not just the phone and the curtains but her childhood. The girl she once was.

For months, she'd dreamed of leaving this room, moving on, setting off on her great Colorado adventure. Nothing was going to stand in the way of those dreams. She couldn't wait to begin the next stage of her life. That was what she wanted. Even if it meant saying good-bye to riding, saying good-bye to Five Star.

Saying good-bye to Ted.

A soft moan escaped her. This—the unable-to-say-goodbye part—wasn't supposed to happen. Ted was her summer boyfriend and, yes, she was crazy about him. Mad about him. Wild about him. But Erika wasn't a crazy-mad-wild kind of girl. She would leave, she would miss him—and as she had just told her bedroom, she'd be back.

By the time she returned to Mendham, he would probably be

gone himself. Just as she was growing and changing and moving on, he would be, too. How much longer would he be pumping gas? Surely he'd grow sick of it and find something else to do, someplace else to be.

Her phone rang, and she sprang across the room to answer it. She hoped it was Laura, someone she could whine to, even though she wasn't sure what she had to whine about. "Hello?"

"Hi," Ted said.

Instead of being disappointed that the caller wasn't Laura, she felt her mouth spread in a giddy smile and her breath catch in her throat. After all these weeks, after so much time spent with him, after spending the past few minutes persuading herself that she wasn't really in love with him, she still responded to the sound of his voice like someone intoxicated by love. "Hi," she said.

"I'm just about finished at work."

"Do you want me to pick you up?" she offered.

"Nah. I smell like axle grease. I've got to shower before I'll let you near me."

"I'm sure you smell fine."

"I'll smell fine after I shower. Wanna come by later?"

"Sure."

"I was thinking maybe we could take in a movie."

"Is anything good playing?"

He didn't immediately answer. They'd already seen every half-way decent movie that had come out that summer. "*Encino Man?*" he suggested.

"Yuck."

He laughed. "So, what do you want to do?"

"We could just hang out," she said. "Go driving or something."

"Okay. Why don't you come by my house in about an hour? I should be smelling less greasy by then."

"Sure."

"I wish . . ." he hesitated.

"What?"

"I wish you didn't have to do all the driving."

"That's okay," she said. "I don't mind." She honestly didn't. At some point in the future, she might get tired of driving, but the novelty hadn't worn off yet.

She knew what Ted was really saying, though: he wished he had a car. She wanted to reassure him, to tell him it didn't matter to her that she had a car and he didn't. But he probably didn't want to hear that. Guys wanted cars. They wanted jobs that didn't leave them smelling like axle grease. They liked to impress girls.

She was already so impressed by Ted—by his artistic talent, his devotion to the animals his family raised, his devotion to his family. He didn't need a car to make her heart swoon over him.

"Go shower," she said. "I'll pick you up in an hour."

"My parents are thinking of moving to Maine," he told her.

Their big drive had so far taken them only as far as the Country Coffee House, where they'd ordered sandwiches and sodas. Under the table, Erika had slipped off her flip-flops and perched her feet on Ted's lap. Every now and then, he'd let one hand drop beneath the table and give her toes a squeeze.

"Maine? Why?"

"Money?" he half said, half asked. "New Jersey is so freaking expensive. You know they love going up there. My dad's thinking of making it permanent."

"Wow." She nibbled the corner of her chicken sandwich, thoughtful. "What will you do if they move there?"

"I don't want to live in Maine," he said. "Too cold. I'll find some-place else to live." He grinned. "I hear Colorado is nice."

He seemed to be joking, and she dutifully responded with a laugh. But what if he was serious? What if he moved to Colorado Springs with her?

On the one hand, this was not part of her plan. She wanted to concentrate on college, not on Ted. She wanted to try new things, not continue with the old. She wanted to be open, unencumbered, moving on.

On the other hand . . . This was Ted. Sweet, funny, intense, smart, sexy Ted. Who she was *not* in love with, she reminded herself firmly. Mad-crazy-wild about, perhaps, but not *in love with*.

She didn't want to think about it. Didn't want to think about his following her to Colorado, didn't want to think about saying good-bye to him. Her sweaters might be packed, but she wasn't ready to leave town yet. That major step was weeks away. She spent too much time thinking about the future; at that moment, she only wanted to think about the present.

Once they'd finished their sandwiches, she slid her feet back into her sandals and they drove off. She cruised past the high school, past India Brook Park, past Village Pizza. They didn't see any of their friends' cars at any of those places, so they just kept driving, hot wind blasting them through the Wagoneer's open windows.

Erika's reflexes must have kicked in, because without con-sciously thinking about it she wound up driving to the stable where Five Star boarded. "Let's go say hi to my baby," she said.

Ted seemed satisfied with that choice. Once she'd pulled into the lot near the barn, he got out and joined her at the front bumper. The sky still held the last traces of daylight, but spot-lights had been turned on near the barn entrance and out in the corral, where a few young riding students were trotting in a circle, practicing their posting.

Erika strode directly to the barn, Ted falling into step beside her. Inside, the ceiling lights spilled a yellow light over the stalls, some empty, some occupied by snorting, munching horses. Erika knew a few of the other horses and liked them fine. But Five Star was her one and only. She headed straight for his stall.

As soon as he saw her approach, he thrust his head out and gave a happy whinny. "Hey, baby," she cooed, rubbing his nose. He exhaled, warm and moist, onto her hand. "You remember Ted, don't you, honey?"

Ted gave the horse a perfunctory nod. Erika knew he was humoring her, and she appreciated his effort.

"Have you been a good boy today?" she asked Five Star, still rubbing his nose and then resting her head against his cheek. "You're my sweetheart, aren't you."

Five Star bobbed his head, his mane flopping along his neck.

"I'm going to miss you when I leave for college," she confided to the horse. "I'm going to cry when I have to say good-bye."

"Are you going to cry when you have to say good-bye to me?" Ted asked. His tone was light, but she heard a solemnity underlining the words. He meant the question seriously. He wanted to know if she would miss him as much as she missed Five Star.

"I will be a wreck," she promised. That wasn't a lie. She would miss Ted—assuming he didn't do something totally nuts like follow her out to Colorado. She *knew* Five Star wouldn't follow her out to Colorado. And it wasn't just Five Star she would miss. It was riding. It was the entire life she'd been living since she first climbed onto the back of a pony at the age of six.

But she'd decided to stay focused on the present. And the present meant Ted and her and a tranquil summer evening, with crickets singing and a light breeze stirring the air and stars just beginning to poke through the darkening sky.

She gave Five Star a final pat, and she and Ted left the barn and climbed back into the Jeep. *Live in the now*, she told herself, then smiled at him. His face was so beautiful to her, his eyes so seductive, his sweet smile a thin veil barely concealing determination and desire—and he smelled so good, nothing at all like axle grease.

Tomorrow didn't exist yet. Colorado was far away in time as well as miles. *Now* was Ted and her and a night full of possibilities.

You have dreamed of this moment for weeks. For years. Probably for your entire life. You have visualized it in lines, in angles and loops, in vivid color. In blind shadows and blinding light. You have imagined it. You have lived it in your mind, in your soul.

Erika Fredell is the girl of your heart, and you want her so much. She is the perfect girl for you, and you want this to be as perfect as she is.

You're scared that it won't be. You're scared shitless.

They wound up back at his house on Pleasant Hill Road, in the backseat of the Wagoneer, where so many of their nights ended. This time he was under her. She straddled him, her knees digging gently into his sides. He had his hands molded to the sweet, tight curves of her butt, massaging her through the thin fabric of her shorts.

He was as hard as granite beneath her. He knew she had to feel his arousal, given where she was sitting, but she'd felt it plenty of other nights when they'd been tangled up on the tan leather seat. A few times she'd *really* felt it, slipping her hand inside his shorts and making him absolutely crazy.

Tonight her hands were on his shoulders. She lowered herself to kiss him and then lifted her head, then sank onto him again, kissing him again.

Yeah. He was absolutely crazy, thanks to her.

"Ted?" she whispered.

"Mmm." Crazy enough that grunting was about all he could manage.

"Ted," she said again, straightening her elbows and lifting herself up.

Hell of a time to want to start a conversation. "What?"

"I want you."

"I want you, too." He gave her ass a gentle squeeze, guiding her so she could feel just how much he wanted her. Not that he'd push, not that he'd pressure. He wouldn't, and she knew it. She knew she could drive him to the raw edge, and he'd stagger into his parents' dark, sleeping house and work it all out in the bathroom. If that was what she wanted, that was what he'd do. Even if you didn't love a girl, you couldn't force more on her than she could handle. It just wasn't right.

And if you *did* love her, not forcing her was about more than right and wrong. It was about love. About letting her know she was safe with you. About letting her know that no matter what, she could trust you.

"I mean it," she said, then kissed him again, warm and wet. "Tonight. Now."

His brain was so fuzzy with lust, it took him a minute to understand what she was actually saying. She wanted him. Tonight. Now.

"Are you sure?"

"Do you have a condom?"

He laughed. He wasn't exactly a boy scout but he believed in being prepared. Damn straight he had a condom.

She wasn't laughing. She was smiling, though, a mysterious smile that added a shimmer to her eyes. A question. Maybe a hint of doubt.

"Are you sure?" he asked again, this time dead serious.

She answered by sitting higher, gripping the bottom edge of her shirt and tugging it up, over her head and off.

He had seen her breasts before—they'd done a lot of making-out this summer—but their beauty never failed to move him. Her half-Latina blood enabled her to tan easily, but her breasts were pale, the color of the moon and just as round. He reached up to caress them and she closed her eyes and sighed. And gave her hips a little hitch that took his arousal to an entirely new level.

She lowered herself against him and kissed his neck. He sighed and slid his hands down her back and inside the waistband of her shorts. She shoved at his shirt, trying to push it up. But since she was lying on top of him, her body pressed to him, she couldn't remove it.

Some rearranging was necessary. He hated easing her off him, but he'd never be able to get naked as long as she had him pinned to the seat.

Pinned. Oh, God, she had him pinned. No referee necessary. No three-count required. He was lost, and defeat had never felt so good.

He shifted against the seat, wriggling out from under her and sitting up. He practically tore his shirt pulling it off, but he wanted her touching his chest. He wanted her touching every inch of him.

She fell back on her knees. In the stillness of the car, he heard her respiration and his own, a little ragged. He resisted the urge to press her back and bury his face in the hollow between her breasts, and instead studied her face, searching one last time for hesitation, for fear.

What he saw was trust. Passion. Transparent faith.

Earlier that evening, when she'd been talking about how much she would miss her horse, he'd felt—all right, it was stupid, but he'd felt jealous. He'd been certain, as they'd stood by Five Star's stall, that she really would miss the damned horse more than she missed him. But now, reading the yearning in her face, he knew it was no contest. She loved Five Star, but she *loved* Ted. Loved him enough to give him all of herself, this incredible gift, this essential proof of her love.

A strand of her hair was stuck to her cheek and he stroked it away. "Erika," he murmured. It was easier to talk when she wasn't on top of him. Easier to think.

She nodded.

"This is—I mean, this is your first time."

She nodded again.

"I don't want to hurt you. But it might hurt."

She grinned. "I'll be fine."

He smiled, too. This was really happening. She wasn't backing down. She was, if anything, more enthusiastic than he was. Not that she loved him more than he loved her right at that instant. That would be impossible.

He dug into the pocket of his shorts, pulled out his wallet, and removed the little foil packet he had stashed there. Then he stuffed his wallet back into his pocket and shimmied out of his shorts and boxers. Erika's gaze dropped briefly, then rose to his face again.

Still no hesitation. No doubt. Still that cute, wicked smile.

She rose higher on her knees and slid her shorts down, nothing more than to give in to the impatient demands of his body, but he had to close his eyes for a moment, just to regain control. She was so unbearably beautiful, he could lose it just from looking at her.

Deep breaths. Frantic mental messages to his body to maintain some semblance of control, to last long enough to make this good for her.

Her clothes heaped on the floor of the Wagoneer, she leaned back, straightened her legs as much as the seat would allow, and welcomed him into her embrace. He lowered himself into her waiting arms, between her waiting thighs. Colors swirled within his head, Erika's colors. The honey-brown of her hair, the honey-gold of her skin except for those creamy places where the sun never touched her. The tawny pink of her lips. Shadows the color of night between her breasts, along the edges of her collarbones, her hip bones. The white of her teeth, the red of her tongue as she opened her mouth to his kisses. The endless, depthless dark of her body as he felt her tense slightly, her eyes squeezing shut and her legs flexing around him.

He wanted nothing more than to obey the impatient demand of instinct, but he did his best to hold back. He kissed her forehead, twirled his fingers through her hair, struggled to remain still, to keep breathing until he knew she was with him. After a moment, she opened her eyes and gave an almost imperceptible nod.

"I love you, Erika," he whispered. Nothing he'd ever said was as true as that. "I love you."

She circled her arms around his shoulders and her legs around his hips. And then he was moving, rocking, burning up. His existence was reduced to heat and a throbbing, lush pain, it was all sensation, it was skin and flesh and breath. And love.

I know the perfect girl for you . . .

And here she was. Beneath him. Surrounding him. Giving him everything she had and taking everything he could give her.

In his mind, the night exploded with light. In his heart, the world exploded with love.

Ten

"ARE YOU OKAY?"

His voice reached Erika as if from a distance, passing through layers of mist. She lay under him, damp with sweat and physically drained.

And happy. Rapturous. Blissful. "I'm fine," she said, then mustered what little energy she had to raise her head and kiss him.

She loved the way he looked, both sated and worried. She'd had no idea what she was doing, let alone whether she was doing it right. But he seemed pretty pleased, all in all. And if they did this again—*when* they did it again—he could tell her what to do, how to make it better for him.

She definitely wanted to do it again. Not tonight, though. It hadn't exactly hurt, but she was feeling a little sore.

She loved the feel of him cuddled up against her. They kissed some more, sleepy, easy kisses. She didn't have the strength for anything more fervent than that, and apparently neither did he. Sweat had turned his hair into a mess of curls, making him look boyish and innocent.

He had a gorgeous body. Not that Erika had seen so many naked guys in her life that she had any basis for comparison, but she'd seen artwork. Sculptures. She'd seen those professional wrestlers on TV in their skimpy animal-print Speedos. Ted was less muscle-bound than rippling Greek statues and buffoonish professional wrestlers. He was lankier, bonier, more natural. And absolutely gorgeous.

Too gorgeous to sound so dismal about her own ending to what they had just done. "You didn't. . . ."

"Ted." She brushed her fingertips over his lips, as if she could rearrange them into a smile.

He shifted slightly, managing to squeeze himself against the back of the seat without pushing her onto the floor. He wedged one arm under and around her, holding her close. "Would it be okay if I just . . . I mean, I don't want to hurt you."

She knew instinctively that he could never hurt her. "Would what be okay?" she asked.

He glided his free hand down her body. Down. "Tell me if this hurts."

"It doesn't hurt." Far from that, she felt renewed heat rising inside her, heat and spiraling tension. Her hips twitched, her abdomen clenched. "Ted," she gasped as her body seized, released in a luscious cascade of sensation. She gasped and wrapped her fingers around his hand, which had made her feel so good.

He went still, just holding her, resting his palm against her and waiting for the pulses to subside. She turned her face against his shoulder. She wanted to crawl inside his skin, become a part of him.

He had said he loved her. She knew she loved him.

She couldn't bring herself to speak the words. If she said them, everything would change. She would have to rethink the entire path of her life. If she loved him, how could she leave him? How could she go to Colorado without him? How could she attend college and explore the world and do everything she wanted to do?

If she didn't say the words, if she didn't acknowledge the emotion, maybe it would go away. She could continue to view Ted as her wonderful, funny, handsome boyfriend until it was time to leave. And then she would leave.

They were only eighteen. Too young to be in love.

If she told herself that enough times, maybe she could convince herself it was true.

They made love almost every night after that. Ted would work at the gas station, Erika would spend her day at the stable or packing more boxes and suitcases for college or visiting with Laura and Allyson and her other friends, and in the evening she and Ted would be together. Whatever they did—eat, go to the movies, watch TV, drive down to the shore for an afternoon—they ended their time together in the backseat of the Wagoneer, naked, breathless, learning each other's bodies, bringing each other pleasure.

Each time was better than the previous time. Each time she and Ted made love, she learned how to read and react to his moves, how to adjust, how to take chances and trust that he wouldn't let her fall. How to soar and how to land safely, cradled in his arms.

Each time, she lay beside him afterward, her feet caught on the door handle and her head cushioned by his arm, and thought, *How will I leave him? How can I?*

She never gave voice to that question, and he never raised it himself—until one night in mid-August, when her departure date was within sight. She was snuggled up to him, her eyes closed and her heartbeat gradually slowing as their bodies cooled, when he said, "Marry me."

She flinched, her eyes popping open. "What are you, crazy?"

He didn't look crazy. He looked earnest and pensive. "I love you, Erika. I want us to stay together. You don't have to go to Colorado. You could stay here and go to Rutgers, or Princeton— or, I don't know, there are so many colleges in the area. We could get married and you could still—"

"I can't," she cut him off. Of course she *could* go to Rutgers or Princeton . . . but that wasn't part of her plan. Marriage wasn't part of her plan. "We're just kids, Ted. We're too young to get married."

"I will never love anyone the way I love you," he said, sounding even more earnest. His certainty scared her a little.

"We're too young," she repeated. "I can't even think about marriage right now. You shouldn't be thinking about it, either." He looked so hurt, she added, "If it's meant to be, we'll wind up together."

"I know it's meant to be," he said.

"Then my going to Colorado isn't going to ruin anything. We'll stay in touch and see each other on school breaks, and we'll grow up a little." She cupped her hand over his cheek, trying to coax a smile out of him. "Come on, Ted. You know we're too young to be talking about marriage."

He didn't look persuaded, but at least he didn't argue anymore.

She should have been relieved. She *was* relieved. But as soon as he stopped talking about marriage, she found herself worrying the idea like a bruise she couldn't stop touching. Of course marrying him was a preposterous idea, but . . . what if? What if she could sleep in his arms every night and wake up to his laughter every morning? What if they could cook dinners side by side in a cozy little kitchen and sit side by side on the sofa while they watched *Law & Order* or MTV, and then retire to their bedroom and make love in a real bed, not in the backseat of a car?

It wasn't what she wanted. It wouldn't work. They were too young.

But still . . . she couldn't escape a tug of wistfulness when she thought about it. It was such a lovely idea. And Ted . . .

Don't say it, she warned herself. *Don't say you love him. If you don't acknowledge it, maybe it won't really be true.*

"Marriage?" Laura squealed. "Oh, God, that's so romantic!"

This was not what Erika needed to hear from her friend. They were seated on the floor of her bedroom, which looked decimated, so much stuff packed away, a few boxes already shipped out west. Ted had gotten a couple of days off at the gas station and traveled up to Maine with his parents, who were apparently serious about moving to East Machias. He'd shown her where it was on a map—a speck of a town, not far from the ocean and not far from the Canadian border. Housing was less expensive there—a hell of a lot cheaper than housing in northern New Jersey, which wasn't saying much. Ninety-five percent of the country probably had housing cheaper than in northern New Jersey.

She was glad Ted was gone for a couple of days. She needed a chance to clear her head, to think about his proposal. To talk to Laura.

Laura was hogging the bowl of pretzels, and Erika reached out and grabbed a handful, then settled against her bed, which she was using as a backrest. "I know you think he's perfect for me," she said between bites of pretzel. "But we're only eighteen."

"So say yes and set the date for four years from now. Can I be your maid of honor?"

"He's *serious*, Laura," Erika scolded. Laura seemed much too tickled by the idea. "He wants to marry me so I won't go to Colorado."

Laura munched thoughtfully and shifted her butt against the carpet. Erika's desk couldn't be as comfortable to lean against as the bed, but if they sat side by side they wouldn't be able to see each other. And Laura wouldn't be able to hog the pretzels as effectively. Finally, she asked, "Do you want to go to Colorado?"

"Of course I do."

"More than you want to be with Ted?"

That question had no *of course* answer. "The timing sucks," she said. "If I'd just graduated from college instead of high school, this would be a no-brainer."

"Would it?"

Erika toyed with the last pretzel in her hand. She slid one finger through the salted loop, then realized it was her ring finger she'd slid through. She knew for a certainty that she wasn't ready to place a wedding band on that finger. But in four years . . .

In four years she would be a college graduate, and Ted wouldn't. In four years she'd be eager to travel, to explore, to move on to even greater challenges. In four years she would be someone else. So would Ted.

In four years, she might meet someone else. So might he.

Nothing about this was a no-brainer.

"You can keep the relationship going while you're away, if you want," Laura reminded her. "You can write letters, call each other. I mean, just because you're moving away doesn't mean you have to break up."

"Right." Erika wished she felt as certain as Laura sounded.

"You're going to stay in touch with me, right? You can stay in touch with him, too."

Erika snorted. Sure, she could stay in touch with Laura, and Allyson, and all her other friends. But she wasn't sleeping with any of them. She wasn't dreaming about any of them. None of them had ever held her in their arms and peered into her face with eyes so beautiful they made her heart ache and said, "I love you."

"I don't want to hurt him," she said.

Laura regarded her thoughtfully. "Sounds as if you've already made up your mind on how this is going to go."

"I'm going to leave him?" Erika guessed. "I'm going to break up with him?"

"Sounds like."

A few tears escaped Erika's eyes, skittering down her cheeks and getting caught in her lip, adding their salt to the salt of the pretzels she'd been nibbling. "What if no one else ever loves me as much as he does?"

"What if *you* never love anyone else as much as you love him?" Laura shot back.

I don't love him, Erika wanted to say, but she couldn't lie to Laura. She did love Ted. And she was going to leave him.

That's it. She's gone.

You play everything over and over in your mind, a continuous loop of torture. You play that last time, just before she left, and she said, "We're going to be two thousand miles apart, Ted, so really, we should both be free to see other people." You told her you didn't want to see other people and she kissed your cheek and said, "We'll always be friends."

You play that moment over and over, that awful scene, that fatal cut. You play it over and over until your brain wants to burst out of your skull.

You play the mix tape she gave you just before she left. Phish, Spin Doctors, Helen Reddy, a sweet, soulful Fleetwood Mac love song. Songs you listened to with her all summer, songs you sang in your choir-trained voice. Songs you made out to. Songs you made love to. You play the tape over and over, you play the summer over and over. You torture yourself with the sounds, the memories, the loneliness of everything you lost when she left.

You lie on the old blue sofa in the living room. The room is gloomy; the trees outside the windows block the late summer sunlight, and that's fine with you. You don't want light. You want the quiet dark of a movie theater so you can play the film of you and Erika over and over in your mind.

You don't eat. You don't talk. You don't move. You just lie there, wallowing in the memory of every moment you spent with her. Especially those last moments.

"We'll stay in touch," she told you. "I'll always care about you. But let's just be friends."

No. Let's not just be friends. "I will never date you again," you tell her. And you mean it. You mean it with all your heart.

Your shriveling shell of a heart.

"You're eighteen years old," your father says. "You've got your whole life ahead of you. The world is full of girls. You'll find someone else."

No. You never will.

"Maybe you should see a doctor," your mother says. "I think you're coming down with something."

Yeah, you're coming down. Down in the world. Down into the darkness that is the end of love.

After a few days, you somehow find the strength to go to work. You sit inside the gas station, staring past the candy racks and the stacks of newspapers to the pumps on the other side of the glass wall, waiting for a car to drive in so you'll have something to do. Thinking maybe an old Wagoneer festooned with horse show stickers will pull in, and Erika will climb out and race to the building, throw open the door and say, "I was wrong to leave you! I love you! I came back."

Volvo wagons stop at the pump. Dodge Caravans filled with little kids in soccer uniforms. Mercedes coupes. Trucks bearing the logos of house painters, lawn services, plumbers. Lincoln Town Cars with tinted windows.

Never a Jeep Wagoneer with wood siding and horse show stickers. Your mother is right. You are sick. You're dying.

Erika's first letter arrived about two weeks after she'd left for college. When he saw it waiting for him on the kitchen table after he got home from the gas station—saw the return address, the Colorado Springs postmark, her familiar handwriting—he thought he just might not die, after all.

He resisted the urge to tear the envelope open right there in the kitchen, with Spot sniffing at his heels and his mother peeling carrots at the sink. Instead, he carried the letter up the stairs to his bedroom, climbed onto his bunk, and held it in his hands. Stared at it. Let it lie on his chest in the hope that it might seep some magical power through his shirt and his ribcage and into his heart.

He listened to the stillness around him, then heard a creak above him, in the attic. One of the ghosts, he thought with a smile. The ghosts Erika insisted didn't exist.

Hell, he'd practically become a ghost himself these past two weeks. If she didn't believe in ghosts, she should have come back to New Jersey and checked out Ted Skala, the haunted guy, the walking dead.

Finally, when he was calm enough to open the envelope without shredding it and damaging its contents, he slid his finger under the flap, shook out the letter, unfolded it, and read.

She was doing well, she said. Colorado Springs was awesome. He wouldn't believe how beautiful the mountains were. Some of the kids in her dorm said they'd teach her how to ski. Apparently you couldn't live in Colorado Springs and not know how to ski. It defied the laws of nature or something. Besides, she said, if she wasn't going to do show jumping, she needed to find some other sport that would give her the sense of flying.

Her classes were interesting. She was especially enjoying her psychology class, and she thought she might major in psych, although she didn't have to choose a major until the end of her sophomore year. She was also taking a fine arts class, and she had a newfound respect for Ted's drawing ability. She wished she had half his talent.

Her roommate was great and she was making lots of friends. The sky was bigger in Colorado, she reported. She couldn't explain it; she knew logically that the sky above Colorado was the same sky as the one above New Jersey, but everything felt bigger out there, wilder, brighter. More open.

She sounded so damned happy he wanted to weep.

He didn't. He just felt his heart shrivel a little bit more, shrinking into a dark, wrinkled raisin in his chest.

She *had* written to him, he reminded himself. She was obviously thinking of him. She wanted to share her experiences with him. The letter was a *good* thing.

What could he write back to her? "Hey, Fred—I'm still pumping gas in New Jersey."

He read the letter again, and then a third time. He analyzed it for hints that she missed him, clues that she still loved him, insinuations that she hadn't completely discarded the notion of marrying him.

Shit. She was having too much fun to marry him. She was growing, learning . . . Christ, she was going to major in psychology.

Once she'd mastered that subject, she would look at him and think, *What a head case.*

He had to write back to her. Not just write back—he had to convince her that his life was as wonderful as hers. But writing didn't come easily to him. He was so much more visual than verbal.

He would draw her a picture.

He heard another creak upstairs in the attic. Maybe the wind had kicked up, maybe the house was settling—that was something two-hundred-year-old houses liked to do—or maybe the ghost was simply letting Ted know he liked the idea. A picture for her, with color, with detail, with brilliance and emotion. A picture that expressed everything he couldn't write in words. He would send it to her, and she would know his feelings for her were a hell of a lot stronger than her feelings for the mountains and the big sky and her psychology class.

He started planning out the drawing the next day at work. He spent large chunks of each day sitting behind the counter at the gas station, doing nothing, simply being present in case someone pulled up to the pump or wandered inside to buy a scratch ticket or a pack of smokes. If he was idle and the mechanics needed his assistance in the garage bay, he'd help them, but they didn't ask him for help too often because if they did they'd have to pay him a hell of a lot more. He wasn't earning mechanic wages, so they couldn't really expect him to be a mechanic.

For a guy who was naturally restless, sitting behind the counter wasn't exactly fun. He whiled away the time reading the newspaper, listening to music, straightening the bags of potato chips on the chrome shelves. But he'd rather be drawing. Thinking. Creating.

His picture had to be spectacular. It had to express everything he felt for Erika. It had to dazzle her.

Them. Of course, it would depict them. In bed. Making love. Their bodies intertwined. Not pornographic, not tawdry but beautiful. Over the days, he stole spare minutes when he could, plied his colored pencils, poured himself into the drawing.

Not just him and Erika. Animals, too. He always drew animals. She loved horses. He'd grown up with sheep and geese, ducks and rabbits. He added donkeys to the drawing. They were kind of like horses, but also like the farm animals he'd taken care of throughout his youth. Donkeys had spirit. They were strong, energetic, stubborn. Like him. Like his passion for her.

Somehow, he managed to intertwine them with the lovers in the bed. He added color, shading. Lines, shapes, intricacies. No rushing, no shortcuts. This was his masterpiece, for the woman he loved.

After a week, he was satisfied with what he'd created. More than satisfied—he was proud. His drawing was amazing. She would love it, and she would love him.

He had an early shift and was able to leave the gas station mid-afternoon, before the post office closed. He had no idea how to ship the drawing; he couldn't fold it to fit inside an envelope. He hoped the post office would know how to package it.

The postal clerk, a middle-aged woman with frosted blond hair and a double chin, gasped when she saw the drawing. "That is beautiful," she said.

"I have to send it to Colorado," he told her. "I don't know how to pack it. I don't want to fold it."

"Absolutely not. You can't fold it." She circled the counter to a corner of the room where packing supplies were on display and pulled a rugged cardboard tube from a rack. "This is what you need for a drawing that beautiful," she said, carrying it with her back to her side of the counter.

Ted watched as she meticulously rolled the drawing, making sure not to crease or dent it or bend the corners. In her pale blue post office shirt with the fake tie at her neck, she looked like the antithesis of Erika. Surely her taste differed from Erika's. If she thought the drawing was beautiful, Erika might hate it.

Even so, Ted absorbed the clerk's compliment like blotting paper soaking up a spill. "It's for the love of my life," he confessed, smiling when he realized how gooey that sounded. He didn't owe her any explanations; he didn't have to prove himself to her. But she thought his drawing was beautiful, and once she'd rolled it for him, she inserted it into the tube with the care of a mother laying her baby in its crib. She was his accomplice, his partner in this essential act. She understood its import, and she was honoring his drawing, and him, and his love.

He hoped Erika would honor it as well. He hoped she would look at it and realize he wasn't just a loser working at a gas station. He was an artist. She had inspired him to create this masterpiece that depicted how much he loved her. He hoped she would pull the drawing from the tube, gasp, and murmur, "That is beautiful."

And then she would get on a plane and fly to Newark, and drive up to Mendham, and charge into the gas station and say, "I love you, too."

The wait was excruciating. Ted alternated between lying on his bunk listening to the mix tape Erika had given him and lying on the blue sofa in the living room and lapsing into dark, depressed moods. When in the grip of one of those dark moods, he had no appetite, and he lost weight he couldn't afford to lose. When he listened to the tape, though, he felt Erika's nearness. Surely she'd chosen the songs for the tape to communicate with him, just as he was using his artistic ability to communicate with her.

He listened to Christine McVie's flute-like voice singing, "I love you, I love you, like never before," and he thought, *This is Erika's message to me. I haven't lost her.*

A week after he mailed the drawing, she phoned. Hearing her voice was like injecting a powerful drug into his veins. It jolted him, heated his entire body, wrenched him into another place. "Hey, Ted," she said.

"Hey, Fred." As gobsmacked as he was, he did his best to sound cool and nonchalant. "How's it going?"

"I just got the drawing you sent me. That was so sweet."

So sweet? So sweet? He'd poured his soul into that drawing. His heart. Every last ounce of emotion. Every bit of love and passion and yearning. He'd killed himself over that drawing, and she thought it was *sweet?*

He wanted to cry. Or bang the phone against the wall until it broke, until it was smashed into as many pieces as he was.

Sweet. Jesus freaking Christ.

"Yeah, well . . ." he said in a deceptively calm voice. "So, how are you?"

She told him exactly how she was: Fantastic. Terrific. Never been better. She told him about her classes and her roommate and the kegger she'd been to last Saturday night. She told him about how she and all her wonderful new friends had gone hiking and they were going to teach her how to ski, and she was so happy to be trying new things. She told him that as much as she'd loved riding, she was welcoming the changes in her life, the different challenges of these activities.

Ted knew what she was trying to communicate: not the sentiments of the Fleetwood Mac song, not that she loved him like never before, but that she was glad to be gone, glad to be embracing all that was new and different in Colorado. Glad not to have stayed home in New Jersey, living the life she'd lived for eighteen years. Glad not to have stayed with Ted.

"That is really cool," Becky said. She and a few other girls had gathered in Erika's dorm room to admire Ted's drawing. No one had been around when Erika had retrieved the mysterious cylindrical shipment from the package room at the campus center. She'd seen the return address and freaked out a little; what could Ted have sent her in a tube-shaped mailer?

She'd wanted to open it right away, but she'd carried it back to her dorm room before prying open one end and sliding out the drawing. And then she'd freaked out a little more, because it was the most astonishing drawing Ted had ever done. Vivid, visceral, an explosion of line and color—and passion. Two lovers in bed, surrounded by all that imagery.

He'd drawn it for her. Gone to all that effort, for her.

Would any other boy ever do so much for her? Would she ever meet another boy as devoted to her as Ted was?

Someone as obsessed by her? Someone determined to cling to what had been rather than open himself to what lay ahead? Someone who refused to step outside his safety zone and see what else the world had to offer?

She'd stared at the drawing and tears had spilled down her cheeks. Crying over Ted came easily to her. He had the key that unlocked all her emotions, and his power over her frightened her. She'd been smart to leave him. If she'd stayed with him, she would have given him control over her hopes and dreams. She would have become Ted's woman, rather than her own. She would have lost herself.

She'd spread the drawing out on her bed, hurried down the

hall to the bathroom, and washed her face. Once she'd regained her composure, she'd returned to her room and phoned him. ""I just got the drawing you sent me," she'd told him when he answered. "That was so sweet."

He hadn't sounded exactly thrilled to hear her voice. She wondered why. She couldn't believe he hated her after he'd drawn such a magnificent picture and sent it to her. Maybe he'd wanted her to say something else.

She'd said what was in her heart: it was so sweet that he'd done this.

And she'd realized, as they'd talked on the phone, that staying connected over two thousand miles was next to impossible. She'd spoken honestly yet sensed that she'd said the wrong thing. He'd sounded clipped and chilly. She couldn't see him, couldn't gauge what he was thinking. She couldn't read his feelings in his eyes, the way she could when they were together.

The more she'd talked, the colder he'd sounded. He didn't want to hear about the hike she and a few schoolmates had taken up Pike's Peak. He clearly felt as removed from her as she did from him.

"Who sent it to you?" Adrienne asked.

Erika set aside her memory of her phone conversation with Ted and basked in the oohs and ahhs of her college friends as they admired the drawing. "My—a friend of mine," she said. Ted wasn't her boyfriend. He wasn't her love. She'd told him when she'd left for Colorado that she wanted them to be just friends.

After talking to him, she doubted they were even that.

Eleven

MAINE IS LIKE NEW JERSEY, *only colder, more rugged, more forested, less congested and the people have tart Yankee accents.*

All right, it's nothing like New Jersey, except for the one thing that matters to you: Erika isn't there.

You help your parents move up to Maine, figuring the change of scenery will be good for you. You want to get away from all the places that remind you of her: the high school, your friends' houses, the stable where her precious Five Star boards. Ghosts may be able to travel up the road from the cemetery to the house you grew up in, but if you're lucky, the ghost of your love affair will not be able to travel all the way to East Machias.

You still write to her, of course. Sometimes you send her a drawing. You and she are still "friends," whatever the hell that means. You know what it means to you: you are still so sick in love with her that you'll take whatever scrap she tosses your way. What it means to her is that she occasionally drops you a line and she doesn't hang up when you phone her.

You sign up for some college courses. Maybe that will impress her. Maybe all she ever wanted from you was a little ambition, some proof that you didn't expect to spend the rest of your life pumping

*gas and wiping dead bugs off windshields. You always had ambi-
tion—if you weren't ambitious, you wouldn't have aimed your
sights on a girl as classy as Erika Fredell. You just didn't know what
you wanted to do with your life.*

Other than love her.

*There's a branch of Maine's state university system in Machias, so
you sign up and hand over a check. You wander around the campus,
sit in on a few classes and think, What am I doing? Why am I here?
How the hell am I supposed to sit still for ninety minutes while this
tweedy windbag takes twenty minutes to define macroeconomics—
yeah, it's the study of broad economic systems, you get it already.
How are you supposed to wait patiently while that militantly funky
woman spends half the art class talking about shading? You get
that, too.*

*This isn't the place for you. Going to college to get Erika to love
you isn't going to cut it.*

*She used to love you just for who you were. She used to think the
fact that you were reasonably intelligent and fun and utterly
devoted to her was enough.*

When did it stop being enough?

Winter came earlier to Colorado than it did to New Jersey. As
much as Erika missed riding, she was glad she wasn't pursuing
the rigorous training schedule she used to have back home. She
would have had to start riding indoors by early November.

Instead, weeks before Thanksgiving, she found herself on a
bunny slope, strapped into rented ski boots, perched on rented
skis and gripping rented poles. And feeling like a toddler learning
to take her first faltering steps.

"Just tell me what to do," she said to Becky, who owned her
own equipment—not just skis, boots, poles, and a helmet, but

fancy insulated gloves and a form-fitting jacket that made her look sleek and slim, unlike Erika's puffy down parka. "I've ridden horses. I made nationals. I'm sure I can do this."

"It's not exactly the same thing," Becky pointed out.

"This hill is hardly even sloping!"

"That's the point. The first thing you need to learn is how to fall."

"I don't want to fall."

"Doesn't matter. You *will* fall, and you need to learn how to fall without hurting yourself."

Two minutes later, Erika fell. The hill might have been about as steep as a typical highway ramp, but the snow was awfully slippery and the skis were unwieldy. At least *her* skis were. Becky's skis were obviously vastly superior. They never seemed to slide out from under her, even when she was zigzagging and making sharp turns and hunching into a tuck position.

She ordered Erika to angle her skis so they were nearly touching in front of her. Becky called this "snow-plowing." Erika called it "skiing cross-eyed."

"It will slow you down," Becky explained, and Erika wanted to argue that she didn't want to go slow. She was used to cantering on horses, galloping on them, flying over fences on them.

But she was the novice here, the East Coast chick in Rocky Mountain country, and she obeyed Becky and Adrienne and the other kids from her dorm who had dragged her off to this mountain for her first attempt at skiing.

Her years of riding had taught her a thing or two about balance, at least. And she was blessed with fearlessness. If she fell, she fell. Sooner or later, she'd make it down the hill without falling. And without angling her skis to slow her down.

She and her friends spent all of Saturday at the slope, which made sense since their lift tickets were good for the entire day. By early afternoon, Erika was actually using the ski lift rather than gliding up to the top of the bunny hill on a tow line. She was a long way from qualified for the double black diamond trails, but she made it down the green trail, escorted by two of her friends, and she fell only twice. At the bottom, she immediately slid over to the lift line to ride up again. She would master skiing the way she'd mastered riding.

She didn't fall at all during her last run of the day. She began to feel comfortable enough to straighten her skis out and add a little speed to her descent. The dry mountain wind stung her cheeks and fanned through her newly cropped hair—she'd decided to try a new style, and she loved the freedom of not having those long, heavy tresses hanging down her back.

New hairstyle. New sport. New life.

Just what she'd wanted when she'd left Mendham.

And yet.

Like an ember that refused to die but continued to glow and send a thread of smoke into the air when the rest of the fire had been reduced to cold, gray ash, there was a part of her that refused to let go of the old life. It had nothing to do with horses, nothing to do with her parents and their comfortable house and the bathroom she'd had all to herself once her sister had left for college. Nothing to do with Allyson and Laura and all her other friends, who'd scattered to other colleges but who managed to stay in touch with phone calls and email.

It was Ted. She couldn't seem to let go of Ted. He was that ember, that spark, still glowing, still hot. Still capable of warming her, or burning her.

Like the long, thick hair she'd once had, he was a weight on her, holding her back. She wanted to move on. She wanted to be Erika, the Colorado ski queen instead of Erika, the New Jersey horse show queen.

She wanted not to be always thinking of him, wondering what he was doing, how he was feeling, whether he still believed they ought to be married. He wanted to marry the old Erika, and she wasn't that person anymore.

Her friends insisted on toasting her success on skis that night when they ended up at a frat house party, drinking cheap beer from plastic cups. "Look at you," one of the guys said as he hoisted his cup in her direction. "A whole day on skis, and you're not in a full-body cast. I'd call that a success."

"Not even a broken leg," one of the girls pointed out.

"Or a totaled knee. I totaled my knee the third time I skied."

"There's a real confidence booster," Erika joked. "Now I can't wait to get back on skis again."

The truth was, she couldn't. The more beer she drank, the more eager she was to return to the slopes. Before the end of the school year, she was determined to qualify for black diamond.

Ted would never understand this, she thought. He'd mastered wrestling, but that was completely different. Wrestling was combat, but it wasn't death-defying, or life-affirming. It was about winning, not about soaring.

He wouldn't understand anything about her anymore. Not her excitement about her studies—intro psychology utterly captivated her, and the level of analysis in her literature class was so much more advanced than those superficial high school discussions about *Julius Caesar* and *Silas Marner*.

He wouldn't understand. He wouldn't know her anymore.

Thinking about that stubborn, glowing ember made her want to cry. She had to extinguish it.

"Hi," she said the next morning. Her head was aching, maybe from the beer she'd drunk last night but more likely from tension. This was not going to be an easy conversation.

"Hey, Fred," Ted greeted her. "How's it going?"

Just do it. Put out that ember before it ignites and burns down your world. "Ted, we've got to stop calling each other."

He said nothing.

"Are you there?"

"I'm here." His voice was low, hard.

"I'm sorry, Ted. Really. But I just can't make this work long-distance. It's crazy." *I'm skiing now*, she wanted to say, as if that explained everything. *My hair is short. I'm someone new.* "You're a great guy, and I don't want to hurt you. But I just can't do this any longer."

Another long silence stretched between them. Closing her eyes, she could visualize the cables stretching across the continent, across the Great Plains, over the Appalachians, north along the coastline to Maine, where he'd moved with his parents. Brilliant inventors had created telephones, engineers had designed grids, laborers had sweated and toiled to string the wires and lay the cables that connected her to Ted right now. And all that effort, all that labor, led to this: silence.

Finally he spoke. "Wow, Fred. That is a really ballsy move."

Not what she'd expected. She'd thought he would plead with her, argue with her, insist that she was wrong, remind her of how much he loved her. Not call her "ballsy."

"Why?" she asked.

"'Because I'm a sure thing. And you're letting me go. I will never be with you again, I could never be this hurt again."

Then silence once more, and she realized the line was dead. She stopped visualizing the cables and instead focused her gaze to the pile of drawings on her desk, the drawings Ted had sent her since she'd left for college. Beautiful drawings, hilarious drawings, somber drawings, and each of them a piece of his soul, captured on paper and presented to her. Gifts, all of them, from the boy who'd been a sure thing. The sure thing she'd just cut out of her life. The ember she'd doused.

She lowered the phone, wiped her eyes before her tears could fall, and slid the drawings into a folder, which she placed carefully into a drawer of her desk for safekeeping.

She might have broken up with Ted, the first boy she'd ever really cared about, the boy with the sexy green eyes and the sweet, hot kisses, the boy who had taught her about wrestling and sex and love. She might have broken up with him—but she wasn't ready to let go of his drawings.

"Yo, Skala," his friend Dave said. "What do you think of Tempe?"

Ted didn't think much of anything these days. He couldn't let himself think of Erika; it hurt too much. And what else was there to think of? His future? Yeah, right. Life in Jonesboro, Maine, population fifty, a few miles down Route One from his parents' home in East Machias? Oh, there was a lot to think about there. Love, sex, work, the meaning of life? Thinking about those things hurt too much.

Right now, all he could really wrap his mind around was the six-pack of Budweiser he and Dave were working their way through. Dave was a few years older than Ted. Now that Ted had quit college and was no longer a student, he and Dave were practically equals—other than the fact that Dave could walk into a store and buy a six-pack of Bud and Ted couldn't.

"What's Tempe?" he asked. "Some kind of sushi?"

"It's a city in Arizona. I'm heading out there. Time for a change of scenery. What do you think?"

"Arizona? That's like the other end of the world."

"It's sunny there, all the time. And there's work there. Why don't you join me?"

Ted tipped the can of beer against his lips and let the sour fizz wash over his tongue. What the hell would he do in Tempe, Arizona? Besides enjoy the sunshine?

Work sounded good.

And what was keeping him back east? His parents were okay, happily settled in Maine, and if they needed anything, his brothers and sister were around. There was nothing to hold him here, nothing that called to him. Nothing that meant anything to him.

"They got beer in this town called Tempe?" he asked Dave with a grin.

"They got everything."

"How long a drive is it?"

"Drive, nothing. I can score us some airplane tickets. We can fly out there, have a look around, try our luck with employment. There's a university there, too—Arizona State."

"I'm done with college," Ted protested.

"Yeah, but there are many thousands of undergraduate girls who aren't done with college there."

Girls. Like he wanted to hook up with anyone.

He *did* want to hook up with someone. *Anyone.* Anyone who wasn't Erika Fredell, anyone who could make him forget her, anyone who could heal the festering wound she'd left in his heart.

"Airplane tickets, huh."

"Gratis," Dave promised him.

"So how long a flight is it?"

"I don't know. You can't fly there direct. These tickets I can score for us, we'd have to change planes in Denver."

Ted might not have known where Tempe was, but he sure as hell knew where Denver was. In Colorado. In the state where Colorado Springs was located, and Colorado College, and Erika.

Don't be an ass, he scolded himself. *That's over. She's over. You're over her.*

Even if he was over her, though, they could still see each other. As former classmates, right? For old time's sake.

And maybe she'd see him and realize she'd been wrong. Maybe she'd see him and think, *What an idiot I've been. Ted is the only man I've ever loved, or ever will love.*

Stranger things had been known to happen.

"Really?" he said to Dave. "You can score free tickets?"

"Why did you agree to do this?" Becky asked as they merged onto I-85 north, heading toward the Denver Airport.

Seated next to her in the passenger seat, Erika sighed. *Good question,* she thought. Becky and the girls in the backseat deserved a good answer.

That it was a sunny winter day and they didn't have anything better to do than spend more than an hour cruising up to the Denver Airport was *not* a good answer. That after spending so many months in Colorado, Erika was hungry to hear a New Jersey accent was *not* a good answer.

That she'd spent hours last night thumbing through the folder of Ted's drawings, trying to convince herself that she was truly over him, and that she thought seeing him would nail that conviction down was not a good answer.

But she *was* over him. And he was over her. He'd said he would never be with her again. When he'd phoned a couple of nights ago and informed her that he had a two-hour layover at the airport in Denver, she remembered his telling her he would never be with her again. She figured he wanted to see her, just to be sure.

She wanted to be sure, too.

"We're friends," she said.

"I'm your friend," Adrienne commented from the backseat. "Would you drive an hour to see me?"

"In a heartbeat," Erika said, meaning it.

"Okay, so you want to see this friend," Anna said placidly. "Sounds good to me."

"Oh, come on. He was more than a friend, wasn't he?" Becky asked. "You showed us that picture he sent you, with the couple going at it."

Erika wanted to scold Becky for her mocking tone. That picture was awesome; all the girls who'd seen it had agreed that it was. She and Ted had never been "a couple going at it." They'd been in love. That love was over, but out of respect for what had once been, she had to travel up to Denver to see Ted.

So it was an outing with her friends. They'd go to the airport, and then, once Ted was on his plane and flying off to wherever—she recalled him mentioning somewhere in Arizona—she and the girls would cruise into Denver and check out a club or two. Or they'd drive back to campus and stop in at one of the frat houses. Or whatever.

It was important for her to see Ted. Important for her to assure herself that he was all right after she'd broken up with him. Important for her to assure herself that *she* was all right, even if the breakup had been at her instigation.

Denver International Airport was a maze of roads, connectors, and parking lots all weaving around a building that looked like a circus tent designed by Dr. Seuss. "Those points are supposed to represent the mountains," Anna explained, pointing to the swoops and peaks of the main building. It didn't remind Erika of mountains, but she was in no state of mind to assess the architectural daring of the building.

In a matter of minutes, she would be seeing Ted. For the first time since she'd broken up with him—for the first time since she'd said good-bye to him before heading off to Colorado—she would be seeing the boy who'd been her first love. Her palms felt clammy and her heart pounded more fiercely than it ever had when she'd been about to ride in a horse show, ski down a slope, or take an exam.

Like her exams in school, this was a test. But unlike her exams, she had no idea what she was being tested on, no concept of how to study for it, and no confidence that she'd pass.

Becky cruised into the short-term garage, took a ticket, and drove up and down the aisles until she found a parking space. *You'll pass,* Erika told herself, mustering the same poise and steadiness that had seen her through so many riding competitions in her youth. *You'll ace it.*

"Do they sell margaritas in the airport?" Adrienne wondered aloud as they sauntered to the crosswalk and into the terminal building.

"Not to nineteen-year-olds," Becky told her.

Erika didn't want a drink. She just wanted to get this reunion over with, so she could be sure she'd done the right thing in breaking up with Ted. So she could get on with her life.

"Which airline is he on?" Becky asked her.

They studied the monitor and figured out which gate he was at. Passing through security was easy, and they hiked down the endless corridor to his terminal. Erika ran her fingers through her hair, casually, so her friends wouldn't notice that she was preening. If she'd been alone, she would have ducked into a restroom to check her reflection in a mirror. But she wasn't alone. And that was a good thing. She needed her friends with her for support.

Fifteen minutes of newsstands, souvenir shops, and food courts later, they reached the gate where Ted would be arriving. "I can't wait to see this guy," Becky confided to Anna and Adrienne in a whisper loud enough for Erika to hear.

"Yeah, I bet you'd love Erika's castoffs," Anna teased.

"I just want to see if he's hot."

"Cut it out, you guys," Erika lashed out. Closing her eyes, she took a deep breath. *You're going to clear the fence,* she assured herself. *You're going to soar.*

Then she opened her eyes and saw him, filing through the door with the other deplaning passengers.

He looked . . . good. He was dressed in a blue mock turtleneck that clung to his torso, hinting at a chest that had added a bit of muscle and heft. Nicely battered jeans—some newly gained muscle in his legs, too. His hair was relatively neat, his smile restrained. He was no longer the gangly high school boy she'd had a crush on. He looked . . .

Really good.

In his hand was an adorable stuffed teddy bear.

Oh, God. A teddy bear. Friends didn't give friends teddy bears, did they?

Becky, Adrienne, and Anna must have noticed the teddy bear when Erika did. Anna nudged her in the ribs with her elbow, and Becky whispered, "Uh-oh. I think he thinks it's Valentine's Day."

"Isn't that *special,*" Adrienne added.

Erika allowed herself a tight grin, acknowledging her friends' snide assessments even though she felt . . . ambivalent. Torn. A touch disloyal. The teddy bear *was* special—it looked like an expensive one. And it was sweet. And kind of desperate.

She shouldn't have come to the airport. She'd broken up with Ted, and she should have left things as they were: done. Finished. *No más.*

But now here she was, flanked by her friends as if they were her seconds in a duel. Looking at Ted was like losing a duel. The memories stabbed her, pierced her, cut straight to her heart. If his stare had been any more pointed, she would have been literally bleeding.

He veered away from the stream of passengers and approached her where she stood among the rows of chairs in the gate waiting area. "Hey, Fred," he said.

"Hey." Her stomach contracted with nerves. With sorrow. Telling him to stop calling her had been easy enough when he'd been two thousand miles away. Now he was just inches away. Close enough to give her a brief hug, which he did. Close enough to kiss her, which he didn't. "These are my friends, Anna, Adrienne, and Becky," she introduced them. "And this—" she addressed her friends "—is Ted."

He barely acknowledged them. His eyes remained on her, his brows dipping slightly. "You cut your hair."

Behind her, her girlfriends laughed.

She gave her head a toss. She loved how light it felt without all that long hair spilling down her back, and the way the clipped ends fluttered like a silky fringe around her face. "Do you like it?"

Stupid question. His expression told her he didn't.

And she didn't care. She wasn't dressing or styling herself to impress him. His opinion of her new coiffure was irrelevant.

She'd never had to struggle to talk to Ted before. But now the words didn't come. Her life was as altered as her hairdo, and he wasn't a part of it. "So," she said brightly. "You're moving to— where was it? Tucson?"

"Tempe. My friend Dave has a place lined up for us . . ." He dug into the pocket of his jeans and pulled out a scrap of paper. "Here's the phone number where I'll be living."

Erika took the paper from him. Such a small piece of paper, yet she nearly staggered from the sadness she felt when she gazed at the digits. Why would she need his phone number? They could barely speak to each other face to face.

She tucked the paper into her purse and forced a smile. "So what are you going to be doing there?"

"I don't know. There are lots of job opportunities. I'll land something."

"That'll be nice." God, this was agony. She'd meant what she said. She wanted Ted to find a good job, something more stimulating—and financially rewarding—than working as a lowly gas jockey at a service station. She wanted him to succeed, to be happy, to figure out what he was meant to do and then to do it.

But *nice*? She and Ted weren't engaging in small talk. They were engaging in microscopic talk.

Her friends must have sensed how uncomfortable she was. "We really should go, Erika," Becky said. "I'm parked in the short-term lot. I don't want to get a ticket."

Erika knew Becky wouldn't get a ticket as long as she handed over whatever amount of money the parking lot attendant charged. But Becky was giving her an excuse to leave, and she gratefully grabbed it. "You've got to catch your next flight, too," she said to Ted.

"Yeah." He still hadn't smiled. Not once. "Okay. You'd better go." Belatedly, he seemed to remember the teddy bear in his hand.

"This is for you," he said, passing it to her as if it were a hot potato he didn't want to get caught holding.

The bear's surface was soft plush. She suppressed the urge to give it a hug. "Thank you."

"Yeah. Well."

"Good-bye, Ted."

"Good-bye, Erika."

She peered into his face, searching for something. Not a smile—she'd relinquished that hope. But maybe a softening. A hint of forgiveness. An acknowledgment that things really were finished between them.

Nothing. Just the steely coldness of his eyes, the grim set of his mouth, the sharp angles of his nose and jaw. As cute as he'd been in high school, he was cuter now. Hell, he was gorgeous.

But she didn't feel that warm tingle he used to stir inside her. She felt only cold. Colder than the snow that blanketed so much of Colorado. The cold of grief and loss and death.

"Erika?" Anna called to her.

She spun from Ted and walked resolutely away, her friends flanking her. Anna bowed toward her and murmured, "Wow, that was weird."

"Really awkward," Becky added.

"You okay?"

"Sure," Erika lied.

"What are you going to do with the teddy bear?" Adrienne asked, and Anna and Becky started to laugh again.

"You could name him Lost Cause."

"Give Up," Anna suggested.

"Take a Hint," Becky chimed in.

"Take a Hike."

Erika joined their laughter. But none of it seemed funny.

Shit.

You watch her walk away with her friends, whispering and giggling. She doesn't even look like Erika anymore, with that short hairstyle and the snug jeans and sweater and the stylish parka with fur trimming the hood, and the fancy boots. Not her riding boots but shin-high and constructed of some sort of rugged animal hide, like what you'd expect to see on Eskimos. Who was she? Who had she turned into?

And come on, what did you expect? That she'd see you in the airport and suddenly remember everything you'd been to each other, every magical moment of your romance? That she'd race into your arms and say, "Oh, Ted, I've missed you so much! I broke up with you because I thought I'd never see you again—but now I've seen you and I realize what a fool I've been. Take me back!"

Yes. That was exactly what you expected.

You are the biggest moron who ever walked the planet.

It's over, you tell yourself. It's over, over, over. Get it through your skull, man. It's over.

Tempe was not New Jersey. It was warm and arid and brown. From the moment he landed in Phoenix, he knew he'd traveled more than a bunch of miles. He'd entered another world, just like Erika had when she'd left for college.

The apartment Dave found for them was cheap but clean, no little six-legged critters scampering across the kitchen floor or hiding in the bathroom. The furniture that came with the place had clearly started its life elsewhere. Nothing matched. But there were two beds in the bedroom, a sofa and a couple of tables in the living room, a Formica-topped table and chairs in the kitchen. And a phone. Just in case Erika decided to call him.

It's over, he told himself. He'd seen her and realized she was not his Erika anymore. She was someone else, and it was *over* . . . and still, he looked at the phone and wondered if she would ever make use of the number he'd given her.

Within a week of arriving in Tempe, he had landed a job as a telemarketer. He sat in a tiny cubicle in a vast call center, wearing a headset, making calls, taking calls. Not the most stimulating job in the world, but it provided him with an income. He was getting a regular wage and paying rent and utilities. Nineteen years old, and he was a grown-up.

She's just a college kid living off the largesse of her parents, he thought disdainfully. *I'm a man, making my own way. Check this out, Fred. I'm a man.*

His days developed a routine, more of a schedule than he'd had since graduating from high school. He woke early, showered, shaved, slugged down some coffee, and went to the call center. He put in his hours. He came home, sometimes stopping on his way to grab some take-out fast food but more often preparing his own dinners to save money. He wasn't eating the way he ate when his mother did the cooking, but he got pretty good at grilling burgers and hotdogs, and peanut-butter sandwiches and salads fell within his competency range.

Dave didn't adapt to Tempe as well as Ted did. Not long after Ted started his job at the call center, Dave decided the desert wasn't for him and took off, leaving Ted on his own. Day by day, he went to work, he came home, he budgeted his money, he made ends meet. Barely, but he did it. Yeah, he was a man. Putting in the time and earning a living.

As soon as he entered the apartment each evening—before he opened his mail, before he hit the bathroom, before he ate—he checked the answering machine attached to his phone. *Call me,*

Erika. Call and let me tell you how much of a man I am. I'm putting it all together. I'm an adult. You would be so impressed. You would see that I've gotten my act together. I'm not a loser pumping gas. Call me.

She never did. The rare times the light on the answering machine flashed, he'd dive across the kitchen, punch the button, and listen breathlessly to some stupid message from the landlord about how garbage not tied in thick plastic bags might attract vermin to the Dumpster, so please make sure you tie your garbage bag before you toss it into the bin.

No calls from Erika. None.

Asshole, she's not going to call you.

Some nights he crawled into bed and lay awake for hours, imagining the stars scattered across the broad desert sky. As a child, he used to recite the poem, "Starlight, star bright, first star I see tonight," and send his wishes into the heavens. Now he imagined the stars as surfaces he could bounce messages off. If he sent a message to a star, would it bounce at the correct angle and somehow reach Erika in Colorado? He lay alone, listening to the silence and sending his wishes skyward: *Call me, Erika. Love me as much as I love you.*

The stars failed him. Or else they passed his messages to her and she failed him.

On nights that he was too restless and lonely to lie in bed beaming messages to the stars, he would wander over to Arizona State University. The campus soon became his destination of choice. It took him little time to obtain a fake ID; when necessary, he became Matt Hackett, born three years before Ted Skala. He could buy liquor. He could hang out at frat houses, smoke weed, listen to music, pick up girls.

None of them was Erika.

He tried to convince himself that was a good thing. If they weren't like Erika, they wouldn't be able to touch him the way she had. They wouldn't be able to reach inside him and claim his heart. They wouldn't be able to hurt him.

He would never let anyone hurt him again. He would never let anyone get that close to him, under his skin, into his soul.

Still, he wanted Erika to know how cool he was, how self-sufficient, how mature. She wasn't the only one going to frat parties. Not only was he going to frat parties, too, but he was also working. Earning money. Paying freaking taxes. Contributing to Social Security. He wanted her to know he was making something of himself.

But he wouldn't call her. Somewhere inside him, he had a teardrop's worth of pride, and that pride kept him from calling.

Instead, he waited for her to call him.

No calls. No messages. No contact.

It's over, Skala. She's gone. It's over.

The teddy bear was adorable. But Erika's friends had made fun of it, and she suspected they were also making sense. A teddy bear couldn't bring her and Ted back together. She didn't *want* them back together.

And *he* didn't want them back together, either. He'd told her he would never be with her again. She had to take him at his word.

She tossed the teddy bear onto the shelf in her closet and tried to forget it was there. She tried to forget Ted, too. Tried to forget how wistful he'd looked in the airport. He'd exuded a potent mixture of emotions as he'd stood with her at the gate. Hope. Fear. Bravado. Sentimentality. Condemnation.

He'd hated her hair. He hadn't had to say it; she'd sensed it.

She told herself that what Ted Skala thought of her hair, or anything else, didn't matter. He was now living in Tempe, Arizona, of all places—she had no idea why, and she told herself that didn't matter, either. What mattered was that he was moving on with his life. Like her, he was breaking away from home and the past and their adolescent love. He was embracing new adventures.

Teddy bear or no teddy bear, he was kissing the past goodbye, turning his back on what had once been and opening himself to the world that awaited him beyond the safe, cozy confines of Mendham. This was a good thing. She should be happy for him.

Every now and then, she glimpsed the bear as she rummaged through the clutter on her closet shelf for a scarf or a pair of gloves. She saw the plush brown doll sitting in the corner, staring at her with an accusatory expression that reminded her too much of the way Ted had stared at her in the airport. "I should throw you out," she muttered, shoving the bear deeper in to the closet. "I should donate you to a children's hospital or a shelter or something."

But she didn't. She couldn't get rid of the bear any more than she could get rid of the letters and drawings Ted had sent her. They all remained safely in a folder inside her desk, except for the first one. She'd framed that one.

Because it was a beautiful piece of artwork, she told herself. Because it was worthy of display. Not because Ted had drawn it for her.

Moving on with your life didn't mean you had to forget about what you'd lived so far. She could remember Ted, remember how precious their love had been. Remember the nights in the backseat of the Wagoneer, when he'd been so gentle and careful with her, when he'd accepted her gift of herself and treated it as a priceless treasure. Remember their long walks and their long talks and even their long, companionable silences, when the only sound was the music spilling from the Wagoneer's radio. Phish. Spin Doctors. Fleetwood Mac, that gorgeous, tender ballad: *I love you, I love you, like never before* . . .

Oh, hell. She *wanted* to forget. She just couldn't.

Twelve

YOUR FATHER WAS RIGHT. The world is full of girls.

Girls at Arizona State. Girls with sun-streaked hair and sun-baked skin who study all day and party all night. Girls whose names and faces melt into a sweet blur, thanks to the recreational ingestion of booze and grass. They're just as hammered as you are, so it all works out somehow.

You party with them during the night, and during the day you learn how to balance a checkbook and how to deliver what your boss is asking of you. When work at the call center begins to pall, you land another job, this time as a salesman at a Dodge dealership. Not such a huge leap from pumping gas, when you think about it. Cars are cars.

You've never done sales before, but you're friendly and helpful and clearheaded on the job. Dealing with all those numbers—negotiating the prices for accessory packages, calculating sales tax—doesn't come easily to you, but if you can balance your checkbook, you can figure out how much to charge for floor mats without losing the dealership its profit. You're the youngest salesman, and your colleagues all remind you of your friends' fathers—beefy, responsible heads-of-household, guys who've gained enough weight since their high school days that their hands have become plump and they have to wear their school rings on their cocktail-hotdog pinkies.

These are not guys you'd do a number with after work. They aren't guys you could sit down and discuss Soundgarden and Alice in Chains with. They probably wouldn't know what to make of the drawings you did late at night when you weren't lost in a happy haze at some campus party, drawings of laughing donkeys and desert flowers, flowing lines and vibrant colors.

But the guys at the Dodge dealership accept you as a fellow sales associate. An adult. A man.

And you get a business card. A business card! With your name printed on it, along with the Dodge logo and the dealer's address and phone number.

Your own freaking business card!

If that's not a sign of success, you don't know what is.

As weeks passed without a phone message from Erika, Ted stopped racing to the answering machine the minute he entered his apartment. She wasn't going to call. He got that. It was over. Done. *Stick a fork in it, Skala—it's cooked.*

But then she surprised him by sending him a postcard. He didn't always remember to check his mailbox, a narrow rectangular receptacle with a locked door, one of many in a panel attached to the apartment building's wall near the front entry. Sometimes he'd unlock the mailbox door and swing it open, and dozens of commercial mailings would spill out. He'd realize that days had passed since he'd last looked inside the box.

This was one of those days. When he turned the lock, the mailbox's skinny silver door practically burst open, releasing a blizzard of fliers, glossy catalogues, and take-out restaurant menus. He gathered the scattered mailings from the floor in front of the mailboxes, carried them to the trash can, and, one by one, tossed them.

If he'd discarded them all together, he might have missed Erika's postcard mixed in with the junk mail.

He read it. Read it again. *Shit.* It didn't say anything.

Sure, it said *something.* She was busy, hoped he was enjoying Tempe, blah-blah-blah. Like he cared. Like this mattered.

He tossed the postcard on the kitchen counter once he'd entered his apartment. En route to the bedroom, he emptied the pockets of the neat khakis he had to wear for work and tossed his keys, change, and wallet onto the dresser. As he reached for a pair of shorts, his gaze snagged on his wallet.

He had a business card. She wanted to know how he was doing? Hell, he'd show her how he was doing. Nineteen years old, and he had his own business card. If that didn't impress her . . .

He didn't question why he wanted to impress her. Instead, he slid the card into an envelope along with a note telling her he was now working as an auto salesman and doing well. He didn't even mention the business card. Let her open the envelope and find it in there, and think, *Wow! Ted has a business card! He's a man and he's going places!*

Eventually, the place he went was Seattle. Selling cars wasn't for him. He was into art, not commerce. He heard the pot was as good in Seattle as it was in Tempe, and the air wasn't as dry. And the music scene up there was supposedly phenomenal. He'd listened to the mix tape Erika had made for him so many times he could sing all the songs, in order, from memory.

Enough. Time to move on. Time to stop listening to her music and start listening to his own.

So he bought a one-way ticket from Greyhound, packed up the

few possessions he'd accrued since arriving in Tempe, and headed north. Seattle was as cold and damp as Tempe was hot and dry, and after a while in the great Northwest, he headed back south, over the border, down to Costa Rica.

He was young and the world was full of girls.

He fell in with a shaggy expat named Bob who hadn't quite lost the West Virginia twang in his voice and who scrapped and scrounged for food. "You wanna learn how to surf?" he offered Ted. "I can teach you that. You wanna learn how to catch a turtle and turn it into soup? I can teach you that, too."

"I'd rather learn how to surf," Ted said.

So Bob taught him how to surf.

Conquering the waves convinced Ted he could conquer anything. He could stand on a narrow board and not lose his balance, even if a ten-foot roller tried to crush him. He wasn't quite as daring as Bob, or as crazy, but he figured if the waves couldn't destroy him, nothing could.

Not even a broken heart. Especially not a broken heart. You just had to learn to protect yourself, keep your wits about you, maintain your footing when the board was slick with seawater and the ocean was foaming all around you.

At one time, he hadn't been able to do that. Now, he could.

Costa Rica was full of girls, but he avoided a lot of them for the simple reason that they were Latina. He'd once loved a girl who was half Latina, whose skin turned bronze at the first hint of sunshine, who had dozens of cousins living in Colombia, who could speak Spanish like a native when the atmosphere was right. He'd once loved a girl whose name began with a vowel, so he avoided girls whose names began with vowels. Eva, Irina, Olivia, Ursula— no, thanks. He learned to read the potential danger in certain ocean conditions and stay on dry land, and he knew to avoid potential danger in relationships.

"Life is about two things," Bob once told him, pushing the long wet snarls of his hair back from his face as he and Ted lugged their boards across the sand after a day of surfing. "Survival, and getting wrecked. Sometimes you need to get wrecked if you want to survive. Sometimes, seems like the whole point of survival is to get your hands on some booze or weed and get yourself wrecked. They go hand in hand."

Not exactly Ted's philosophy, although he respected Bob's hard-won take on the world. Ted's philosophy was that the best way to survive was to protect yourself. Take chances with your body if you want, but protect your heart. Vulnerability equaled death, so don't ever let yourself be vulnerable.

He'd had his heart broken once. He was never going to let that happen again.

Thirteen

THIS IS WHAT LIFE IS ALL ABOUT, Erika thought, stretching languidly beneath the Caribbean sun. The heat baked her, the sand beneath her towel cradled her, and the salt-laden breezes blowing in off the water reminded her, with each gust, of how much she loved the ocean.

Four years in landlocked Colorado hadn't changed her that much. She was still a Jersey girl, in love with the shore. She'd learned to ski in college, and after graduation she'd worked for a season in Vail, catering to the wealthy skiers and joining them on the slopes whenever she had a day off. But mastering the slopes had been only one adventure. She'd wanted more.

So she'd learned how to sail and joined the crew of a sailboat for a transatlantic trip. Finally the expression "learning the ropes" made sense to her. She'd learned what a sheet was, and a shroud, a halyard, and a forestay. She'd learned enough different knots to qualify for a Boy Scout merit badge, and she'd learned how to clip her vest to a railing so she wouldn't get knocked overboard by a swell. She'd worked her ass off and loved every minute of it—the calms, the storms, the blisters that turned into callus across her palms. The way her skin and hair wore the scent of the sea as if it were perfume.

She wasn't a thrill seeker, she assured herself. She was just . . .
someone who'd grown up vaulting over fences on the back of a
horse. Tearing down a mountain on a pair of narrow polyure-
thane slats or sailing across the ocean in a streamlined fiberglass
bathtub, powered by wind against canvas, seemed natural to her.

Lying on a beach on St. Barts, with a Jameson on the rocks
within reach of her left hand and a neglected book within reach
of her right, offered a different sort of exhilaration than galloping
across a field or sailing across the ocean. But she deserved this
vacation, just as she deserved the Cartier watch circling her wrist.
She was thirty-four years old, and she was a vice president at one
of the world's biggest financial corporations.

What a long, strange trip, she thought with a smile.

There had been her return to New York City from Europe after
the transatlantic sail, when she'd decided to become an actress.
She'd given herself a year, attended auditions with hundreds of
other young women—gorgeous women, staggeringly talented
women, women who'd graduated from Juilliard and Carnegie-
Mellon and the Tisch School of the Arts at NYU and actually
knew what they were doing on stage. Women who were willing to
starve and wait tables for years and sacrifice their entire lives for
the chance to appear in a thirty-second commercial for mouth-
wash or to be cast as a juror on *Law & Order*. Erika didn't want it
enough. She'd given it a year and moved on.

Her degree in psychology had helped her a bit with acting, and
it helped her even more once she landed a job as a recruiter, evaluating job candidates. That had led to a job at an investment bank.
After a few years there, she'd decided she needed another chal-
lenge, something new to get her blood pumping. Business school.

She wasn't going to be just another drone, though, learning
marketing and accounting and winding up in an inner office,

pushing papers around for no other reason than that someone was paying her big bucks to do so. In her riding days, she'd been a jumper. She wanted to clear some fences in business school, too. So she'd enrolled in the Thunderbird International School of Management, studied in Arizona and Mexico, and earned a degree in international business.

She'd had some good jobs before landing her current position. But now she'd reached a pinnacle, the business equivalent of making nationals. She was thirty-four years old, she had an apartment in Manhattan—a tiny one, but all hers—and her life was complete.

Almost.

Her eyes were feeling the sun through her lids, so she rolled over onto her stomach, careful not to knock over her drink or bury her book in the sand. The heat baked her back and she sighed. Really, she told herself, she didn't need more. If she'd wanted a man in her life, she could have had one.

She *had* had one—more than one. There were always dates, always guys. Always opportunities for romance. She worked with rich, powerful men. She hung out in neighborhood clubs full of funky, arty men. Friends set her up.

She remembered one recent blind date with a banker. He'd been such a cool guy—suave, poised, successful. He'd traveled the world, like her. He spoke several languages, like her. They'd gone to an expensive restaurant and he'd ordered something weird— frog legs, she recalled with a smile—and described the two-bedroom, two-bath apartment he'd just bought in Manhattan, and he'd told her he needed help decorating it.

A come-on if ever she'd heard one. A sign of genuine interest, a bid for a second date, or at the very least a hint that he'd like her to come to his apartment.

She'd sat across the linen-covered table from him, eating something far less exotic than frog's legs—she couldn't remember what, even though she remembered what *he'd* ordered—and imagining herself living in his two-bedroom, two-bath apartment. Decorated by her. With a kitchen big enough to prepare a gourmet feast in, big enough for her friends to keep her company while she fixed that gourmet feast. A couple of kids running around underfoot, too. Beautiful kids who'd gotten into top-ranked private schools.

It had been a glorious image—except that she couldn't find the suave, multilingual banker anywhere in the picture. In her imagination, she'd loved the kitchen and the kids. Not the man.

She was okay with that. If she never fell in love, so be it. She could always go to a sperm bank or find a willing male friend to provide a share of the genes if she wanted to have a baby.

Which she did, she admitted silently, reaching for the Jameson. The glass was filmed with sweat, the lime-flavored whisky cool against her tongue and warm going down her throat. She would love to become a mother.

But she just couldn't seem to fall in love with a man.

She'd fallen in love once. So many years ago. Falling in love with Ted had seemed so easy—but she'd been young then, too young even to understand what love was about. The giddy joy of being desired? The satisfaction of knowing this one person was all yours? The sweaty, clumsy sex in the backseat of an old Jeep Wagoneer? The security of having someone to hold hands with, to hang out with, to talk with for hours? To talk about nothing with, all the while knowing that "nothing" was everything?

First love. Puppy love. All well and good when a girl was eighteen years old. But now . . .

Now she was a hot-shot VP. Competent, confident, content. To accept a man into her life would be to change the life she had, which she really liked the way it was. To love someone would mean to lose a part of herself. Which part was she supposed to sacrifice? What, of the many things that gave her pleasure, would she be expected to give up in order to make room for love?

A two-bedroom, two-bath apartment would be terrific. But her tiny studio apartment near Gramercy Park was also terrific. And it was all hers.

Maybe he was crazy to contact her. It had been so long. Why pick open a wound that had successfully healed? Why risk the pain, the possibility of infection? Erika had left a scar, but not a disfiguring one. Just because she was living across the river from him in Manhattan wasn't reason enough for him to suggest that they get together.

He had a full life. A good job, finally. His position at East River Marketing was more than a job, or even a career. It was a calling. It tapped into his artistic talents. It satisfied his constant need for change. It demanded that he work hard—and when he was passionate about something, he loved working hard. One day he'd be occupied devising a strategy to convey not just what a cable network was but what it meant to consumers. The next day he'd be busy designing a concept that embodied a national magazine. Sometimes the deadlines were so intense he didn't bother to eat. He didn't skip meals merely because he was pressed for time; he stopped eating because during those pulse-pounding marathon stretches at work when everything was due yesterday, he became another creature, not quite human. All his energy, all his concentration had to be about the client, the assignment, the commission. He would live on soy lattes for days and not even miss the experience of chewing.

Work was great. His social life was also great. He was in a

relationship. Three solid years with a fantastic woman, sharing a comfortable apartment in Brooklyn, just across the bridge from Manhattan. She was beautiful, smart, good-natured . . . everything he wanted in a woman.

And yet . . . something was missing. Something wasn't quite right.

She wanted to get married. He didn't blame her. They were in their thirties, and she had that biological clock thing going, and—well, three years was a long time for a couple to be together without taking the next step.

Ted wanted to take the next step. But something held him back. Something nagged at him, whispering in the darkest recesses of his soul that if Marissa wasn't the one, he shouldn't marry her. And it whispered that she wasn't the one.

He hated the feeling of limbo. He hated becoming a cliché: the guy who couldn't commit. He wanted to do right by her. But . . . something was missing.

He knew what that something was.

What was the current jargon word? *Closure.* He needed closure with Erika.

Stupid. He *had* closure with her. They'd had closure when she told him, just before leaving for college, that she wanted them to be friends. And when she'd broken up with him definitively over the phone. And when she'd driven up to Denver to meet him at the airport, and he'd seen with his own eyes that she was no longer the girl he'd remembered, the long-haired, golden-skinned girl he'd been so madly in love with. And in every cold, clipped communication they'd shared since then, the few times they'd run into each other at gatherings of the old gang in Mendham, when they'd chatted politely for as little time as possible before gravitating to opposite ends of the room.

If closure was the same thing as having a door slam shut, that door had slammed shut on him enough times to get the point across.

But.

Something was missing.

Someone from the old Mendham group—Allyson, maybe—had provided him with Erika's email address. *What the hell,* he thought. *Just see her and make sure that door is not just shut but locked and bolted.* So he sent her a note and suggested they meet somewhere for a drink, for old time's sake.

A few days later she replied: *Sure.*

He asked her to name the place, and she recommended Fanelli's Cafe, downtown in SoHo. They set a time and a date.

He had never really believed in ghosts, even though he'd had fun pretending his childhood home was haunted. Now he did believe in ghosts, because suddenly he found himself haunted by the ghost of the lovesick boy he'd once been, pining for a girl who'd walked away from him.

He wasn't pining, he assured himself. He was just exorcising a ghost.

Darting between the raindrops the day of their meeting, he arrived at the corner bistro on time. He surveyed the pub and didn't see her. She'd picked the place; he figured she would have chosen someplace convenient for her. If he could get there on time when he lived in Brooklyn, surely she could get there on time from her Manhattan apartment.

All right, so she was running a little late. No big deal. He sauntered down to the far end of the bar and settled on an empty stool that gave him a good view of the place. He'd be able to see her the moment she entered—before she saw him. This would give him a chance to assess her, and to brace himself.

The bartender approached, a skinny, pretty boy with an air about him. Ted realized the stool he sat on was prime real estate; he'd have to order a drink if he wanted to stay there. He asked for a Budweiser.

Waiting for her gave him too much time. Time to wonder whether he was overdressed or underdressed. He'd chosen cords and a polo shirt, neat but not prissy. He'd dressed in a way he hoped would communicate that he was prosperous, content, cool.

Christ. You're still trying to impress her. Maybe you ought to give her one of your business cards, while you're at it.

The minutes ticked by. He nursed his beer. The voices around him melted into a blur of sound. The door opened to admit patrons. None was Erika.

He was trying to impress her, and she'd stood him up. Talk about a door slamming in his face. He decided that if she hadn't arrived by the time he'd finished his beer, he'd leave a note with the bartender. A ten-dollar bill and a note inviting her to have a drink on him. That would be gentlemanly.

And cool. Impressively cool.

A note saying, *Maybe next time.* Only there wouldn't be a next time. He'd accept the meaning behind her absence. Finally, *finally,* it would be over for him. He'd purge her from his mind once and for all. He promised himself he would.

The door opened again, and that promise flew out into the drizzly night as Erika stepped inside.

She was beautiful.

Of course she was beautiful. He knew she was beautiful. She'd been beautiful at sixteen, when she'd been the new girl in their high school sophomore class. She'd been beautiful at eighteen, when she'd become his girlfriend. She'd been beautiful when she'd ridden horses, when she'd danced, when she'd lain beneath him in the backseat of the Wagoneer, opening her body and her soul to him. She'd even been beautiful in the Denver airport, with her hair cropped short and her college friends snickering about the loser boyfriend who'd flown halfway across the country with a teddy bear in his hands.

She was beautiful now, her hair glistening with drops of rain, her slim body decked out in a white tank top and a black jumpsuit, her throat circled by a chunky black necklace. She still had the ramrod posture she'd had in high school, the same long, slim legs, the same generous breasts. The same gentle brown eyes and golden skin and intoxicating smile.

She searched the room with her gaze, eventually spotting him. She worked her way to his end of the bar in strong, decisive strides, and he realized she wasn't nervous at all. Her gait intimidated him as much as her beauty and poise.

Her smile didn't intimidate him, though. It was young, sweet, eager. She seemed truly happy to see him. A big difference from that time in the airport, he thought as he smiled back at her. As long as she kept smiling, he'd be able to think of her not as the girl of his dreams, the one that got away—pick a cliché, any cliché—but as a chic, together woman.

Who was heading straight toward him. Who had spotted the empty stool next to him and bee-lined to it. As if she was genuinely glad to be there, with him.

"Hey," he greeted her, as she settled onto the stool. His gaze ran the length of her and he blurted out his reaction. "Wow."

"I know. Wow." Her smile grew even wider and warmer, and then she started babbling about how she didn't have any money with her, she'd left her wallet at home, she'd thought about going back to get it but she didn't want to be late—hell, she was already nearly half an hour late—and she'd been at the gym, and . . .

"Don't worry about it," he said, taking those words to heart. She shouldn't worry about not having any money with her. He shouldn't worry about sitting with her in this bar. She was a friend—a gorgeous woman, yes, but also a friend. Someone who'd known him when he was a kid, when he was a jerk, when he was lost and struggling. He wasn't lost and struggling anymore, and Marissa didn't think he was a jerk most of the time.

This was good. Seeing Erika was good. Sitting next to her, catching a whiff of her perfume . . . It was all good.

Talking to her was good, too. There had been a lot of passion in their relationship, plenty of emotional peaks and chasms, but there had also been friendship. They used to talk about everything—their families, music, work, animals, their hopes and dreams. And here they were, having a beer together and talking. To Ted's surprise, talking to Erika after all these years proved to be easy.

She told him about her job. He told her about his job at East River—and he recognized that the pleasure came not from impressing her with his fancy title and his exalted responsibilities but simply from sharing with her the things that comprised his life. He didn't *have* to impress her. This was Erika. Someone who knew him, knew his strengths and his weaknesses, knew his history. Someone whose voice was like a beloved song, one that evoked memories of all the times he'd enjoyed that song in the past but also could be appreciated for its beauty in the present.

Beyond friendship, though . . . He wanted to kiss her.

He'd arranged to see her because he'd hoped to straighten out his head and make sure he was completely over her. And maybe he was over that old love, the wild, tangled, jumping-off-a-cliff love they'd had so many years ago. The attraction he felt toward her now was entirely different. It was the attraction of a man to a gorgeous, smart, radiant woman.

A woman as familiar as an old song, but as new as a melody he was hearing for the first time.

"So," he asked, "are you seeing anyone?"

"I'm seeing lots of people," she said casually.

Her answer pleased and dismayed him. Pleased him because she was apparently not involved with anyone. She was free, unattached, available.

Dismayed him because he was *not* free, unattached, or available. And he shouldn't be thinking about how he wanted to cup his hands around her smooth, dewy cheeks and draw her face to his, and kiss her and kiss her and kiss her until the bar they were in vanished and the voices of all the other drinkers and diners faded into the rainy night sky and all that existed was Ted and Erika and their endless kisses.

Instead, he had to answer her question about whether he was seeing someone. He had to answer honestly, because he had never lied to Erika and he wasn't about to start lying now.

"I'm sort of . . . well, yeah."

As soon as the words were out of his mouth, he felt as if he had lost his footing. He remembered those times when he'd been learning to surf, down in the tropical heat of Costa Rica, with that crazy stoner Bob bouncing on a board next to him, instructing him on how to sense the wave, how to time its approach, how to start paddling with your hands and then hoist yourself to your feet and ride it in. How many times had he misjudged the wave? How many times had he managed to stand on the board and ride it a few thrilling feet, only to have the damned thing slip out from under him?

That was how he felt now: that something was slipping out from under his feet, and he was about to plunge into a surging, frothing wave. Bob had also taught him never to fight the wave but just to let it toss him around until it tired itself out, at which point he would rise to the surface. He always did, but sometimes he'd had to hold his breath for so long he was certain his lungs would burst. Sometimes the ocean just kept playing with him, spinning and tumbling him, and he was sure he would drown. And he would open his eyes and see the sky just above the surface of the water, the air so close, his life so close—and he would fight the tide and force his way up, toward that light.

Then he would be alive again, breathing once more. Wheezing air into his lungs would revive him, and his vision would clear. He would feel the hot sun sizzling on his wet shoulders and scalp, and he'd grab his board and climb back onto it, wondering whether he could trust it not to slip out from under him again.

At that moment, seated so close to Erika, he wanted to climb back onto the board. But he was still under water, being tossed and agitated like a T-shirt in a washing machine. He couldn't, shouldn't, *mustn't* want to kiss her. Not when he was in another relationship. Not when he was supposedly in love with someone else.

"This has been great, Fred, but I'm afraid I've got to hit the road," he said, surprising himself by resorting to the old nickname he used to call her.

She seemed surprised too, whether by his use of her nickname or his abrupt announcement that he had to run, he didn't know. But if they'd stayed there any longer, he would have given in to the thundering urge to kiss her, and that would have been wrong. Reckless. Like trying to surf through a riptide.

While he settled up with the bartender, he and Erika exchanged a bunch of platitudes about how lovely it was to have gotten together. He dared to touch his hand to the small of her back as they wove through the crowd to the exit. Feeling its graceful curve made him want to gather her into his arms. But then, he'd want to gather her into his arms even if he hadn't touched her.

He had to get away from her. He had to go home and straighten things out. He needed to plant his feet on dry land until he regained his equilibrium.

Outside, rain fell in a gentle shower from the purple-black sky. She thanked him yet again for the drink. He considered ribbing her about her having conveniently left her wallet at home, but he wasn't in a joking mood.

His yearning trounced his good sense and he pulled her into his arms. God, she felt good. More than before, he knew he had to get away. "Take care, Erika," he said.

"You, too."

Was that a good-bye? A have-a-good-life kind of farewell? He didn't want to analyze it. Instead, he released her, took a cautious step back, and smiled at her. Her responding smile was breathtaking. Raindrops shimmered on her cheeks like clear, tiny pearls.

Then she turned and strode down the street, looking so elegant, so poised, so together. It took all his willpower not to chase after her and say, "Damn it, Erika, let's try again and see if we can get it right this time."

As she turned the corner and disappeared from view, he thought he heard another door click shut. But maybe, just maybe that noise was the sound of a key twisting in a lock, turning the bolt so that the door might open again.

Fourteen

ERIKA LAY ON HER BED in her studio apartment, staring at the ceiling. What was wrong with her? Why had she stood in the rain weeping as if she were at a funeral? She'd had a beer with Ted. It wasn't the first time, and now that they were both living in the New York City area, it probably wouldn't be the last time.

Hell, the next time they got together, maybe he would bring his significant other.

A choked sound emerged from her, and she tried to convince herself it wasn't a sob. Surely she couldn't be crying over Ted. Not now. Not when their relationship had died sixteen years ago.

It hadn't just died. She'd killed it.

And maybe that was why she'd bawled like a mourner at a funeral. The funeral had been for her first love.

Her *only* love. All the men she'd dated since college, all those eligible bachelors her friends had set her up with, all the colleagues at her various jobs over the years who'd leaned across her desk and murmured, "Why don't we continue this discussion over drinks after work . . ." None of them had ever touched her heart. None of them had ever made her cry.

Ted did.

All right. She'd killed their relationship—but if she hadn't, it would have died, anyway. They'd been too young. She hadn't been ready to make the kind of commitment Ted had demanded of her, and if he were honest he'd admit he hadn't been ready, either. He'd been caught up in the romance of it, the feverish excitement. But if she'd accepted his proposal that long-ago summer when they'd been teenagers, he would ultimately have grown to hate her. She would have tied him down, prevented him from finding out what he was meant to do. The job at East River—his "calling"—would never have called. How could he have taken the journey that brought him to that wonderful position, to the wonderful life he was living now, if he'd had Erika hanging like an albatross around his neck?

She'd done him a favor by breaking up with him. One of them had had to take that awful step, and she'd been the one to take it. But it had benefited him as much as her.

Maybe more than her. He seemed so happy now. So poised.

So sexy.

Another of those weird choking hiccup sounds caught in her throat. She swallowed, tasting the salt of unshed tears, and pushed herself to sit. Her hair was still damp from her trip home in the rain, and it was drying in tangled waves. She shoved a heavy lock of it back from her cheek, decided the moisture on her skin was from her hair and not from crying, and reached for her phone. Allyson's number was on speed dial, and she pressed the buttons and waited.

"Hey, Erika," her old friend greeted her. "What's up?"

"I had a drink with Ted this evening," Erika said, skipping past the niceties and diving straight into the heart of things. She and Allyson didn't require small talk.

"Ted? As in Skala?"

"How many Teds are there in my life?"

"Right," Allyson said. "There's always been just one. So, you had a drink with him, huh."

"A beer at Fanelli's."

"Nice." Allyson sounded a little snarky, but also amused.

"He's in a relationship. He's been with her for a long time."

"Well," Allyson said, sounding less snide than cautious now. "Good for him. I think. Did you meet her?"

"No, he left her home." Yet another sob rose into Erika's throat, and she couldn't keep this one from escaping. "He's the one, Allyson. He's always been the one."

Now Allyson sounded truly sympathetic. "Don't confuse what you were feeling sixteen years ago with who he is now."

"That's the thing. Sixteen years ago, he was a kid. We both were. Now he's a man. He's solid, he's grown up, he's got a career . . . he's everything I wasn't ready for sixteen years ago, everything *he* wasn't ready for."

"Honey, there are lots of other solid, grown-up men with careers out there. I've introduced you to a few of them myself."

"But they aren't Ted. They aren't the guy I fell in love with. The guy I learned all about love with. Ted was my soul mate."

"And you think he still is?"

"It doesn't matter what I think. He's with another woman. And . . ." She drifted off, remembering.

"And?"

The words echoed in her skull, harsh and bruising. "He said, 'I will never be with you again.'"

"When did he say that? Tonight?"

"When I broke up with him in college."

"That was a long time ago."

"He said I hurt him too badly. He couldn't bear ever to be hurt that badly again, so he would never love me again."

"Maybe he's changed his mind."

Erika laughed through her tears. "That's not the kind of thing you change your mind about. Like he'd say, 'Oh, I thought about it recently, and I decided you didn't hurt me that badly after all.' I stabbed him in the heart, Allyson. He'll never forgive me for what I did." *And I'll never forgive myself,* she added silently.

"But he had a drink with you. Who initiated that?"

"He did," Erika conceded.

"So? Why would he have asked you to meet him for a drink if he didn't want at least *something* to do with you?"

"A drink with an old friend is meaningless."

"Not to you, it isn't. And maybe not to him, either. Like you said, he's your soul mate."

"*Was,*" Erika corrected her.

Allyson fell silent for a moment. "Remember the old days when you used to ride?"

"Yeah, I think I have a few memories of that." It was Erika's turn to be snarky.

"So, a horse threw you. What did you do?"

"Don't give me platitudes, Allyson. I know how to ride. I know how to pick myself up and dust myself off. But if a horse said to me, 'You will never ride me again, because you hurt me too much,' I wouldn't get back on that horse again."

"I'm not talking about Mr. Ed," Allyson retorted. "I'm talking about you. Figure out what you want, Erika. Set a goal and go after it. You know how to do that. If he's really tight with his current girlfriend, you'll wish him well and move on. But don't be so defeatist. You never know about these things."

With a few final sniffles and a brief enough-about-me change of topic so Allyson could whine about all the petty annoyances of her life, Erika ended the call. After tossing her cell phone onto her night table, she sank back onto the bed, stared at the high ceiling above her, and took a few deep breaths. Then she sat up again and leveled her gaze on the wall beside her closet. A framed picture hung there, of two lovers in bed, with donkeys watching them.

Why had he drawn donkeys on that picture? He'd always liked donkeys, and she'd loved horses, and . . . who knew? The drawing had worked. It had moved her enough to frame it. She'd stashed it in her parents' house while she'd been sailing across the ocean, and while she'd been sharing a flat with two other girls during her year of menial labor and theater auditions, and when she'd headed out west to attend business school. Once she'd moved into her quaint little apartment in a grand pre-war building in Gramercy Park, however, she'd retrieved the drawing from the depths of the closet in the guest room of her parents' home. She'd brought the drawing back to New York and hung it on the wall.

Not because she loved Ted or missed him, she'd told herself at the time, but because it was a work of art. A work of genius. Intriguing and odd and beautiful.

She stared at it now, stared at the intertwined lovers at its center, and tried to figure out what she wanted. To get back together with Ted?

Getting back together with him was impossible.

If she couldn't have him, if she couldn't go back and reclaim what she'd tossed away all those years ago . . . what else did she want?

To find another man who could make her feel the way Ted had. A man she could trust as much as she'd trusted Ted. A man who could make her laugh the way he did, and who could see through her shit and call her on it and keep her honest. A man with bed-room eyes and strong arms and big, sturdy shoulders, the kind of shoulders a woman knew she could lean on. A man with an artis-tic streak, an abundance of energy, and the intelligence and wit to conquer worlds.

Another Ted. That was what she wanted. Either another Ted or no one at all, which had suited her fine until that evening.

She shouldn't have agreed to meet him for that drink. She'd been perfectly content until he'd reentered her life and reminded her of what it was like to be in love.

Being on the receiving end of a breakup can be agony. But being on the giving end wasn't exactly a walk in the park, either. When you use a knife to whittle away a space between yourself and some-one else, you are as likely to nick yourself as to cut the other person. You both wind up bleeding.

Ted had never thought of that when Erika had broken up with him all those years ago. He'd been so deeply wounded, so angry, so utterly certain that she was wrong and he was right. He'd never wasted an instant imagining what she might be experiencing, whether hurting him had hurt her as well.

Breaking up with Marissa hurt. The waves of her pain washed over him and dragged him under. "What do you mean, it's over?" she wailed. "How can you just end things like this?"

He gazed around the living room of their Brooklyn apartment. It was nicely decorated, mostly reflecting Marissa's taste—which she had in abundance. No complaint about the choices she'd made, the shades on the windows, the area rugs, the old sofas jazzed up with colorful accent pillows. Ted was artistic; he knew how to make a room look good, but he'd left her to her own devices, figuring she'd turn the apartment into a warm, welcoming residence.

Or maybe he'd allowed her to decorate the place because he hadn't been fully invested in it. Maybe he'd been thinking, *Marissa can't fix up my heart, but she can fix up the apartment.*

"I'm sorry," he said, realizing at once how feeble that sounded. "I never wanted to hurt you, but—"

She froze him with a lethal look, then took a sharp, quick gulp from the glass of Stoli she'd poured herself. "If you didn't want to hurt me," she snapped, "we wouldn't be having this conversation."

"I'm not doing this because I *want* to." He sighed, accepting that he was hurting her, despite his protestations. "I really hoped this would work out, babe, but—"

"Don't call me babe."

He sighed again. At that moment, he would have liked nothing more than to be at that neighborhood bar in SoHo with Erika. After so many years, after the pain and the resentment and the silence, he'd still felt more comfortable with her than he'd ever felt with Marissa. "If we were meant to be, we would have been there by now. I wasn't sure. You kept asking me when I would take the next step, and I kept telling you I didn't know. That was the truth. I didn't know."

"And now you know? Now you know you'll never take that step?"

"I'm sorry, but . . . yes."

"Stop saying 'I'm sorry.'"

Okay. No *babe*, no *I'm sorry*. Maybe he should ask her for a list of prohibited words and phrases.

He tried again, selecting his words carefully. "There's always been . . . *something* . . . holding me back." The truth was, there had always been *someone*, not *something*. Until he'd seen Erika, though, he'd thought it was something. What, he hadn't been sure of. A block, a wall he couldn't get around, a gate he couldn't unlatch. Something holding him back, preventing him from opening his heart again.

The fear of getting hurt the way he'd been hurt by Erika. The fear of allowing himself to be that vulnerable ever again. The knowledge that a person who'd survived one heart attack was less likely to survive another.

If he broke up with Marissa—no *if* about that; it wouldn't be fair to continue with her, feeling the way he did—*when* he broke up with Marissa, he would want to see Erika again. Yet he would never allow himself to be vulnerable to her the way he'd been vulnerable years ago. He didn't want the second heart attack. If she broke up with him again, it would kill him.

But he wanted her. There was no question in his mind about that. Ever since he'd seen her sweep into Fanelli's, her face glittering with raindrops, her eyes so wide and warm and her body . . . Christ, her body.

He wanted her. He wanted to make love to her properly, not like a breathless kid but like a man. Slowly. Gently. Wildly. He wanted to make her melt and moan his name. He wanted to do it right.

For all he knew, she had no interest in him other than as an old high school classmate, someone to have a beer with while reminiscing about the good old days. He might break up with Marissa and wind up with nothing, no one. Erika might say, "Ted, you asshole. I broke up with you. Remember?"

But he couldn't stay with Marissa, not feeling the way he did. Love wasn't like buying a car; you didn't accept the red sedan because the silver sedan wasn't in stock.

"It's for your own sake," he told Marissa, knowing she'd want to add that to her list of things he mustn't say, but saying it anyway. "It's for your own good. You deserve a guy who can give you one hundred percent. I can't. I've tried, but I can't."

"I hate you," she said.

He didn't blame her.

And he knew there was nothing he could do to make things better for her. Leaving her was for the best. She might not realize that now, but maybe—hopefully—she would someday.

And maybe someday, he'd realize that Erika's having broken up with him sixteen years ago had been for the best, too.

A few weeks later, she heard from Ted again.

She'd needed those few weeks to screw her head on right. To remember that she and Ted were just friends, that he was in a relationship, that if he wanted to see her again, it was probably because their last meeting had been kind of short and they hadn't really finished catching up.

And that was fine, she assured herself. Her bout of tears after she'd seen him at Fanelli's had been one of those weird hormonal things, nothing more. A reaction to the comprehension that she was no longer the naïve young girl she'd been so many years ago. A pang of nostalgia, nothing more.

That was what she'd told her mother during their most recent phone call. Her parents had moved to Florida. They'd reached the stage in their life where the occasional hurricane seemed less of a hassle than the frequent snowstorm, and Erika was happy to have a warm place to visit when the New York winters dug their icy claws into her.

After her mother caught her up on what was going on in her parents' life, Erika filled her mother in on developments at work, what she liked and didn't like about her new job. "We're so proud of you," her mother said repeatedly.

Erika smiled. Her parents were always proud of her. They'd been proud of her equestrian achievements, proud of her good grades, proud of her for graduating from a top-notch college and business school. Even proud of her for sailing across the Atlantic, although they'd also panicked and tried to talk her out of that escapade. Once she'd flown home and they'd seen for themselves how much the experience had changed her, how it had made her even more independent, more confident of her abilities, more joyfully fearless, they'd allowed that perhaps it hadn't been the stupidest thing she'd ever done. "We can say that now that you're home, safe and sound," her father had conceded.

"So," she told her mother, "Guess who I had a drink with not long ago? Ted Skala."

"Ted?" Although her mother was down in Florida, Erika could picture her mother's startled expression as if she were sitting just a few feet away in Erika's apartment. She could picture the arcs of her mother's eyebrows, the circle of her lips shaping an O of surprise. "He's in New York?"

"Working in Manhattan, living in Brooklyn. It was great seeing him, Mom. He grew up."

"We're all getting older," her mother said with a melodramatic sigh. "So. Ted Skala. What's he been up to?"

Erika told her mother about his job.

Her mother sounded duly impressed. "He always had a lot on the ball," she said. "Not taking the route everyone else took, but he was a smart boy and a hard worker. That summer, he was working two jobs, wasn't he? Caddying at Somerset and working at the gas station. Definitely a hard worker." Her parents had always honored hard work. Her father, after all, had started his life in the humble environment of the working-class Bronx, earned scholarships and wound up a stockbroker on Wall Street. Her mother had been an immigrant who hadn't even understood English when she'd arrived in New York, but she'd found work teaching Wall Street executives how to speak Spanish so they could communicate more effectively with their business associates south of the border. Neither of her parents had started out with much, but thanks to hard work they'd wound up affluent. "He has a work ethic, that boy," she said of Ted.

"He's not a boy anymore," Erika pointed out.

"And? Are you going to see him again?"

"He's in a relationship, Mom," Erika said. The night she'd met him at Fanelli's, and burst into tears, and raced home and wept on the phone to Allyson, she wouldn't have been able to say that so calmly. But time had passed, and the inexplicable, turbulent emotions of that night had vanished like a storm blown out to sea. Ted was an old friend. A mature friend. Period.

"So he's in a relationship. Are you going to see him again?"

"Mom," she said firmly. "It's a relationship of long standing. They've been together for years. They're *living* together."

"He isn't married to her, is he?" her mother asked.

Erika didn't want to venture too far in the direction her mother was heading.

Her mother apparently did. "If she was the woman for him, they'd be married by now. They're not married."

As if Ted's being a typical commitment-phobic guy meant he could possibly be interested in seeing Erika again—interested in her as something other than an old, mature friend.

He had told her, years ago, that he would never love her again. He would never trust her not to hurt him the way she had before. She accepted that. She respected it. The fact that he wasn't married had nothing to do with her.

Thus, she was a little surprised when he phoned a few days later and suggested they get together for a drink and a bite. Not exactly a formal invitation to dinner, but a step beyond their last meeting, which had been just a drink. Not a bite.

"Fanelli's?" she suggested. "They have a food menu there, tables in the back . . ."

"I was thinking someplace a little nicer, maybe? Is there someplace in your neighborhood? I don't know downtown that well."

"How about the White Horse Tavern?" she asked.

"Sure. Fine."

They settled on a date and a time and said good-bye. This time, Erika promised herself, she would be ready. Seeing Ted as he was now, so handsome and manly and confident, wouldn't be a shock. Knowing that he was seeking only friendship with her, that he was already taken, that they were just two old—*mature*—friends getting together, that nothing more than a fun night out would come of it, that he would be returning to his girlfriend afterward, or perhaps even bringing his girlfriend with him, and that Erika would be returning to her own happily single life, the life she'd chosen for herself, the life she wanted . . .

She would be ready.

Fifteen

THIS TIME YOU'LL BE READY. *You know she's beautiful. You know the risks. You know she broke your heart before, and you'll keep your heart well protected, as you always do, you'll keep that most fragile part of your soul buried in an impermeable bunker so she can't break it again.*

You'll be careful. You'll ride the wave, but you won't hot-dog it. You can do that. You know how to surf, and this time you'll have your board with you.

You're a single man now.

Not because of Erika, you tell yourself. You ended things with Marissa for Marissa's sake, not because you wanted to see Erika again but because after seeing her once, you'd acknowledged that you've always been seeing her. She's never left you. You've never been free to give yourself to anyone else. You know that now. You've tried to ignore it, but it's there.

So you'll climb on your board and paddle out and hope a nice roller rises up and carries you along for a ride. Erika had always been the one who craved adventure, but now it's your turn. And she's your adventure.

You'll enjoy the experience, have fun, learn something. Get a little wet when the wave breaks over you.

But you won't drown. You'll be careful. You'll be ready.

Erika's cell phone rang while she was walking to the White Horse Tavern. Without breaking stride, she plucked the phone from her purse and flipped it open. "Hello?"

She'd expected the caller might be Ted, telling her he was running late—something she would deserve, given how long she'd made him wait for her at Fanelli's while she'd dried her hair, put on makeup and realized, halfway to the bar, that she'd left her wallet at home. Or it might be Ted telling her he couldn't make it at all. Something might have come up. His girlfriend might be ill. Maybe she was vomiting unexpectedly. Maybe she was nauseous and late and . . . Oh, for God's sake, Erika!

"Hi," an unfamiliar male voice came through the phone. "This is Bill. I'm a friend of Sarah's . . ."

Erika nodded, then realized he couldn't see her. "Hi," she said. Sarah was a colleague at work. A happily married colleague who seemed determined that Erika become her neighbor in the joyous nation of holy matrimony. To that end, Sarah directed every single man she knew under the age of fifty in Erika's direction.

"Sarah said we ought to get together. She also said to tell you I'm not a loser." He laughed.

Erika laughed, too. "Sarah doesn't know losers," she said, silently admitting that every guy Sarah had ever set her up with had been reasonably decent. A few sevens and eights, and no one below a five.

"So, how about it? Should we meet somewhere for a drink?"

The White Horse Tavern was just up the block. She could see Ted standing just outside the entry, tall and broad-shouldered, his

dark hair neat and his gaze searching the street, watching for her.
"Tell you what," she said to Bill. "I can't talk right now, but why
don't you give me a call next week and we'll set something up?"

"I'll do that," he promised. "From what Sarah's told me about
you, I'm looking forward to meeting you."

"Great. I'll speak to you next week." She said good-bye, folded
her phone shut and crossed the street.

Ted spotted her and smiled.

"Hey, Fred!" a man shouted—not Ted. She glanced around,
figuring someone actually named Fred might be in the area, and
spotted one of her old high school friends jogging toward her
from the other end of the street.

Weird that Ryan should show up just at that moment, less than
a minute after she'd agreed to a blind date with Sarah's friend Bill.
It was as if the world had conspired to surround her with guys.

Yes, that was it. The world wanted to remind her that Ted
wasn't the one and only man in her life, that he hadn't been her
one and only man for sixteen years, that he never would be her
one and only man. Ryan charged down the sidewalk, barreled
into her and wrapped her in a bear hug when she was just a few
feet from Ted. "Hey, what's up?" Ryan asked.

She peered over his shoulder and her eyes met Ted's. His smile
deepened, as if he and she were sharing a secret joke.

She wished she knew what the joke was. In that instant, in that
secret exchange of smiles, she wanted to know everything about
him, to share everything with him.

Ryan released her, turned and saw Ted. "Hey, Skala!" They did
the guy thing, bumping fists, slapping shoulders. "Small world,
huh? Half our high school is hanging in Manhattan these days.
You guys headed in there?" He gestured toward the White Horse
Tavern.

"Yeah," Ted said. "We're going to have something to eat."

Don't invite Ryan to join us, Erika thought, then chastised herself. Of course Ryan could join them if he wanted. He was just another old, mature friend.

He beamed at both of them. "Cool. You two have a drink in my honor, okay?" He socked Ted in the shoulder once more, gave Erika a parting squeeze and continued jogging down the street. Erika wished she didn't feel so relieved that she and Ted would not have him as a chaperone for the evening.

Ted gave her another quiet smile. He held open the inn's door, then touched his hand to the small of her back and ushered her inside. Like a gentleman. Like a date.

He's not a date, she chanted silently. *He's got a girlfriend. We're just old friends.*

Don't push it, he ordered himself. *Don't rush into anything. This is just a fun ride. Nothing serious. Nothing real.*

As he picked at his salad and Erika described what she'd done all day, he contemplated telling her that he was now a single man. But the words got stuck in his throat. Erika looked so vibrant, so stunningly beautiful—he didn't want Marissa barging in on the evening. Mentioning her, even in the context of the fact that she was no longer in his life, would be an intrusion.

Or maybe that wasn't why he couldn't bring himself to tell Erika about his newfound available status. Maybe he was just being cautious. Self-protective. As long as Erika thought he was still in a relationship, a buffer would remain between them. And as much as Ted desired her, as much as he wanted to knock the dishes and glasses from the table with a single swipe of his arm, and then lean across that cozy linen-covered square and kiss her, he needed that buffer.

She had hurt him, after all. More than hurt him—she'd demolished him. Devastated him. *Take it slow, Skala,* he told himself. *Don't let her get close enough to hurt you again.*

Not that he had any reason to think she wanted to get that close. She was chatting away as if they were long-lost friends. Nothing suggestive in her behavior. Nothing seductive.

Hell, she didn't have to *do* anything to be seductive. She just had to exist. He'd gotten a crush on her the first time he'd seen her, back in tenth grade. And here he was, eighteen years later, still with a crush on her.

Keep your distance, Skala.

He'd kept his distance with Marissa, even when they'd been living together. He'd always kept his distance with every woman. The tactic had been successful. He'd been enjoying a good life, no romantic crises, no lacerating pain, no crippling injuries. Women came and went. Sometimes they came and stayed for three years, and he tried, really tried to breach that distance. But he couldn't. And when the breakup occurred, he felt . . . regretful. Apologetic. Sad to think he might be the one inflicting pain.

But he didn't suffer the pain himself. When Erika had broken up with him all those years ago, he'd suffered enough pain to last a lifetime. He would never, ever love a woman the way he'd loved her.

He wouldn't even love *her* the way he'd loved her.

So what was he doing having dinner with her?

Playing with fire? Testing his willpower? *Nostalgia,* he tried to convince himself. *Good times for old times' sake.*

He just wished she wasn't so freaking gorgeous, and exuberant, and funny. And—damn it—seductive.

When she was done talking about her work and asking him about his, they talked about Ryan, and Laura, and Allyson, and some of the other friends from their old high school crowd. They discussed the free Shakespeare plays that would be staged at Central Park that summer, the annual Nathan's Fourth of July frankfurter-eating contest at Coney Island next week, and the fireworks the city would blast over the Hudson River—a much more fitting way to celebrate Independence Day than stuffing one's face with wieners, in Erika's opinion. She'd insisted that he taste her chicken, and he'd poked a bite of his steak into her mouth, and he told himself that her eating off his fork and his eating off hers didn't mean anything.

When they were done she suggested they go dancing. He was far from ready to end the night, so he said sure. "I know this great club near here—Atomic Slims," she told him.

"Sounds good." He led her out of the restaurant. The sidewalk had grown crowded with pedestrians enjoying the balmy summer night, and he took her elbow so he wouldn't lose her in the crowd.

No. He took her elbow because he wanted to touch her. Because he felt the same way he'd felt when he'd seen her at Fanelli's. He wanted to kiss her. He wanted to hold her. He was strong, his defenses in place, his heart untouchable—but man, Erika pushed his buttons. All these years later, she still inspired an adolescent lust in him. He wanted her.

The wave was building behind him. *Catch it,* he ordered himself. *Ride it in.* The worst that could happen would be that he got tossed and wound up with a mouth full of sand.

"'I don't know what it is about you," he said, "but it's like you've been etched in the forefront of my mind for the past sixteen years. And I can't get you out."

She said nothing. He could feel the tension ripple through her—a catch in her gait, a shift in her shoulders, a tilt to her head. She seemed deep in thought.

A mouth full of sand, he thought bitterly. He could practically taste the grit against his teeth.

Her silence continued

Christ. He shouldn't have said anything. She was going to hurt him again—except no, he wasn't going to let her. He could actually feel something inside him contracting, withdrawing, folding into a protective tuck. He assured himself that he was safe. Invulnerable. She wouldn't destroy him again.

They reached the end of the street. A red light stopped them from stepping off the curb, and she turned to him, her eyes churning with emotions he couldn't read. "I don't know why we're here, Ted," she said. Her voice was low but he could hear her clearly despite the traffic noises, the clamor of voices around them, the dull rumble of a plane arching into the sky above them. "I don't know why, but there's a reason this is happening."

What's happening? he wondered. *What does she think is happening?*

"I wasn't ready for you sixteen years ago," she said. "But . . . I'm here now."

When you're surfing and your board slides out from under you, you plunge into the water. It bubbles and spirals around your head, and your hair swirls into your eyes, and for a few seconds you aren't sure which way is up. And if you're unlucky, you wind up with that mouth full of sand.

But other times, your hair is swept back and you look up and the sky is right there, just inches of water above you, close enough for you to reach through the surface and touch. And you shoot up into the sunlight and take a deep, cleansing breath.

That was what he felt like—a surfer bursting into the air and filling his lungs with the air they craved, the air that was the very essence of life.

I'm here now, Erika had said. She might not be here tomorrow, or next week. She still had the power to destroy him if he opened himself up too much. But for now . . .

I'm here.

She was there. And so was he.

Erika was still mulling over her confession to Ted, and his to her, as they entered Atomic Slims. She hadn't expected things to get so honest so fast. She'd been planning to go on a date with Sarah's friend Bill just minutes before she'd met up with Ted at the White Horse Tavern. And Ted was in a relationship, for God's sake. This evening was supposed to be about two old friends getting together, nothing more. Some good times, some reminiscences, some catching up. Period.

But then he'd hit her with his solemn words about her being etched into his mind for sixteen years, and she'd hit him with her words about how things happened for a reason and, whatever else had transpired over those sixteen years, she was with him now. *With him.* That sounded almost scary.

Yet she didn't feel scared. She'd conquered mountains, she'd conquered oceans, and these days she was conquering the financial world. Surely she had the courage to be *with* Ted long enough to find out what exactly was going on.

Atomic Slims was a postage stamp of a club, the dance floor a tiny square crammed with people. Erika loved dancing in the center of a mob. She grabbed Ted's hand and dragged him out onto the floor. As they began to move to the music, she found herself remembering another dance floor sixteen years ago, when he'd been in a tux and she'd been in a pastel gown that had supposedly made her look slim and graceful, and they'd been dancing with other people. And she'd secretly wished she was dancing with him.

Now she didn't have to wish. There was no secret. They danced. They touched. They laughed. Their gazes collided and they discovered they were both singing along to whatever song was playing. Exhausted after a few numbers, they fought their way to the bar and Erika treated everyone within shouting distance to a beer. She was a vice president of a major financial corporation, and this time she'd remembered to bring her wallet. She could splurge.

She was in a festive mood. She and Ted had given each other a glimpse of their souls and they'd survived. More than survived; they were exulting in the moment, the reality of their being together for this one evening. She wanted to dance with him forever, but that was impossible. So she'd dance with him now, and drink, and celebrate.

After she and Ted had quenched their thirst, they returned to the minuscule dance floor and let the music wash over them. And because she was so happy, so delighted to be with him, she wrapped her arms around him in a spontaneous hug.

His arms closed around her, and he looked as ecstatic as she felt.

And she thought, *I am with him. And that's exactly where I want to be.*

Sixteen

From: Ted Skala
To: Erika Fredell
   Crazy night.

From: Erika Fredell
To: Ted Skala
   Kind of an incredible night, actually. I'd like to see you again, maybe under less crazy circumstances. I'm feeling pretty vulnerable writing this, but I don't want to make the same mistake twice with you.

From: Ted Skala
To: Erika Fredell
   I've been thinking about last night and everything we talked about . . . Where from here, huh?

From: Erika Fredell
To: Ted Skala
   I know. Where from here . . .
   Here is what I think. I think if we did nothing we'd regret it. But to have no regrets, to go for it, you have to flip your life upside down. Which is huge, I know.
   I do think certain things in life are out of our control.

The notion that certain things in life were out of her control scared the hell out of Erika. What she'd loved about riding was the confidence that she could control a thousand-pound beast as it stormed down a track and launched itself over a fence. What she'd loved about sailing was that she could control a boat's response to gale winds and tides. What she'd loved about skiing was that, no matter how steep the slope or how icy the snow, she could control her speed with a mere turn of her ankles, a bend of her knees, a shift in her weight.

But she couldn't control her feelings for Ted. Not this time.

Why had she been able to control her feelings so much more effectively when she'd been younger? She was an adult now. She was experienced. She had a clear idea of the direction she wanted her life to take. She knew what mattered to her.

Having a partner, a significant other, a man in her life hadn't mattered . . . until Ted invaded her life.

Where from here?

He had a girlfriend. Thinking about that caused a sour taste to rise in Erika's mouth. She hated the possibility that she could be a home-wrecker. Not that he was married. Not that Erika could be named as a co-respondent in divorce proceedings. But she prided herself on being ethical when it came to relationships. If a guy was taken, she stayed away.

If Ted was taken, why had he gone dancing with her? Why had he looked at her the way he had, all night long, and touched her, and hugged her? Why had he told her she was etched into his mind?

Where from here? Nowhere, she thought grimly. Dancing half the night away with him had been lovely, but she hadn't forgotten the words he'd spoken so many years ago. Those words were etched just as deeply into her mind: *I will never be with you again, I could never be this hurt again.*

So where from here?

Ted knew he should tell her he was single. But trust was so damned hard.

He'd found an apartment in Hoboken and moved out of the place in Brooklyn he'd been sharing with Marissa. He checked on her a few times and she told him to bug off. He imagined she would recover quickly enough from their breakup. Even when they'd been together, when she'd been pushing for more of a commitment from him, he'd never sensed that she was any more in love with him than he was with her.

She'd wanted a baby and she'd been anxious about her age. He'd been the boyfriend at hand. He'd liked her, obviously. You didn't stay with a woman for three years if you didn't like her. But he hadn't wanted to have a child with her. Maybe if he'd loved her more, he would have been willing. But . . .

He didn't do *in love*.

So she'd have to find another sperm donor, and he had no doubt she would. She was beautiful, smart, all that.

His new apartment was no great shakes. It had what it needed and not much more. Maybe if he were a vice president at a big bank, he could afford an apartment in Manhattan. East River Marketing was a great place to work, but Hoboken was more in his price range. Just across the Hudson River from Manhattan, the one-time scruffy blue-collar enclave was deep in the throes of gentrification. Fortunately not completely gentrified, or Ted might not have been able to afford Hoboken, either.

Although he worked in Manhattan, it had always seemed like a magical place, just beyond his reach. Emerald City. El Dorado. He was a New Jersey boy, the kid who pumped gas instead of going to college. Manhattan was the sort of place where a princess like Erika would live.

He tried to picture her apartment. She'd mentioned, somewhere along the line, that she lived in Gramercy Park. What little he knew about the Gramercy Park area was that it was ritzy, full of grand old buildings bordering an actual park that was so exclusive, only residents of the neighborhood were allowed to enter it. The park was surrounded by a high wrought-iron fence, and residents got keys or pass cards or something. He imagined her living in one of those grand old buildings, in an apartment with nine-foot ceilings, parquet floors, and a wood-burning fireplace. One bedroom at least, maybe two, and a bathroom—or two—with marble counters and a claw-foot tub. He pictured ornate chandeliers and decorative moldings and windowsills wide enough to hold potted geraniums.

What did bank vice presidents earn? Enough to pay for such an apartment, he assumed.

Could he go to her apartment and keep his defenses up? Could he visit her there, make love to her there, spend the night with her there, and leave the next morning with his heart intact? Could she destroy him all over again if he let her?

God, yes.

If he let her.

That weekend, they went to Coney Island, Brooklyn's answer to the honky-tonk boardwalks along the Jersey Shore. They strolled along the boardwalk, inhaling the distinct blend of scents: ocean, coconut-perfumed sunscreen, cotton candy, and the hot grease of pizza and fried bread; and listening to a symphony of beach sounds: the wind, the surf pounding against the sand, the electronic beeps and boings emerging from the arcades, the shrieks of thousands upon thousands of people romping in the ocean, shouting to one another across the beach, screaming on the Ferris wheel, the roller coaster, and the Tilt-A-Whirl.

Summer had officially arrived, and Erika felt her skin soaking in the sun's baking rays. Although her coloring was fair for a half-Latina woman—her father's Northern European genes seemed to have trumped her mother's South American genes—Erika tanned easily. By the end of the day, her bare arms and her legs below the hems of her shorts were sure to be a rich tawny hue.

Next to her, Ted frequently paused to peek into a kiosk or an arcade, clearly tempted to try his luck shooting an air rifle at a moving target in one booth or to rack up points on one of the elaborate pinball machines in another. But he never gave in to the temptation. He shambled along, his hair glinting beneath the sun, his hands in the pockets of his loose-fitting shorts.

Erika wished he would take her hand.

She wished she wasn't wishing for that. They were just friends, after all—although she found it odd that he would choose to spend a Saturday afternoon with her rather than his girlfriend. She could tell by the pensive line of his mouth and the way he kept gazing out toward the horizon that he had something on his mind. So many years later, she was still able to read Ted. Today, she could tell that he was not in the most carefree of moods, despite his having chosen to ride the subway to Coney Island with her.

He motioned with his chin toward a food stand. "You hungry?"

She shrugged. She could use some food, but not the oily, fatty, sugary junk most of the vendors were offering. The stand he had gestured toward sold Italian ices. Not oily or fatty. "Sure," she said.

She got a cup of lemon ice, and he bought himself a large, doughy pretzel dotted with crystals of salt. They found an empty bench facing the ocean and sat. Ted propped his feet on the railing bordering the boardwalk and stared out at the ocean.

He took a bite of his pretzel, chewed and swallowed. "What?" Erika goaded him.

He glanced at her and laughed. "*What? What?* Remember when I proved how wrong you were about saying 'What?'"

She laughed, too. "Oh, yes." They'd been in high school then, and she'd explained her theory about why girls always said, "What?" when someone told them something they wanted to hear. If a guy said, "You're looking good," a girl would say, "What?" If he said, "I love you," she'd say, "What?" The reason, Erika had explained, was that the girl wanted to hear the guy say it again. Ted had contemplated her theory for a few minutes, then abruptly called her the foulest, most obscene word a guy could ever call a girl. "What!" she'd erupted, shocked that he could say such a thing. "There goes your theory," he'd said.

"You didn't say anything," she pointed out now. "That's why I said 'what.' I feel like there's something you want to say, but you aren't saying it."

"Hmm." He ate some more of his pretzel. Erika tried not to stare at his beautifully chiseled profile, the angles of his jaw as he chewed, the sexy glint in his eyes, half closed against the glaring sun.

She shouldn't push him. She had no right to know his secrets, no right to ask him more than he wanted to volunteer. But she couldn't help herself. "So? Are you going to say it?"

"I'm single."

"Single what?"

"Single, as in unattached."

Erika's heart gave a little stutter. She shouldn't have been happy to hear this, but she was. More than happy. She was delirious.

She tried to tamp down her joy. Just because Ted was unattached didn't mean he had any intention of attaching himself to her. He'd told her he would never love her again, and she believed him.

She shunted aside all thoughts of herself and focused on him. "Are you okay?"

"Now that I'm eating this pretzel, yeah," he said. "I was starving."

"No—I mean about the breakup."

"Oh." He shifted on the hard slats of the bench and broke off a curved loop of his pretzel. "Yeah."

"You were with her for a long time."

He shrugged. "It wasn't going where she wanted it to go, so I felt breaking up was the only fair thing to do."

"Is *she* all right?"

"She's probably better off now than she was when we were together."

Erika refrained from arguing that he was a damned good catch and that no sane woman would feel she was better off without him than with him. "Did you have to move out?"

"Yeah. I found a place in Hoboken. Most of our stuff was hers, so the move wasn't too hard."

"When did all this happen?"

He shot her a glance, then turned his gaze back to the horizon. "Before we went dancing the other night."

She wondered why he hadn't told her then. Maybe he *had* told her, sort of. He'd told her she was etched into his mind. And he'd hugged her on the dance floor, and she'd felt so connected to him, as if a circuit had been closed, sending an electric current through her. She hadn't dared to ask then if the current had spun through him, too—because she'd thought he was still with his girlfriend.

But he hadn't been.

Where from here?

She counseled herself not to ask any more questions. She'd asked more than she should have, and he'd been generous enough to answer. To press him for more would be unfair. She should be satisfied with the knowledge that he was now available, that if there was any chance that he would change his mind about never being with her again, the odds had just risen a percentage or two. And that was good enough for now.

"I need to have the shit scared out of me," she announced, slurping her rapidly melting Italian ice. "As soon as we finish our snack, we should go on the Cyclone. Or the Tilt-A-Whirl. Which do you want to go on?"

"Which one will we be less likely to puke from?"

"Don't be a wuss. The Tilt-A-Whirl it is."

From: Erika Fredell
To: Ted Skala

Who knows why this is happening now? I can't answer that question for you, and I can't tell you what's going to happen next. I can only tell you how I feel when I'm with you, which is really nice and comfortable, peaceful and secure.

We need to be clearheaded and honest, and the right things will happen.

I'd love to be lying down under a tree. I'm still dizzy from that flippin' tilt-a-whirl.

Ted reread the email she'd sent him the day after their Coney Island outing, and then read it a third time. He was dizzy, too, and the Tilt-A-Whirl had nothing to do with it.

He hadn't meant to tell her he was a single man.

He hadn't meant to want her so much.

He slouched on the sofa, his BlackBerry in one hand and a cold Budweiser and the remote control in the other. He pressed the channel button and the screen flipped through a sequence of shows: a blast of sitcom laughter, a cloying advertising jingle, a ranting pundit, two eerily good-looking people running down a dark alley, a Yankees game. He stopped channel-surfing and let the Yankees invade his living room. They were playing the Red Sox, which meant it would be an intense, meaningful game. But he couldn't bring himself to care about the outcome.

You're setting yourself up for disaster, Skala. This is Erika we're talking about. Erika Fredell, who tore your heart out of your chest and crushed it beneath the cold, hard heels of her knee-high riding boots. Erika, whose friends laughed at you when you flew like a lovesick headcase to Denver and gave her a stuffed teddy bear. Erika, who you knocked yourself out trying to impress, and who was never impressed.

Erika, who said no when you asked her to marry you.

Erika, who wounded you so badly, you swore you'd never trust a woman that way again.

Across the room, Derek Jeter hit an RBI double and Ted couldn't even rouse himself to cheer along with the crowds at Yankee Stadium. He angled the beer bottle against his mouth and let a few long swallows of beer slide down his throat, then sighed. How was he going to protect himself from Erika?

For years, he'd done fine. He'd lived here and there, wound up back in New Jersey, built a career for himself in New York, brick by brick. He'd been with women. He'd had relationships. And he hadn't let anyone hurt him.

He'd decided to contact Erika last month only because Marissa had deserved something and he needed to figure out if he was the one to provide it. Not just a baby but a commitment. An acceptance that the past was over and he was fully healed, and the time had come to shed at least one layer of his protective armor.

Not just for Marissa but for himself, he'd had to ascertain that he was truly over Erika. So he'd gotten in touch and agreed to meet her at that SoHo bar.

And damn it, he'd discovered that he wasn't over her.

How long could a love hang on? Wasn't love like a flower that shriveled and died if you didn't water it? Wasn't it like a fire that burned itself out if you didn't add more fuel?

He would run out of bad metaphors for love before his love for Erika died.

The inning ended with Jeter stranded at third base, and Ted closed his eyes. The television screen was replaced by the screen of his imagination, his memory—and Erika was the star of the show being broadcast there. Erika on the boardwalk at Coney Island, with the wind rolling off the ocean and lifting her hair. Her long, beautiful hair, not that ghastly short hair she'd had at the airport in Denver. She'd looked fine in short hair—she was so beautiful, she'd look fine bald—but he'd hated that haircut because it had represented the new person she'd become, her rejection of who she'd been.

Who she'd been was Ted's girl. When she'd hacked off her hair, she might as well have been hacking him out of her life.

But her hair was long again, long the way it had been during that magical summer so many years ago. The Coney Island sun had lifted the golden highlights to the surface as it had darkened her skin.

You swore off Latina women, Skala. Don't you remember?

He laughed, even though he felt more miserable than amused. Yeah, he'd sworn off Latina women, and now the prima Latina was back in his life.

He tossed the remote control onto the scuffed coffee table in front of him and lifted his BlackBerry. A few clicks brought up his saved emails and he read what she'd written to him: *We need to be clearheaded and honest, and the right things will happen.*

How could she be so sure of that? The right things hadn't happened the last time they were together.

But he hadn't been clearheaded then. Honest, yes—and damn it, she'd been as honest as he was. But his head had been about as clear as gouache, a paint he particularly liked working with because it was so opaque. Beautiful stuff, dense with color. But not the least bit clear.

He'd been dense. Intense. He'd loved her obsessively, and then when she'd left him, he'd cleared his head by smoking his way through Tempe, Seattle, and Costa Rica, where Bob, that crazy old surfer dude, had kept him happily stoned when they weren't riding the waves, and sometimes when they were.

Clearheaded then, no. Now? Now a voice inside him warned that he was being too clearheaded. He didn't trust that voice. It was the voice that lured him into taking risks, some of which turned out pretty damned good, some not so good.

He drained his bottle, the cold, bitter beverage cleansing him. Okay, he was going to be clearheaded. Not in spite of having just chugged a bottle of beer but because of it, he thought with a grin.

Clear thoughts: He wanted Erika. Wanted her as much as he'd wanted her in high school. No, he wanted her more now than he'd wanted her then. Now she was a woman. She'd always been cool and confident, but now she was seasoned. She'd seen the world. All those adventures she'd dreamed of, she'd lived, and experience was like a unique element in her blood. She radiated strength and self-knowledge.

She was just . . . amazing.

Clear thoughts, he reminded himself.

He wanted her. He wanted to kiss her. He wanted to lie with her, on top of her, underneath her. He wanted to envelop her. He wanted to feel her skin against his skin. He wanted to feel her hair raining down onto his face. He wanted to come inside her and feel her coming around him.

Christ. Think about Erika for more than a minute and his brain zoomed south to take up residence in his groin.

Clear thoughts. He wanted her. He wanted hot sex with her. Surely he could have hot sex with her while keeping a cool head, couldn't he? He could give her his body while protecting his heart.

He read her email one more time. Neither of them knew why this was happening now, or what would happen next. But whatever it was, she was up for it. He sure as hell wasn't going to let her be more daring than he was.

He clicked her number and listened to the purr of her phone ringing on the other end. "Hello?"

"Let's go on a date," he said.

Seventeen

TED HAD ASKED HER TO PICK A TIME and day for their date. Easier said than done. Her schedule was so insane. Work made impossible demands on her, and she was departing tomorrow on a long-planned trip to Sun Valley. But she'd planned to leave work a little early the day before her trip, so that seemed like a good evening to get together. He'd agreed to pick her up at her apartment at six.

That he'd offered to come to her home was important to her. It meant this was really, truly a date, not just a casual after-work get-together. Meeting him someplace straight from work might have been easier—she wouldn't have had the time to fuss with her hair and her lipstick, and she wouldn't have had to fret over what to do if he asked to come upstairs. Her apartment was so small— just one room, a glorified bedroom that also served as a living room, dining room, den, and office.

She and Ted were still figuring things out. If this was indeed a date, it was their first, or at least their first in sixteen years. She wasn't about to invite him into her bedroom.

Not that she wasn't tempted. If she asked the doorman to allow Ted to come upstairs, they might never reach the wine bar. She might just yank him across the threshhold, slam the door, shove him onto the bed, and have her way with him. She had been embarrassing herself with nearly constant X-rated fantasies about him ever since their outing to Coney Island. Something about riding the Tilt-A-Whirl with a sexy man could make a woman incredibly horny.

She laughed, then gave her head a shake, wishing she could throw off such thoughts the way a dog could throw off water by shaking its body. Their meeting at Fanelli's had been a get-together, their outing to Coney Island a lark. She was *not* going to bring Ted upstairs. Their history notwithstanding, they weren't going to pick up where they'd left off sixteen years ago. Ted was not going to gain easy access to her bed with a wink and a dazzling smile.

Her intercom buzzer sounded, and she abandoned her efforts to tame the summer frizz from her hair. When she lifted the intercom receiver, the doorman reported that a gentleman named "Ted Scallop" was asking for her. "Tell him I'll be right down," she said, then returned to the bathroom for one final inspection of herself in the mirror. Her dress was new—she'd bought it just for tonight—and it looked fresh and flattering without being obvious. She checked inside her purse to make sure she had her wallet with her—even if this was a date, she wasn't going to leave her wallet behind again—and then left the apartment, locking up behind her.

Ted wasn't in the lobby, but the doorman nodded toward the building's glass front door and she spotted Ted outside, leaning against the mailbox and thumb-typing text into his BlackBerry. She thanked the doorman and swept out of the building.

"Hi, Erika," Ted said without looking up.

She grinned at his ability to sense her presence without even looking at her. Had he caught a whiff of her perfume? Or was he just so attuned to her that he felt her nearness subliminally?

He looked wonderful. Not just in an objective sense, not just as a guy good-looking enough to turn heads, but as *Ted,* the man she was going on a date with. The man who had once been the boy she'd loved.

She *had* loved him back then. She'd thought and thought about it, recalling every detail of their summer together, remembering the flutter she'd felt in her heart and her gut every time she saw him, every time she heard his voice on the phone. Every time they were together—and when they were apart, too.

She'd loved him but talked herself out of it.

To this day, she didn't regret her decision to break up with him. The timing had been wrong then. Now, it was perfect. Everything about this moment—the way Ted looked leaning casually against the mailbox in a jacket, an oxford shirt open at the collar, tailored slacks that reminded her of the strength in those wrestler's legs, and his eyes as green and full of life as the ocean at Coney Island had been last Saturday—was perfect.

Except for the fact that he had told her he would never love her again.

He'd asked her out on a *date,* for God's sake. Maybe he didn't love her. Maybe he couldn't love her. But they had this evening, this moment. If it wasn't perfect, it might well be as close to perfect as she could hope for.

At last he tucked his BlackBerry into a pocket and gave her a full appraisal—and a shimmering smile. "I like your necklace," he said.

She had to touch her hand to her throat to remember what necklace she'd chosen. All that time donning her new dress and fussing with her hair and eyeliner, and she couldn't even remember what she looked like. The necklace was one of her chunky, artsy pieces. She had only two kinds of jewelry: classic, demure, daughter-of-a-stockbroker adornments and wild, brash stuff. She wondered what Ted would think of the elegant strand of cultured pearls sitting in her jewelry box upstairs.

"Is there a good place around here?" he asked. "This is your turf. Where should we go?"

"Do we want food or drinks? Or both?"

"Both," he said, then made a hand gesture she interpreted to mean that she should lead the way.

She didn't want to lead the way. She wanted to hold his hand. Better yet, she wanted him to arch his arm around her and hold her close as they walked down the street. This wasn't just a date, she thought; it was a *first* date, and their history didn't seem to matter. He kept his hands in his pockets and she kept hers at her sides. They felt empty, hollow.

First date. "This place is nice," she said as the approached a cozy wine bar. "We can get drinks and snacks."

"Perfect." He held the door open for her and she stepped inside.

The hostess, a thin young woman with cheekbones sharp enough to draw blood, led them to a small round table. A single pink rose stood in a bud vase at the center of the table, next to it a jittery flame dancing on the tip of a wick dipping into a well of oil in a blown-glass bowl. Erika focused on the flower and the lamp because it was easier on her nerves than focusing on Ted. He looked too damned good. And she couldn't erase from her memory bank those dooming words he'd once spoken.

I will never be with you again.

He asked her how her day was, and she told him. "It was busy. Demanding. Okay," she concluded with a sigh.

"Just okay?"

Another waif-like woman came to take their order. Unemployed actresses, Erika deduced—both the server and the hostess.

Unless they were unemployed models. They were certainly skinny enough.

Ted skimmed the wine list, then handed it to Erika. "I don't see any Budweiser here," he joked. "You order."

She requested a Pinot Grigio and Ted requested a platter of fruit and cheese for them to munch on. As soon as the waitress sashayed away in what definitely resembled a runway saunter, he narrowed his gaze on Erika. "Why just okay? I thought this was your dream job."

"I thought so, too," she admitted. "I shouldn't even be talking about this, but . . . well, the economy is doing its dying swan routine. Some of the big financial companies are going to take a hit, and my company might be one of them."

"Really." Ted seemed not surprised but concerned. His gaze warmed with sympathy. "How bad a hit?"

"I don't know. There'll probably be layoffs. I don't think I'm at risk, but do I want to be there while everyone else is getting sacked?"

"Everyone?"

"Well, no." She realized she was overstating things a bit, but sharing her worries with Ted was such a relief. She hadn't been able to discuss them with anyone else. Her father, a Wall Street veteran, might have offered good insights, but if she told her parents, they'd fret about her. And she couldn't talk about the shaky economy with her colleagues, who were all feeling the tremors beneath their feet as strongly as she was.

But she could confide in Ted, whose insights were every bit as valid as anything her father might have to say. He talked about how riding the economy these days was like riding the Tilt-A-Whirl—or, more aptly, riding a wave. "You think your footing is secure and you're balanced, and then suddenly a wave you can't even see knocks you over. It's nothing you did, nothing you can prepare for. It just happens."

The conversation flowed as smoothly as poured wine. They sipped their Pinot Grigio, nibbled on grapes and slivers of brie spread on whole-wheat crackers, and Erika gazed into Ted's eyes and saw the boy she'd loved as a high school girl and the man he'd grown into. He had changed—and hadn't changed. It was like having double vision, seeing the past and the present all in one person and feeling her own past and present colliding. Who she was then, who she was now. How she'd felt then, how she felt now.

He'd been easy to talk to then, too—at least until the end, when the talk had revolved around her leaving him. But even as she'd broken up with him, she'd trusted him. She'd believed he was always speaking from his heart, regardless of the fact that his heart was shattered. She'd hurt him, and he'd told her, as honestly as he'd always spoken to her: *I will never be with you again. I could never be this hurt again.*

She had loved him then. Loved him as well as an eighteen-year-old girl with a horizon yawning open in front of her could love a boy not standing on that horizon. It had been an immature love, an incomplete love, an unprepared love. But it had been love.

And now?

It was love. She was falling in love with Ted Skala all over again. Not with the boy he'd been then, but with the man he was today. As she listened to his words, as she nodded and laughed and offered reasonable responses to his comments, a part of her brain was sending out frenzied signals, like one of those car alarms that switched from a beeping horn to a siren wail to a screech. Ted was breaking and entering her heart, and her mind was emitting a deafening warning: *He will never be with you again. Not that way. You hurt him too badly.*

If she loved him—no *if* about it—then he could hurt her as badly as she'd hurt him. And then they'd be even. Maybe that was the best she could hope for.

Because suddenly, finally, she comprehended what he'd experienced all those years ago, when she'd abandoned him and set out on her own path. What he'd felt then, what she was feeling now, was crazy. It was obsessive. It was magical. It was scary.

It was love.

"So, you're going where tomorrow?"

"Sun Valley," she told him. They'd finished eating and drinking and left the wine bar. Above them the sky stretched lavender, a color she always associated with summer evenings in Manhattan, and the air was warm without being oppressive. Unlike SoHo, Gramercy Park radiated a dignified calm: young couples strolled along the sidewalk pushing elaborate strollers, elderly couples leaned into each other and moved slowly, their lumbering gaits heavy with age and affection. A few children skimmed past on scooters. The trees surrounding the park at the center of the neighborhood were dense with leaves that fluttered slightly, casting flickering shadows on the ground. "I'm leaving directly from work tomorrow."

"What's in Sun Valley?"

"Ski slopes," she said, then laughed. "Nobody's skiing at the moment, of course. It's beautiful there in the off season. When I was in college, I did a lot of hiking. I really loved the mountains out west. So some friends and I are meeting there to hike and swim and enjoy the resort at discount prices."

"Sounds nice."

"I think the time away from the office will be good for me." *The time away from you will be good for me, too,* she thought. Her heart seemed swollen with love for Ted. She needed to get away, to regain her perspective. To remember that he'd sworn he would never love her again.

"I hope you spend the whole time you're there thinking of me slaving and sweating here in New York, breathing all the bus fumes and trying to keep the economy from going under."

"You're so noble," she teased. "So selfless."

"Yeah, that's me." Abruptly, he took her hand and gave it a tug. She thought he must have noticed a kid on a scooter or a skateboard speeding toward them, and he was pulling her out of the kid's path. But when she glanced over her shoulder, she saw no one. And when she turned back she realized Ted had pulled her to a stoop, the brownstone steps leading to the arched entry of a charming old townhouse.

Before she could question him, he had her in his arms. He bowed his head, touched his mouth to hers, and lingered.

This is love, she thought, wrapping her arms around his strong, solid shoulders and kissing him back.

The kiss seemed to last forever. It wasn't fiery, it wasn't forcing. Just Ted's lips against hers, sweet and gentle, exploring, nibbling, savoring. She tasted tart wine and honey-sweet pears and the heat of her own desire as he quietly seduced her mouth with his.

Then and now, she thought. He'd been a fabulous kisser then, and he was an even better kisser now. She'd been crazy for his kisses then, and she was even crazier for them now.

Oh, she had it bad. This wasn't nostalgia. It was love.

He was the one to end the kiss. If it were up to her, she'd have remained by that townhouse stoop, snuggling into his embrace, kissing and kissing as the night fell over them and the next day arrived. She would have missed work and her flight to Idaho.

But if she'd been the sensible one sixteen years ago, he was the sensible one now. He drew in a deep breath, peered down at her and smiled. Then he took her hand and walked with her the last block to her building. Neither of them spoke. As easily as they could talk, they could just as easily enjoy each other's silence.

At her building, she considered asking him in. She shouldn't; they both had work tomorrow morning, and she still had to pack for her trip, and . . .

And she didn't want her heart broken. Even if that was her fate, she wasn't ready to accept it yet.

But he took the choice away from her by stepping back and saying, "So, I'll see you when you get back."

"Okay." She sounded half-drugged. *Okay. Anything you say, Ted. I'm all yes for you.*

He was still holding her hand, and he lifted it to his lips and pressed a kiss to her palm. Then he folded her fingers around it, as if to make sure his kiss wouldn't slip out of her grasp, and turned and walked away.

She told herself she would sleep on the flight. She sure as hell didn't sleep that night. She was too psyched, too crazed, as dizzy as if she'd just stepped off the Tilt-A-Whirl. As if she was still on it, unable—unwilling—to get off.

She managed to fake her way through work, one eye on her watch and the other on her suitcase, propped in a corner of her office. When her cell phone rang that afternoon, she prayed that it would be Ted.

Instead it was her friend Allyson. "Is there something you want to tell me?" Allyson asked.

Erika was too tired and distracted to figure out what Allyson was demanding. She let out a weary laugh. "No. There's nothing in the world I want to tell you." Another laugh, and she added,

"I told you I'm flying out to Sun Valley this evening, didn't I?"

"Screw Sun Valley. Maybe you don't want to tell me anything, but I want to tell you something."

"What?"

"I just got a text from Ted Skala. It said, and I quote, 'I kissed that girl Erika last night.' Who is *that girl Erika*? Which Erika do you suppose he's talking about?"

Erika laughed again, an eruption of sheer joy. "Oh, Allyson. I'm in love."

Eighteen

THE THOUGHT OF HER OUT WEST, climbing mountains, gives you heartburn. She went out west and climbed mountains before, didn't she? She climbed mountains and stood on snow-capped peaks and surveyed the world spread out below her, and you weren't in that vista. She didn't see you at all.

Go slow, Skala. Be careful. Only one woman in the world can break your heart, and it's Erika Fredell.

If you do nothing else in your entire freaking life, do this: protect yourself. Don't let her hurt you again.

She texted him from Sun Valley. She might be climbing mountains out there, or swimming in the resort pool, or shopping in the boutiques, or just decompressing from the stresses at work, but somehow she managed to keep him in her vista. Her texts were brief and superficial, but he didn't need them to be long and heartfelt. All he needed was to know that she was thinking about him at least half as often as he was thinking about her. That kept him going until she returned home.

Once she did get home, he intended to see her again. He *had* to see her again. Was he supposed to ask her out on more dates? Wasn't that a bit quaint? A bit artificial? After all he and she had been through?

He just wanted to see her, be with her. Absorb her.

His cell rang while he was at his desk. At the second ring, he swiveled away from the artwork he'd been evaluating, checked his cell phone's screen to see who his caller was and smiled. "Hey, Fred," he greeted. "Are you back?"

"Surrounded by skyscrapers instead of mountains. I forgot how noisy Manhattan is."

"You weren't gone that long."

"It felt like forever." She paused, as if she wasn't sure what she'd said. He wasn't sure, either, but he interpreted it the way he wanted to: it felt like forever because she'd missed him. "What did you do while I was gone?" she asked.

"Ate some pizza, went to some orgies, the usual," he joked. "I found this pizza place where they go overboard with the olives. You know those pitted black olives? I love them."

"Then that's the pizza place for you. I hope you enjoyed the orgies as much as the pizza."

"One orgy is just like another. After a while they get boring."

"So," she said, sounding a little breathless. "Are you all booked up on the orgy circuit, or can we get together?"

He smiled again. "I'll cancel the orgies. When are you free?"

"Tonight's a mess. How about tomorrow?"

Was she really going to make him wait another day to see her? "Tomorrow sounds good," he said, hoping he didn't sound as eager as he felt. "When should I pick you up at your place?" *Can I come up to your apartment this time?* he thought but didn't ask. He was curious to see her home. Gramercy Park was one of the fanciest, priciest neighborhoods in New York. A hell of a lot fancier and pricier than his little dive in Hoboken. He needed to know if she was living the life of a Manhattan princess—because if she was . . .

Shit. He was searching for barriers. Hoping for protection. Scrambling for excuses that would allow him to rationalize maintaining his defenses.

Erika wasn't the kind of woman who'd care about whether she lived in a nicer place than he did. All those years ago, she hadn't broken up with him because he pumped gas while she was attending an exclusive private college, right?

Not right. That might have been one of the main reasons she'd broken up with him.

He exhaled, wishing he could force his insecurities out of his mind as easily as he could force the air out of his lungs. Erika was discussing times, and he heard himself promise to be at her place tomorrow at seven.

Screw her fancy apartment, he told himself once the call had ended and he'd stashed his phone back in his pocket. He was going to see her. She wanted to see him. He could protect himself without succumbing to self-doubt. He was a successful man. No one could shake his confidence.

Well, one woman could. But only if he let her. And he wouldn't let her.

She thought about their previous date while she prepared a plate with treats, her own version of tapas. Initially, she'd thought that when the doorman signaled her on the intercom that Ted had arrived, she would ride the elevator down and meet up with him in the lobby—or outside, if he was leaning against the mailbox and texting someone on his BlackBerry. But then she'd remembered the way they'd talked at the wine bar, and the way they'd gazed at each other, and the way she'd felt when he'd kissed her, and she'd resolved that they were ready for the next step. The next several steps.

At least *she* was ready.

Ted's kiss that night, before he'd walked away, convinced her that he was ready, too.

So had the flurry of emails they'd exchanged yesterday and today. Every hour or so, she would check her phone and find another note from him, brief messages, just a few words that implied so much more than they said: he was thinking about her. As much, as often, as she was thinking about him.

She'd left work early and stopped at Whole Foods on her way home to pick up some snacks. Some cheese, some cured meat, and a tub of pitted black olives, because he'd told her he liked them.

When she'd gotten home, she'd changed into casual clothes, fixed her hair, put on some makeup—*it's just Ted,* she'd reminded herself, although she already knew there was nothing *just* about him—and scampered around the apartment, tidying the place up. There were advantages to having an apartment the size of a phone booth, she thought as she plumped the pillows on her bed, which was in full view of the kitchen alcove. No getting around that. He would walk in and see her bed.

A hot shiver skimmed the length of her spine.

It's just Ted, she told herself again. He'd already seen her naked—back when she was a teenage girl with admirably thin legs and perky breasts and every square inch of skin dewy and taut. She shouldn't be apprehensive about his seeing her naked now, even if she was sixteen years older. She was more graceful these days, she assured herself. She knew a little bit more today than she'd known then. She would like to think she might have a better idea of what she was doing and how to please him.

If it came to that. He might stand in the doorway, announce that he had a seven-fifteen reservation somewhere and they'd better leave immediately so they wouldn't be late for it, and never even see the platter of meats and cheeses and black olives she'd prepared, or the wine bottle she'd removed from the refrigerator so it would be chilled but not icy.

When she'd met him at Fanelli's a few weeks ago, she'd been nervous because she hadn't known what to expect or what she wanted. Now that she knew exactly what she wanted, she was twice as nervous.

Her intercom buzzed. She stopped fussing with the platter of snacks, rinsed her hands off so they wouldn't reek of olives, and lifted the receiver. "There's a gentleman here to see you," her doorman reported. "That Ted Scallop fellow again."

Erika laughed and decided not to correct the doorman's mis-pronunciation of Ted's name. "Send him up," she said, then set the receiver back in its cradle and turned to survey the apartment. All right, he wouldn't see the bed right away. He'd have to enter the room first, and with the carefully chosen spread and pillows, her bed could almost pass as a sofa. Not really, but almost.

She sniffed her hands—no olive smell—and then flinched at the jarring sound of her doorbell. *It's just Ted*, she whispered before opening the door.

Seeing him was like getting slapped in the face, only without the pain. The whole time she'd been in Sun Valley she'd thought of him, just as she thought of him pretty much every waking minute when she was home—and most sleeping minutes, too. But still, viewing him, standing before the man she'd loved as a boy and acknowledging her love for him now, was jarring. It lurched her nervous system into a new alignment. It simultane-ously clarified her vision and made her see stars.

"Hey, Fred," he said, stepping into the apartment.

He was inside. She closed the door and promised herself that whatever happened next, whether they left right away or had a nosh and then left, or had a nosh and then didn't leave, would be fine with her.

"This is it?" he asked, gazing around.

"This is what?"

"Your whole apartment?"

"No, actually it's a duplex, only the stairs are invisible. Yes, it's my whole apartment."

He took a few steps further into the room. More accurately, a few steps across the room. Too many steps in any one direction and he'd collide with a wall. He studied the tiny café table and two chairs she had tucked beneath one of the windows, and the area rug, and the wall unit that served as a bureau for her clothes, her computer station, and shelving for books and her TV. He paused to note the cedar chest that doubled as storage and seating—in an apartment this compact, everything doubled as something else— and peered up at the high ceiling, which made the room seem both airier and narrower. After a glance at the framed prints adorning the walls, he gazed for several long seconds at her bed, and then he turned back to her. "It's so cute. It's like a doll's house."

"It's all I could afford," she explained. "I mean, Gramercy Park—half my rent is paying for the address."

He must have sensed defensiveness in her tone. "No, I mean it. It's not what I expected, but it's really cute."

Cute sounded condescending to her. *Dollhouse* sounded . . . cute. "Well, it may not be much, but I don't need much." She hesitated, then asked, "What did you expect?"

"Gramercy Park. Big pre-war, wood-burning fireplace, spectacular views—"

"I have a spectacular view of the Chrysler building," she said, marching him over to the windows. "See?"

He stood beside her, gazing out at the distinctive landmark tower. "Cool."

"You hate it."

"No." He turned to her. "I like it. I thought you were living in a palace or something."

"Apparently, I'm living in a dollhouse."

"I guess that makes you a doll." Grinning, he admired her view of the Chrysler building for a moment longer before he turned his attention back to the artwork with which she'd decorated her walls.

One piece of artwork in particular, hanging between the closet door and the bathroom door, caught his attention. He frowned, moved closer to it, and frowned more deeply. "Holy shit," he murmured, clearly amazed.

She moved to stand beside him and admired the drawing he was staring at. It featured two lovers in bed, flanked by donkeys. It was bright and whimsical, bizarre and unique.

"I can't believe you saved it all these years," he murmured.

"Not just saved it but had it framed."

He shook his head, still apparently stunned. "I was just a kid when I drew it. A very angry kid."

"It doesn't look angry. It looks loving," she said.

"I was an angry kid in love." He moved closer, squinting as he assessed the drawing he'd sent her so many years ago. "I thought it would bring you back to me. I thought you'd see it and think, wow, he loves me that much, and you'd leave Colorado and come home."

She hadn't come home. But she'd kept the drawing, and treasured it. In fact . . . "Come here," she said, taking his hand and ushering him away from the drawing to the wall unit. She opened a bottom drawer, dug beneath her neatly organized files of bills and receipts, and pulled out a portfolio. She unlaced it, flipped it open, and displayed it for him.

The frown came back, a frown not of annoyance but of sheer bewilderment. Inside the portfolio was every letter he'd ever sent her, every note, every drawing. Even a business card he'd mailed her from Tempe, when he'd had a job as a car salesman.

"You saved everything."

"There were times I wondered why," she admitted. "I was moving around so much, doing the transatlantic sail, living in New York, heading out west for graduate school, back here again . . . I was always clearing things out, giving stuff away, donating things to Goodwill so I wouldn't have to move them. But I never got rid of this."

He leafed gingerly through the letters, pausing to skim a few. "Did you ever go back and reread these letters? Was it a thing, like, once a year—time to haul out the crap Ted sent me and remember what an asshole he was?"

She jabbed him playfully in the ribs. "You weren't an asshole. And no, I didn't reread them. But . . ." Her playfulness fled, replaced by anguished honesty. "I had to keep them. I could never throw them out. You were the first boy I ever loved. The first boy who ever loved me. I never wanted to forget that love."

"There were times I wanted to forget that love," he said quietly. "I tried to forget it. But I couldn't."

"It made us who we are, Ted. It's a part of us."

"Yeah." He folded the portfolio shut and placed it carefully next to her computer. His smile was wistful, a poignant expression of both pain and joy as he took her in his arms and kissed her.

They stood beside that pile of letters and drawings, kissing for what felt like an eternity. Ted tangled his hands into Erika's hair, using his thumbs to tilt her chin, sliding his tongue deep into her mouth. He grazed the nape of her neck with his fingertips, warmed her shoulders with his palms, drew his hands forward to the front of her blouse. Kissed her. Fiddled with the blouse's buttons. Kissed her again.

She let his kisses melt her, heat her, flood her with pleasure. She was wistful, too, aware of everything she'd lost when she'd walked away from the first boy she'd ever loved, the first boy who had ever loved her. She'd gained so much by declaring her freedom, learned so much, grown so much—but she'd also lost so much. She'd lost him.

Now she had him back.

As turned on as she was by the brush of his fingers against her skin as he opened one button and then another down the front of her blouse, she was even more turned on by the way he looked at her. She had always believed his eyes had a special power, not just the power to mesmerize her with their beauty but the power to see more than normal people saw. He was an artist; he noticed the lines and shapes of things, the hues and shadings, with a discernment most people didn't possess.

But he also saw *her*. When he looked at her the way he was looking at her right now, she was certain he saw her yearnings, her fears, her soul. When they were young, he had seen in her the person he'd wanted her to be. Now he saw the person she truly was.

She worked her way down the front of his shirt, lingering at each button, teasing him with gentle taps and twists of her fingers against the chest she was baring. Long before she'd really understood her own responses, she'd been transfixed by the sight of him in his wrestling singlet, that clinging Lycra uniform that had exposed so much of his lanky, boyish body.

His body was no longer boyish. His torso was warm and solid, thick with muscle. When his shirt was fully open, she flattened her hands against the surface of his chest, needing to confirm by touch what she could see: that he was a man, strong and sturdy and wanting her. She caressed the firm contours of his shoulders, felt the wild beat of his heart, noted the flexing of his abs as she skimmed her hands down to the waistband of his slacks. When her hands alighted on the button of his fly, he let out a sound that was half a sigh and half a groan.

He kissed her again, a hungry, greedy kiss that swamped her with sensation. How could she open his fly when he was kissing her like this? How could she get him naked—which at that moment was her one and only goal in life? How could she think when his tongue was seducing hers, luring it, subduing it?

She was scarcely aware of the faint chill on her shoulders as he pushed her blouse down her arms and off her. Scarcely aware of the tickle at the center of her back as he flicked open her bra. All too aware of the heat in his hands as he brought them forward to her breasts, cupped beneath them, splayed his fingers over them.

"Fred," he murmured. "Erika."

"Yes." It was all she had to say. All she *could* say.

She was glad her apartment was so small. They had to take only a couple of steps to reach the bed. They tumbled onto it, and it occurred to her that they had never before made love on a bed.

They had never before made *love,* she thought. They'd had sex. And yes, she'd loved Ted, and he'd sworn he loved her. But they'd been too young to comprehend what love meant. It had been an ideal, an abstract concept.

Now it was real. It was destiny.

He kissed her, kissed her, intoxicated her with his kisses. He finished undressing her and helped her finish undressing him. They lay together, bodies pressing close and then moving apart to give their hands room to claim, to touch, to take. Every part of him—shoulders, back, butt, thighs, calves—was as warm and hard as his chest had been. Every part except his erection, which was much, much warmer, much, much harder.

She ran her fingers the length of him. "Do you like this?" she whispered. Back when they'd been teenagers, she had never asked him what he liked. She'd been too shy.

A soft, helpless laugh escaped him. "Even if I were dead, I'd like that," he said. He shifted on the mattress and lowered his mouth to her breast. Twinges of heat shot through her as he nuzzled one breast and then the other. She combed her hands through his hair, holding his head to her, thinking, *Yeah, I like that.* Anything he did to her, everything he did to her . . . yeah, she liked it.

He lifted his head and gazed down at her. "Do you have any idea how beautiful you are?" he asked.

It was a question she couldn't possibly answer. Yes would make her sound arrogant; no would make her sound coy. She liked to look nice, but she wasn't obsessed with her appearance. Yet when she peered up into his eyes, she saw her beauty there. She was beautiful because Ted thought she was beautiful. She was beautiful because he desired her.

"Love me," she murmured.

"I think I can do that," he said, trailing his hand down her body. "Maybe a little better than last time."

Last time. Sixteen years ago. The night before she left for Colorado. That time had been so precious in its own way, so bittersweet. *Good-bye* had shimmered through them that time. It had hovered in the air. It had whispered itself in every kiss.

She prayed that this time would have no *good-bye* in it. Running her hands down his back, gripping his hips, lifting herself off the pillows to nip the hollow of his throat, she prayed that this would be the start of something, not its conclusion.

This time she understood love. She believed in it. She lived it.

This time, he knew what he was doing. They both did.

He played his fingers over her until she moaned with need, her hips twitching, her hands groping, clinging. Then—at last—he joined himself to her, and for a blissful instant her world fell still and silent. Everything was in balance, everything was as it should be. Her and Ted, united.

They moved together, strove together. They sensed each other's needs, adjusted their weight, their rhythm, their breathing until they were one single entity gliding, soaring.

Sensation tore through her, deep, wrenching pulses of pleasure that left her gasping and trembling and blessedly spent. Above her, Ted moaned, lost in his own ecstasy. She held him close, letting him sink into her embrace. His breath was raw against her shoulder. His back was filmed with perspiration.

I love you, Ted Skala.

She didn't dare to speak the words. She was afraid he might not believe her. She had thought she loved him once, and then she'd gone away. Would he trust her if she professed love this time? Better for her to wait, to prove her love to him. Then he would believe her when she spoke the words.

After his respiration returned to normal, he eased off her and flopped down on his back beside her on the bed. "Definitely better than last time," she said.

He laughed and drew her against him, planting a slow, weary kiss on her lips. "I think we're beginning to get the hang of it."

Lying on her side, she traced a wandering line on his chest with her index finger. "I wasn't sure what the plan was for this evening . . ."

"I don't know what *your* plan was. This was *my* plan," he declared.

It had been her plan, too, but she let him assume this had been all his doing. "Anyway, I put together a bite to eat, if you're hungry. Just some snacks, and some wine."

"Sounds good." He released her and raised himself to sit, propping pillows behind his back.

She crossed to the kitchen to get the plate she'd been preparing when he'd arrived. "Guess what I bought, just for you?"

"What?"

She lifted the plate so he could see it. "Pitted black olives."

She'd thought he would smile, but his expression was more meditative than happy. "You bought those for me?"

Had she made a mistake? "You said you liked them."

"Erika." At last the smile came, a slow, deep smile. "You were thinking about me when you bought the olives?"

"Of course."

"Do you think about me a lot?"

"All the time." She admitted it without embarrassment. "It's crazy," she said as she placed the wine bottle, two glasses, and the food on a tray and carried them over to the bed. "All day, all night. You're like something out of a cheesy sci-fi movie. You've taken over my brain."

That made him laugh. He grew solemn again as she joined him on the bed and set the tray down between them. "Do you think about *us*?" he asked.

She could see why he wasn't laughing anymore. This was serious. "Yes," she answered honestly. "I think about *us* a lot."

She reached for the bottle, but he intercepted her and gathered her hand in his. "Are you in love with me?" he asked.

If he hadn't been ready to hear it, he wouldn't have asked. She curled her fingers tightly around his and said, "Yes, Ted. I am in love with you."

He pulled her hand to his mouth and kissed her palm, just as he had the evening before she'd left for Sun Valley. "I've been in love with you for sixteen years," he said. "It's about time you figured this thing out."

When he'd been making love with her, she'd been positive nothing could ever make her feel better than to have him deep inside her, bound to her. But she'd been wrong.

Hearing Ted tell her he loved her was better.

Nineteen

THE LAST TIME he'd been in the Denver airport with Erika had been one of the worst days of his life. He'd stood there with a teddy bear in his hand and his heart on his sleeve, and an entirely new version of Erika had appeared with her entirely new friends. He'd left the airport knowing, even though he hadn't wanted to admit it, that their relationship was dead. He'd tried reviving it, performed romantic CPR on it, pressed the paddles to it, and attempted to shock it back to life. But nothing had worked. The love had been gone.

He probably shouldn't be thinking about that now. But just as he'd sensed ghosts in his childhood home, he sensed the ghost of that ghastly day hovering around him as he and Erika strolled through the concourse in search of a place that might offer palatable food while they waited for their flight back to New York.

The relationship isn't dead, he told himself. *It's the past that's dead. Let the past stay dead.*

They'd flown out to Colorado to attend the wedding of one of Erika's friends in Vail. He had never been to Vail before, and in September the place didn't exactly seem like a ski Mecca. But the mountains were picturesque, and the wedding was fun. And he sensed that Erika hadn't brought him with her just so she wouldn't have to attend the wedding without an escort but because she wanted her friends to meet him. She wanted to present him as the man in her life. She wanted to acknowledge in some public way that the combination of him, her, and a wedding environment worked pretty well.

It was time to slay the Ghost of Denver Airport Past. Things were going amazingly well between him and Erika. They were together whenever they could be, and when they couldn't be, they communicated in a constant flow of text messages and emails. They spent most nights in her shoe-box-sized apartment, which they had both taken to referring to as the Doll House. They spent most nights tangled up together in her bed, having sex, dozing off, then rousing themselves and going at it again. Making love with Erika was like being reborn. It was like bursting into the world, drawing breath into his lungs, seeing and hearing and feeling everything as if for the very first time.

Sometimes he felt like the crazed teenager he'd once been, thinking about sex constantly—not just sex but sex with Erika. Thank God he didn't perform like that crazed teenager anymore. As far as he could tell, he was pleasing her a lot more now than he had then.

"This place looks like it won't give us food poisoning," she said, slowing to a halt in front of moderately upscale eatery. It was enclosed, not part of a food court, and odors of heavy grease weren't emanating from it, so he nodded his agreement and held the door open for her.

They wheeled their bags over to a table and sat. The menu was heavy on the usual—burgers, sandwiches, steaks, pasta. Aware that there would be no food on the airplane, they ordered salads and entrees. Ted requested a beer, Erika a glass of wine.

"Didn't you think the wedding was beautiful?" Erika asked as they waited for their food to arrive. "With the backdrop of the mountains? God, I love Colorado."

He studied her across the table. Her eyes were so animated, shining as she visualized the previous day's extravaganza. He loved everything about her—the beautiful proportions of her features, the flash of her teeth when she smiled, the contours of her cheeks, her blessedly long hair, but especially her eyes, so expressive, so vivid.

Slay the ghost. "So, you want to get married in Colorado?"

If she sensed an ulterior question hiding behind his statement, she didn't acknowledge it. "Speaking hypothetically?" she asked, and he gave a little nod because he wasn't ready to take this past hypothetical yet. "Hypothetically . . . It would be a pain in the ass," she replied. "I mean, it's beautiful, but planning a wedding long-distance is so hard. And so many of the people I'd want to invite are back east. Family, friends . . . I can't see transporting everyone halfway across the continent just so I can have a mountain back-drop. I love Colorado, but I'm a New Yorker now."

"So you'd rather get married in New York. Hypothetically."

"But a wedding in Manhattan would have to be small, because, my God, everything costs so much."

He screwed his courage and pushed to the next level. "What if I'm not talking about a wedding in the abstract, Fred? What if I'm talking about a wedding that would actually take place?"

She stared at him, clearly stunned. He wasn't sure what she read in his expression, because after a long moment, she gave a flustered laugh and shrugged. The waitress arrived with their drinks and salads, and she took the time to thank the young woman before turning her gaze back to Ted. "You're talking about *our* wedding?"

"Well . . ." Was he moving too fast? She looked so rattled. "Sure. Hypothetically."

"*Our* wedding." She took a minute to compose herself. "Okay."

He grinned, aware of the hasty retreat the Ghost of Denver Past was beating. "I mean . . . it's not like I asked you to marry me or anything."

"You asked me to marry you sixteen years ago, in the backseat of the Wagoneer."

"I think there's a statute of limitations on wedding proposals."

She managed a smile. He liked how unbalanced she seemed. Erika was always so poised, so confident. Seeing her eyes flash with a glorious combination of uncertainty and hope and yearning tickled his ego and warmed his soul. "Is a Manhattan wedding all right with you?" she asked.

"It would be perfect." Anyplace would be perfect if Erika was his bride. They could get married at the Waldorf-Astoria. At City Hall. At Grand Central Station, or Central Park. They could get married in the Doll House, although he doubted his immediate family could fit into Erika's apartment, let alone his extended family, her family, and all their friends.

"So . . . I mean, should we discuss this?" she asked.

"Like you said, I asked you to marry me sixteen years ago. I can't back out now." He tapped his beer glass against her wine glass and took a drink. "Looks like I'm stuck," he said, feigning disappointment.

"Because the thing is, I'm thirty-four." She sipped her wine, then dug into her salad, sounding a bit more certain now. "If we're going to have children, we're going to have to get started on that right away. We *are* going to have children, aren't we?"

"Absolutely." The ghost shriveled into dust and vanished into the dry mountain air. No more Denver Past. Only the utterly amazing prospect of having children with Erika. Little Teds. Little Erikas. Lots of them.

"Because once we get married, it might take a while to get pregnant, and suddenly my fortieth birthday is breathing down my back. If we're going to do this, we have to work fast."

"Fine." Fast enough that she couldn't have second thoughts. Fast enough that she couldn't change her mind.

"I know you've taken care of animals, so I think you can handle taking care of children."

"Yeah. Those years of practice with Ba Ba and Bunky were excellent preparation. You should have seen how good I was at changing Bunky's diaper."

Erika swatted at him without making contact. She seemed amused but also serious. "Do we want to stay in the city once we have kids? If we do, are we going to send them to private school? The best private schools have wait lists out the wazoo. Maybe we should get our kids' names on the lists now. This salad isn't half bad, by the way. How's yours?"

"Half bad. We don't have kids yet," he reminded her. "We're not even married yet."

"Well, I guess . . . we need to get moving on that."

"I was thinking . . ." Actually, he hadn't been thinking, at least not consciously, about this. But if they were going to get married—and apparently, after all these years, they finally were—he wanted to do things right. "I was thinking I should go down to Florida and talk to your parents. Ask them for their permission to marry you."

Erika fell back in her chair, apparently even more stunned than before. "That's so old-fashioned," she said, and for a moment he feared he'd said the wrong thing. Then her face broke into a radiant smile. "That's so sweet."

He recalled her phoning him from Colorado after he'd mailed her the drawing of them and the donkeys, and telling him it was so sweet. At the time, he'd thought she'd been patronizing. But she'd saved that drawing, framed it, and to this day had it hanging prominently in her apartment. When Erika said something was sweet, she meant it.

Sweet but also, admittedly, old-fashioned. "I want them to see I'm not the punk pumping gas who gave their daughter a hard time that summer after high school."

"You didn't give me a hard time. *I* gave *you* a hard time."

He couldn't argue that. "I want them to see that I've turned out okay, that I'll take good care of you. That I *can* take good care of you. And that there's nothing I want to do more in this world than take care of you. Except maybe for diapering sheep. That's always been one of my favorite activities."

Her eyes were shining again, and he realized they were glistening with tears. "I'm sure they'd love to hear about how well you diapered Bunky," she said.

They talked about possible Manhattan wedding venues throughout the rest of their meal, then raced down the concourse to their gate to make their flight. As soon as they were belted into their seats, Erika rummaged through her oversized purse and pulled out a pad and pen. The engines rumbled, the flight attendant pantomimed how to use the oxygen mask, and Erika scribbled on the pad and handed it and the pen to him. He read what she'd written: "If we don't live in the city, what kind of house would you like?"

The plane lurched away from the gate. The pilot's voice filled the cabin, offering a folksy report about tailwind speeds and clear skies. Ted jotted, "Enough bedrooms for the kids. Enough acreage for animals." He handed the pad back to her.

"Horses?" she wrote, then passed him the pad.

"And donkeys," he wrote back.

She laughed. "How many kids?" she wrote.

"Not so many that they have to sleep four to a room," he wrote.

She took the pad from him, read what he'd written and laughed again. "I love you," she wrote.

He took the pad from her. "Marry me," he wrote.

"Yes," she wrote.

The plane sped down the runway and lifted into the air, suddenly quiet, smooth, floating. Ted vowed that the Ghost of Denver Past was gone forever.

"I've got an idea," Erika said. She was seated on her bed, an oversized T-shirt covering her and brochures and computer printouts arrayed in neat piles around her. Ted teased her about being a neat freak—and really, she wasn't, but she liked organization. She couldn't imagine arranging a wedding without plans, timelines, flow charts, and everything in neat piles.

That it was the middle of the night didn't faze her. She and Ted had gone out club-hopping, returned to the Doll House after one, and made love. She should have been fast asleep by now, but she was too pumped, her mind humming with adrenaline. She'd recently switched jobs, and every minute she wasn't dealing with her new position in finance, she was plotting the intricate details of her wedding to Ted.

He seemed happy to leave the planning to her. He could handle the large picture, which in this case was *We Will Get Married*. But comparing prices per plate at this restaurant and that hotel and analyzing the benefits of cupcakes over a tiered wedding cake did not appeal to him.

He had returned from Florida a few days ago, after visiting her parents to request their permission to marry Erika and receiving their blessing. He'd barely left their home when Erika's mother had phoned to tell Erika what a courtly gesture he'd made, how impressed she and Erika's father were that Ted was honoring tradition. "I thought you were smart to break up with him all those years ago," Erika's mother told her. "Now, I think you're smart to hang onto him. By the way, I've found some old photos of the two of you, from high school. I'll have Dad scan them and email them to you, if you'd like. You'll enjoy them."

Across the room from her, Ted sat at the tiny café table near the window, sipping a beer. He had on a pair of old jeans and his shirt was unbuttoned, allowing her a tantalizing view of his chest. She should have let him sleep, but her mind was clamoring too loudly for *her* to sleep, and if she wasn't going to sleep, why should he?

"What's your idea?" he asked.

"We should put a photo of us from high school on our wedding invitations. Or our engagement announcements. Or our save-the-date mailings. On *something*. Don't you think that would be cute?"

Something darkened in his face. "What, like, our yearbook photos?"

"A photo of us together. My mother found some pictures of the two of us from Mendham and had my dad email them. Here." She located the folder with the scanned photos in it and extended it to Ted.

The apartment was so small, he almost didn't have to rise from his seat to reach the folder. As soon as he had it, he settled back into the chair and thumbed through the photos. His silence, and the frown that creased a line into the bridge of his nose, informed her that he didn't think her brainstorm was as cute as she did.

"What?" she prodded him. "Don't you think those photos are hilarious?"

He finished flipping through the pictures and tossed the folder onto the table. When he gazed at her, his eyes were the color of a stormy sea. "No, I don't think they're hilarious."

His anger puzzled her. "Granted, I look kind of gawky in them. But you were always adorable, Ted. You were then, and you are now. I know you were kind of skinny back in high school, but—"

"Erika." He glanced toward the window, as if analyzing his words before he uttered them. Eventually he turned back to her, looking just as troubled as before. "I don't want pictures that remind me of how you broke my heart."

Now it was her turn to frown. "That's not what those pictures are. They were taken when we were together. I didn't—I mean, we didn't break up until months later."

"We never broke up," he reminded her. "You broke us up."

"Okay, well, that was a long time ago."

"Yeah." He lifted his beer to drink, all the while eyeing the folder as if it was a venomous spider preparing to spring at him and bite him on the nose. "I look at those photos and remember how much I loved you back then. And how much you didn't love me."

"I did." She spoke carefully, aware of the ground shifting beneath her, the foundation beneath her sliding, growing soft, cracking into deep potholes that could trip her if she wasn't cautious. "I did love you. I just wasn't ready to make a lifelong commitment back then."

"And now you are?"

Indignation flared within her. "Of course I am!" she retorted, no longer cautious. "How can you think I'm not?"

"I remember . . ." He thumped his hand on the folder. "I look at those pictures and I remember that you walked away from me. I was ready to lie down and die for you, and you walked away."

"I was a kid. We both were. Come on, Ted—if I'd agreed to marry you then, we would have been divorced ten years by now. We couldn't have handled marriage then."

"And you're so sure we can now?"

Her outrage increased as his seemed to wane, replaced by bleak resignation. What the hell was wrong with him? They were going to get married. He'd gotten her parents' approval. She had folders stacked all around her on the bed. How could he doubt that this was going to work out?

"You still have no idea how badly you hurt me," he said. His voice was low, tight, as if the hurt was just as acute today as it had been sixteen years ago.

He was right—she had no idea. She could guess, but no one had ever hurt her that badly. She'd lived a lucky life.

"I will never hurt you again," she promised, tamping down her fury over his having the nerve to question her devotion to him. "I love you."

"You loved me then, too. For a while, at least."

"Comparing then with now isn't fair, Ted."

"So why do you want to put these frickin' photos of *then* on our wedding invitations? Christ." He shoved away from the table and stood. "I've got to get out of here."

"Out of where? It's two o'clock in the morning!"

Busy buttoning his shirt and stepping into his shoes, he ignored her question. "I need some air."

"Don't you dare walk out of here!" She leaped to her feet, unsure whether she wanted to block the door or slap his face. "Don't you walk out on me when we're fighting."

"We're not fighting," he snapped, his voice even lower and tauter, as if emotion was twisting his vocal cords. "You're yelling. I'm remembering that I've always loved you more than you loved me."

"That's not true!" Forget slapping him; she wanted to throttle him. She wanted to wrap her hands around his throat and shake him until he came to his senses. "Who the hell are you to tell me how much I love you?"

"Who the hell am I?" He gave her a bitter smile. "I'm the guy you sliced to ribbons sixteen years ago."

She didn't throttle him. Or slap him. Or stand in front of the door, denying him the chance to escape. Instead, she stood paralyzed with rage, and watched as he swung the door open, stepped outside, and slammed it shut behind him.

Three a.m. wasn't the best time in the world to be wandering around Manhattan, but Erika's neighborhood was relatively safe. The actual Gramercy Park, a city block enclosed within a tall wrought-iron fence, was kept locked; only residents of the neighborhood had access to it. So it wasn't full of homeless people or thugs. The expanse stood empty, the manicured grass fading to beige and the trees showing the first tinges of color on their leaves as autumn settled over New York.

Ted stood beside the fence, his hands wrapped around its vertical iron bars as if he were a prisoner pleading for freedom. Of course, he was free. He was on the outside, not trapped in the park. *You are free*, he reminded himself. *You are not trapped.*

Unlike SoHo, or Times Square, or even his own semi-gentrified neighborhood in Hoboken, Gramercy Park wasn't exactly happening at this hour. In the distance, he could hear the hush of cars cruising up and down Park Avenue, and the buzz of the mercury streetlamp casting a rose-hued glow over the park, and miles away the whine of a siren. But here, on this patch of sidewalk less than two blocks from Erika's building, Ted was totally alone.

How could she look at those photos and think they were *cute*?

When he looked at them, he saw his own blindness and stupidity. He saw the trusting, naïve boy he'd once been, a boy so wildly, passionately in love, the universe seemed too small to contain his emotions. He saw a boy so full of trust, he couldn't have conceived of the possibility that Erika could hurt him.

But she had. God, had she ever.

He looked at those photos and saw not just the lovesick fool he'd been but the anguish he'd endured after she'd left. The nights he'd spent curled up on his parents' blue living room sofa, so crippled with grief he could scarcely move, let alone eat or think or *live*. He saw the despair, the loss, the certainty that he would never recover.

He'd recovered. And he'd promised himself he would never let himself become that vulnerable again.

So how did he get here? How did he allow Erika to break through his defenses? How had he fallen under her spell a second time, torn open his soul for her, given her access to his still-wounded heart? What was the point of enduring such agony if you didn't learn from it?

If she broke that heart again, he wouldn't survive. He knew that.

The bars of the fence were cold and hard, denting the skin of his palms. The weight of the long night pressed down on him. He needed sleep, but he couldn't go back to Erika's apartment. Hoboken seemed so far away, though.

Didn't his old high school friend Ryan live in the city? Maybe he could crash on Ryan's couch. He'd spent many Saturday nights crashed on people's couches when he'd been that stupid, naïve kid in the photos Erika had shown him.

But if he called Ryan, and Ryan told him to come over, and he arrived at Ryan's apartment, wherever it was . . . Ryan would ask him questions. "Yeah," he'd have to say, "I'm still a stupid, naïve kid, too dumb to save myself. Can you save me? Do you have an antidote for Erika?"

Right. That would work.

He snorted, forced his fingers to unfurl, and pushed away from the fence. He would walk for a while. Shake off the spell. Regain his footing. Try to find his way back to safety.

As if he could ever be safe from hurt as long as Erika was in his life.

Miles above him, a few brave stars twinkled in the gray-black sky, visible despite all the ambient light New York City emitted. He sent a message upward, aiming at the brightest star and wondering if it would bounce off and somehow reach Erika: *Make me believe. Make me believe that loving you won't destroy me again.*

She'd never received his star-sent messages all those years ago. He realized that she wouldn't receive this one, either.

The bastard!

If she were given to grand gestures, she would have swept all the piles off her bed and let them scatter across the floor. And then she would have stomped all over them. Maybe she would have donned her old riding boots first to maximize the damage.

But she was too tidy, and she'd worked so hard to compile all that wedding information: the notes on restaurants, hotels, florists, photographers. She gathered her piles, stacking everything in order, and placed all the folders inside the drawer where she stored them. The same drawer where she stored all the letters and drawings Ted had sent her so long ago, the letters and drawings she'd never been able to throw away.

By the time she was done clearing her bed, tears were spilling down her cheeks.

How could he accuse her of not loving him enough? How much was enough? Enough to fill an ocean? To flood the planet? Enough to occupy the entire galaxy? What would be enough to reassure him?

I will never be with you again. I could never be this hurt again.

He had said that to her, and for sixteen years she'd believed he meant it. She knew how immeasurably fortunate she was that he'd gotten past it, that he had decided to be with her again. My God, he hadn't just discussed marriage with her. He'd discussed it with *her parents.*

And in spite of all that, he still didn't trust her not to hurt him.

Trust was her bottom line. If he didn't trust her, their relationship was over.

That thought sent a fresh wave of misery crashing over her. She sat on her bed, shaking with sobs, soaking her T-shirt with tears. She couldn't marry someone who didn't trust her—and Ted didn't trust her. It was over, really over.

The worst of it was, she was in dire need of someone to comfort her as she mourned the loss of Ted—and the someone she wanted to comfort her was Ted. She prided herself on being strong and independent, but on those rare occasions she needed a shoulder to cry on, the only shoulder she wanted was Ted's.

The son of a bitch.

She grabbed her cell phone from her night table and speed-dialed Allyson Rhatican. After a couple of rings, Allyson's voice reached her ear, hoarse and sluggish. "H'lo?"

"Allyson, it's me."

"Erika?" Allyson cleared her throat, then cursed. "Do you know what time it is?"

"Two?"

"Three. You woke me up. This better be good."

"It's terrible," Erika said, then started sobbing again.

"Oh, my God." Allyson sounded fully awake now. "Did someone die? Is it your parents? Your sister?"

"No. No one died." Erika struggled to breathe, to flush the tears out of her voice with a few deep sighs. "Ted walked out on me."

"When?"

Erika wasn't sure. It seemed as if he'd only just stormed out the door—and as if he'd been gone forever. "Ten minutes ago?"

"Why? What happened?"

"He doesn't trust me. He doesn't think I love him as much as he loves me. He doesn't think I *can* love him as much as he loves me."

"Oh, Erika." Allyson's voice grew honey-soft and consoling. "He's just scared."

"Scared of marriage? I don't think so. He's wanted to get married since he was eighteen years old."

"Scared of getting hurt."

"*I'm* the one who's hurting right now," Erika protested.

"Yes, and you sound pretty damned scared."

Erika let Allyson's words seep into her. Their truth resonated inside her. She wasn't angry or resentful. She was frightened. More frightened than she'd ever been in her life.

Frightened of losing Ted. Frightened that if she lost him, she would never recover. Frightened that the pain of losing him would destroy her.

Just as frightened as he must be.

"What should I do?" she asked Allyson.

"Dust yourself off," Allyson suggested. "Get back on the horse, and give it a kick, and fly."

Erika thanked Allyson, apologized for waking her, thanked her again, apologized again, and obeyed Allyson's order to shut up and let her go back to sleep. She stared at the phone in her palm, drew in another deep breath to make sure all the weepiness was gone, told herself to get past her abject fear, and speed-dialed Ted's cell phone.

He answered almost at once. "Fred."

"Come home," she said. No sobs in her voice, no panic. Only the truth. "I need you. I love you. Please come home."

"I'm in the lobby," he said. "Tell the doorman to let me in."

If she weren't so wrung out, she might have smiled. "I love you more than you love me," she said.

"That would be impossible." Her intercom buzzed, and, still clutching her cell phone to her ear, she climbed off the bed and grabbed the intercom phone.

"Ms. Fredell?" The overnight doorman's voice was almost as groggy as Allyson's had been. Erika wondered if he'd been sleeping at his desk. "Your fellow is here. Looks as if he might have been crying."

"Good," Erika said. "We'll match. Send him up. And tell him I love him."

The doorman snorted, no doubt embarrassed. She didn't care. He was sending Ted back to her, and for that alone, she loved him, too.

Epilogue

YOU OUGHT TO BE IN THE MOMENT *at a time like this, but so much has happened, so fast, and you feel like you need to review it one last time before the door opens and you enter the next stage of your life.*

Beside you, the woman you love looks like a mess. A gorgeous mess, but definitely not her well-groomed best. You know there are things you're supposed to say to her, and you say them. You hold her hand, rub her back, kiss her fingertips even as she's screaming and cursing and making an all-out spectacle of herself. And instead of being in the moment, you find yourself focused on the diamond on her hand, and you remember that crazy trip you took to Arkansas to dig for a gem at a mine called Crater of Diamonds State Park. You could have taken her to Tiffany's, but no, you had created a unique design for the ring you wanted to give her, so you trekked out to Arkansas to dig for a diamond yourself. And you stood in the hole you'd dug, and suddenly water started rushing into the hole, and you'd thought, I am going to drown because of love.

But you'd already accustomed yourself to that idea, anyway—that loving Erika could kill you. You'd accepted it. Because you loved her more than you loved your own life. Because you couldn't not love her.

You didn't drown. You came home and picked out a stone from a certified dealer and had the ring made.

Seventeen years. Seventeen years from the moment you'd known she was the only woman you would ever love. And now she's next to you, sweating and swearing, and she's never looked more beautiful to you than she does right now.

You gave her the ring in Florida. She'd probably expected to get it in Maine, where you'd gone first, making the rounds of the parents for the holidays. You'd spent a couple of days up in the snows of East Machias—too close to the shoreline to go skiing, but that was okay, this was a family visit, not a ski vacation. Your brothers were there. George pretended to wrestle you, but of course you weren't his puny baby brother anymore. You're as big as he is these days, and he knew that if he took you on, you'd have him pinned in two seconds flat. Josh and Adam and Nancy and their assorted partners, spouses, and children were there, your parents' house was crowded and noisy and Erika kept giving you looks that grew progressively more doubtful, more worried.

But you waited. You wanted to do this right—not with all your nosy, noisy siblings around.

So you flew with her from Maine down to Florida, and she was getting a bit edgy and anxious. You were kind of edgy, too, because her parents—who are really great people but kind of old fashioned— put you in the guest bedroom and her on the convertible sofa in the den, and you were horny as hell. At six-thirty in the morning, you couldn't stand it any longer, so you sneaked into the den and joined her on the sofa—just for a snuggle, you weren't going to get into anything intense with her parents asleep just down the hall. And she started cuddling against you, making you ten times hornier, and you said you wanted to take a walk.

"Alone?" she asked.

"You can join me if you'd like," you said, all casual. Thank God she'd decided to come with you.

She was dressed in pink. The color of the sun rising over the ocean. You had the beach to yourself; everyone else was probably still in bed, visions of sugarplums dancing in their heads. The sand was soft and white, the air sweet and morning-cool, the water as smooth as a mirror.

You couldn't stop looking at her. You couldn't stop thinking that everything you'd ever wanted, everything you'd ever dreamed of, everything you'd ever wished upon a star for—it was here. It was her. Erika.

You were rehearsing in your head how you would phrase the question—as if there were all that many ways of phrasing it—but before you could speak, she launched into a monologue, going on and on about how wasn't it amazing that a year ago you weren't even in each other's lives, and six months ago you'd met at Fanelli's, and as soon as she'd said good-bye to you that day, she'd realized she was in love with you, and how generous fate had been to bring you and her back together—and you're thinking, excuse me, I was the one who got us back together, sending you that email and asking if you'd like to meet for a drink, but okay, give fate all the credit—and she was babbling, and you were wondering if she'd ever stop to catch her breath, only you didn't want her to stop because she was just saying, in so many different ways, that she loved you.

And you realized that yes, there were many ways to phrase the question.

So you finally turned to face her, and she finally shut up, and you said, "You are the only woman I have ever really loved." And you fell to your knees on that warm, white sand and said, "I want to spend the rest of my life with you." And you gave her the ring, which did not have a stone from the Crater of Diamonds State Park in Arkansas, and damn it, if you'd drowned there, it wouldn't have been the worst way to go.

You remember that at your wedding, the first song you and she danced to as husband and wife was "Songbird," by Fleetwood Mac. The song she'd included on the mix tape she'd given you so many years ago. The heartfelt ballad that said everything. "I love you, I love you, I love you like never before . . ."

She's groaning, and you steer your attention back to the hospital room. Floral wallpaper—supposedly soothing, but only one thing would soothe her right now, and it's happening in its own time. There's a doctor in the room, a nurse, a midwife, and everyone is smiling, even Erika when she's not muttering and panting and doing all those breathing things you tell her to do. You want to point out to her that she was the one who insisted you had to start having babies right away, and as it turned out, right away happened on the honeymoon.

Not a bad way to celebrate a wedding.

Even if it meant you wound up spending your first few months of marriage searching for a bigger apartment. Because there was no way you could squeeze a crib into the Doll House. But you found the apartment. Not the house you've talked about in the country, with horses for her and donkeys for you and a dog like Spot, although Erika says if you have a dog it has to be fixed.

The way she's feeling right now, you wonder if she's going to want to have you fixed so she doesn't have to go through this again. You squeeze her hand, wipe a damp cloth over her forehead, kiss her matted hair, and remind her to keep breathing.

"I have to push," she says.

You wish you could push for her. You wish you could take on her pain for her. But she would never let you. She promised you she would never cause you pain again, and she never will. You know that now. She's Erika, wise, beautiful, earthy, brave Erika.

The only woman you've ever really loved.

"It's crowning," the midwife says. "Let's have another big push now, okay?"

And suddenly everything happens so fast, and Erika clutches your hand and scrunches her face and pushes, and you feel as if you're drowning right now, not in a hole in a diamond mine but right here, drowning in love and joy, and the midwife says, "It's a boy."

And your son lets out a cry. And you and Erika start crying, too.

So many years. So much pain, loss, distance. So much love.

They ask you to cut the cord, and you do, and your son is bundled into a blanket and handed into Erika's loving arms. And you think, it was worth it. All those years, all that hurt, but now you have this. You have everything.

It was definitely worth the wait.

Submit Your Own True Romance Story

"The marriage of real-life stories with classic, fictional romance—an amazing concept."

—Peggy Webb, award-winning author
of sixty romance novels

**Do you have the greatest love story never told?
A sexy, steamy, bigger-than-life or just plain
worthwhile love story to tell?**

If so, then here's your chance to share it with us. Your true romance may possibly be selected as the basis for the next book in the TRUE VOWS series, the first-ever Reality-Based Romance™ series.

• Did you meet the love of your life under unusual circumstances that defy the laws of nature and/or have a relationship that flourished against all odds of making it to the altar?

• Did your parents tell you a story so remarkable about themselves that it makes you feel lucky to have ever been born?

• Are you a military wife who stood by her man while he was oceans away, held down the fort at home, then had to rediscover each other upon his return?

• Did you lose a great love and think you would never survive, only for fate to deliver an embarrassment of riches a second or even third time around?

Story submissions are reviewed by TRUE VOWS editors, who are always on the lookout for the next TRUE VOWS Romance.

**Visit www.truevowsbooks.com
to tell us your true romance.**

TRUE VOWS. It's Life . . . Romanticized